# A MATCH MADE IN GOOD HOPE

### CINDY KIRK

WAVERLY
HOUSE

# CONTENTS

# CHAPTER ONE

Valentine's Day sucked.

Katie Ruth Crewes was no stranger to this particular holiday gone bad. It was her own fault she felt so low. She'd set her hopes too high for tonight.

Not that she expected a rom-com-worthy Valentine's Day. Just a nice night with an old friend, maybe ending in a sweet good night kiss at the door. But this was shaping up to be the worst Valentine's Day ever.

No, not the *worst*. That title would always belong to the holiday eight years ago when she'd been part of a Valentine's Day bachelorette weekend in Vegas that had gone very, very wrong.

The bride had gotten alcohol poisoning, the maid of honor lost a small fortune in the casino, and Katie Ruth had—

She shut her eyes against the memory. She'd been a different person back then. Those wild and crazy few years were definitely in the rearview.

Tonight's Valentine's disaster was still very much front and center.

The fact she had a date for the party at Kyle and Eliza Kendrick's home had itself been a cause to rejoice. Last year, when she turned the big 3-0, she'd spent V-Day alone with a pint of Ben & Jerry's, watching *Shakespeare in Love* for the zillionth time.

The sad part was, that had been a better night than some of the ones she'd spent with a man.

She slanted a glance at Dexter Woodard, her date for the evening's festivities. He and Beckett Cross—attorney and restaurateur—were currently engaged in a deep conversation about something to do with physics and mass transfer.

Katie Ruth, well, she was pretending to be interested.

When Beck's wife, Ami, strolled up with two glasses of fruit punch, Katie Ruth flashed a relieved smile. The cavalry had arrived.

Ami handed a crystal cup to Katie Ruth. She listened for a second to the conversation between her husband and Dexter. Then she stepped back and made a come-with-me motion. Apparently, Katie Ruth wasn't the only one bored by biotechnology chatter.

"You look ready to pop." Katie Ruth widened her eyes at the sight of Ami's pregnant belly, covered by the soft red fabric of a wrap dress. "I'm surprised you came this evening."

"It feels good to be out instead of sitting at home wondering if today's the day." Ami, her blond hair pulled back from her face with two sparkling butterfly clips, rested a hand on the mound. "We're all excited to meet him or her."

*All*, Katie Ruth knew, included soon-to-be big sister, two-year-old Sarah Rose.

"I wonder if it'll be a boy or girl." Though Katie Ruth didn't have any children, many of the women she'd gone to high school with were having babies this spring. They usually loved talking about their children or their pregnancies.

Which was why Katie Ruth was surprised when Ami waved the topic aside and leaned close, her voice barely above a whisper. "Eliza mentioned you were bringing a plus one. She didn't say it was Dexter."

Katie Ruth understood Ami's interest. Dexter had gone to high school in Good Hope. Then he'd left for college and built a life elsewhere.

Ami's eyes sparkled with curiosity. "When did he get back?"

"A couple of days ago." Katie Ruth took a sip of fruit punch and kept her tone matter-of-fact. "His mom was recently diagnosed with cancer. Dexter wanted to be here when she has surgery on Monday."

"I hope she'll be okay." Ami's green eyes clouded. "I really like LaDonna. I don't think I've ever seen the woman without a smile on her face."

Katie Ruth nodded. "Dexter has nice parents."

Parents who'd never said a word to Katie Ruth about the scandal affecting her own family.

"I have to say," Ami's red lips curved, "I'm impressed."

Confused, Katie Ruth inclined her head.

"You move fast." Ami chuckled. "The guy barely hits the city limits, and you snag a date for the most romantic evening of the year."

"You misunderstand." Katie Ruth spoke quickly. Knowing how easily rumors could take hold and spread, she needed to make it absolutely clear this wasn't a date. They were simply two friends from high school attending a party together. "It's not like that."

"Not like what?" Eliza Kendrick, hostess of the party and Ami's BFF, interrupted without apology.

Like Ami, Eliza was pregnant, though not due for a couple of months. Instead of looking like a beach ball beneath her stylish black cocktail dress, Eliza's baby bump was more like a cantaloupe.

"Katie Ruth was about to spill how she and Dexter hooked up tonight," Ami told her friend.

Katie Ruth stifled a groan.

Eliza's gray eyes shifted to the man still in conversation with Beck, now gesturing excitedly with his hands as he made a point. "He's certainly changed since high school."

That was the understatement of the year. The tall man, with his athletic build, dark wavy hair and brilliant blue eyes behind stylish eyewear, bore no resemblance to the boy. Back then, Dexter had been a beanpole with glasses that were always slipping down his nose, and he'd had an awkwardness around anyone of the female persuasion.

He'd also been scary-smart and fascinated by anything to do with science and math. He—like Katie Ruth—had led a comfortable existence on the outer fringe of the popular crowd.

As if sensing their assessing gazes, Mr. Geek-Turned-Hunk turned to direct a megawatt smile at their hostess. "Eliza Shaw. Thank you for allowing me to crash your party."

"It's Kendrick now." Eliza smiled even as she continued to openly study him. "And you didn't crash. You came with Katie Ruth."

Dexter offered Katie Ruth a quick smile, then immediately refocused on Eliza. "That's right. Kendrick, not Shaw. I heard you'd gotten married. Congratulations."

"Thank you." Eliza's gaze strayed to where her husband stood, surrounded by friends. She smiled, and any hard edges softened when her gaze settled on Kyle. "It's been an exciting year."

Beck moved to Ami's side and slid an arm around her shoulder. The light kiss he brushed against his wife's cheek had Katie Ruth swallowing a sigh.

The gesture was so sweet.

So romantic.

Dexter remained where he was, a good foot separating him from Katie Ruth. No one looking at them now would think they even knew each other.

"I heard your husband is part of Kendrick Inc." Dexter's tone was one of respect. "That's a huge operation. They've got their fingers in a lot of pies."

Pies that obviously interested—and impressed—Dexter.

Eliza waved away the comment. "I was sorry to hear your mother is having health issues."

"The doctors are hopeful that once they take out the part of the kidney where the tumor is, she'll be fine." Though Dexter's tone remained light, the worry in his eyes had Katie Ruth's irritation easing.

"We'll be keeping her in our prayers," Ami assured him.

Katie Ruth nodded.

Dexter rocked back on the heels of his Ferragamos and cleared his throat. "I appreciate that."

"Now, tell us." Eliza swept a hand in Katie Ruth's direction. "How did you two get together?"

Dexter blinked. "We're not really—"

"She means tonight," Katie Ruth clarified.

"Oh, yes, of course. Katie Ruth and I have kept in contact through social media. And I subscribe to the Open Door." Dexter slanted a glance at Katie Ruth as he mentioned the e-newsletter she edited. "When I mentioned I was coming back to Good Hope for a week, she asked if I wanted to come with her tonight and reconnect."

"Reconnect?" Eliza arched one dark brow, a teasing glint behind her sharp and assessing gaze. "That sounds…intriguing."

Dexter had had the unfortunate tendency to blush when he was younger, Katie Ruth suddenly recalled. Though he kept his composure, she saw the tips of his ears turn red. "That was poorly worded."

"Eliza." Katie Ruth spoke sharply. The woman was toying with him, much like a cat played with a mouse merely for the sport of it. "Cut the guy a break. You knew what he meant."

"Katie Ruth assured me there'd be a lot of people I knew from high school here tonight." Regaining his composure, Dexter gave Katie Ruth a mock salute. "She delivered."

Katie Ruth might not have had any romantic fantasies where Dexter was concerned, but did he have to make it sound as if she was nothing more to him than a vehicle for a party invitation?

*Don't be ridiculous*, Katie Ruth told herself. She and Dexter were friends. Hadn't they chatted comfortably on the drive over to Eliza's house? If he'd failed to offer any compliments about her appearance, well, it was because he saw her as his friend, not his date.

Dexter's gaze slid around the room and came to an abrupt stop. His eyes widened as his gaze shot back to Eliza. "I thought your brother no longer lived in Good Hope."

Ethan must have spotted Dexter at the same time. He grinned and lifted a hand in greeting to his former Science Olympiad partner.

"He's been back for—"

"I'm going to say hello." He was across the parlor before anyone could blink.

"Like Dexter said, tonight is, ah, all about reconnecting." Katie Ruth managed to keep a smile on her face. "If you'll excuse me, I think I'm going to grab more of this amazing fruit punch and mingle."

Katie Ruth took her time refilling her cup. She would admit, just to herself, that while she hadn't assumed—or expected—Dexter to be glued to her side, she *had* thought they'd spend *some* of the evening together.

Right now, she felt like a lonely only in a room full of couples. A pint of Ben & Jerry's and a movie were sounding better by the second.

Across the room, Katie Ruth caught Gladys Bertholf studying her. The ninety-some-year-old knew everything that happened in this small community on the Door County peninsula. Because Katie Ruth had her pride, she abandoned her solitary stance at the punch bowl, smiled brightly at no one in particular and sauntered over to a group gathered by the food.

Eliza and Kyle had gone all out for this party, not only bringing in a bartender and wait staff, but filling the two parlors and foyer with a plethora of roses.

When Katie Ruth had stepped through the door earlier this evening, the sweet scent wafting in the air struck her as oh-so-romantic. Now, the cloying fragrance had her stomach churning.

Out of the corner of her eye, Katie Ruth saw Dexter was now in the midst of a flirtation with Greer Chapin.

Greer's gray silk was the perfect foil for her dark hair. Katie Ruth could see why Dexter appeared mesmerized.

"If you wanted to spend the night talking to everyone else, why did you come with me?" Katie Ruth muttered. It might not be fair, but she wasn't feeling particularly generous right now.

"Pardon?"

A curse rose to Katie Ruth's lips. She immediately swallowed it as she turned to greet Dan Marshall.

*Pastor* Dan Marshall.

A godly man who'd likely never uttered a foul word in his life.

"Did you just arrive?" Despite her almost faux pas, Katie Ruth relaxed, and the smile she offered was genuine.

Dan was a solid guy whom she knew well from her volunteer work at the church. With him, there was never any game-playing. What you saw was what you got. And what you got from this man was all good.

"I walked through the front door less than five minutes ago to find the party in full swing." The minister's brown eyes were warm, and his normally messy cap of brown hair had been recently cut and combed.

"I wasn't sure about coming, but I ran into Kyle earlier today. He made me promise to stop by." He gestured with one hand to the group by the bar. "It feels strange attending a Valentine's party alone."

"Surrounded by couples." Katie Ruth glanced around the room and resisted the urge to sigh.

"You look lovely this evening." Dan studied her short, black-lace sheath dress with a flirty scalloped hem.

The chill, which had seeped into her when Dexter hadn't commented on her new outfit, disappeared in a warm rush of pleasure.

"Thank you. You're looking spiffy yourself." The second the words left her lips, Katie Ruth wished she could pull them back.

The exercise class she'd started teaching at the Good Hope Living Center was clearly having an impact. Seriously, did anyone under the age of eighty even know what *spiffy* meant?

Not to mention there was probably some sort of biblical canon against complimenting a minister.

Dan glanced down at his dark pants and gray shirt. "I should have worn a suit."

Katie Ruth made a dismissive sound. She'd spent her childhood surrounded by men in suits. Dark suits and conservative ties were de rigueur in the death care industry. Until she'd left for college, her parents had owned and operated the Amigone Funeral Home. The funeral directors, including her dad, wouldn't be caught dead in anything but a suit. Pun intended.

Thinking about those days still brought a smile. The mortuary had been called Amigone when her parents had purchased the business, and they'd kept the name. Her parents' quirky sense of humor and love of the absurd were only two of the many reasons she adored them.

Dan glanced around the room as if to reassure himself he fit in, or maybe he was seeing who was here that he knew. Which, if she had to hazard a guess, was probably close to everyone.

Dan shifted his gaze to the bar. They watched business owner Ryder Goodhue down a shot of whiskey, then immediately hold it out for the bartender for a refill. "What's with him?"

With Dexter busy mingling with everyone but her, Katie Ruth

had plenty of time to study the rest of the party guests. "Something is definitely troubling him."

Dan's brow creased in concern as Ryder tossed back the second shot.

Katie Ruth wondered how long it would be until the minister left her to check on Ryder.

"Engaging in a little partner switching this evening, Ms. Crewes?" Dexter's drive-by shot, coupled with a wink and a thumbs-up, had Katie Ruth sucking in a breath.

She didn't have a chance to respond, because Dexter disappeared into the crowd. Feeling Dan's assessing gaze, Katie Ruth rolled her eyes. She'd had lots of practice controlling her reactions to such comments. Still, hearing the barb come from Dexter's lips had been a surprise.

He'd never teased her about her parents. Not once.

Why now?

Beside her, Dan furrowed his brow in confusion. "Who is he?"

"Dexter Woodard. He's an old high school classmate." Katie Ruth fought to keep her tone nonchalant. "We rode to the party together."

Katie Ruth hoped that would be the end of it, but she hadn't realized Ruby and her two friends stood close enough to hear.

The older woman placed a hand on Katie Ruth's arm, her bright blue eyes filled with sympathy. "I'm sure Dexter didn't mean it the way it sounded."

"The way it—" Katherine Spencer, Ruby's close friend, frowned as if not making the connection. Then her eyes widened. "Oh. Oh."

Gladys Bertholf, elder statesman of the threesome at ninety-seven, stepped forward. "The man is a cad. Eliza should toss him to the curb."

"It was a careless remark," Katie Ruth began, but Gladys waved an impatient hand.

"Careless remark, my ass," Gladys muttered.

"Gladys." Ruby gestured with her head toward Dan. "Man of God."

"Don't make a scene." Katherine, steady as they came, gave her friend a warning glance.

"I'm not following." Dan glanced at Katie Ruth, appearing even more puzzled.

Katie Ruth hesitated, then gave a little laugh. "It's nothing. Really."

"Daniel." Gladys fixed those pale blue eyes on him. "Why don't you and Katie Ruth grab some food and enjoy this lovely party?"

"Ah, sure." Dan offered a tentative smile, glanced at the empty glass Katie Ruth held tightly gripped in one hand. "Would you like more punch? Or something to eat?"

The kindness in those dark depths had her returning his smile. It was the question she saw lingering there that had her making the decision to explain.

"I'd love some. While we eat, I'll tell you a story." When her knees went suddenly weak, Katie Ruth slipped a hand around Dan's arm. "Once upon a time…"

# CHAPTER TWO

Dan wasn't sure what to think when Katie Ruth began telling him how much she loved her parents.

He'd never met Mike or Lisa Crewes. They'd moved out of town long before Dan arrived in Good Hope. All he knew was they'd owned the local funeral home and had been embroiled in some sort of scandal.

Edna Peabody, one of the more conservative—and outspoken —members of the congregation, had known the couple. She'd marched into his office spitting fire shortly after he announced he was putting Katie Ruth in charge of the church's youth programs.

When he asked why she objected so vehemently to the appointment, Edna had told him Katie Ruth's parents were not godly people. Though she hadn't offered specifics, he knew she'd have told him if he'd asked. He hadn't asked.

Dan had reminded Edna that Katie Ruth had fabulous credentials and her reputation in the community was above reproach. Not only that, he believed strongly that a person was responsible for their own actions, not the actions of others.

"I may not agree with their decisions, but that doesn't change the fact that my parents are wonderful people." Katie Ruth gazed up at him.

Had her eyes always been that blue? Or was it the light from the chandelier that made them look as lovely as a cloudless, summer sky?

Her blond hair, the color of winter wheat, hung loose to her shoulders in soft curls. Tonight, her full lips were a bright cherry red.

How was it that such a wonderful woman was alone on Valentine's Day?

Katie Ruth leaned close. "Are you listening?"

Ignoring the intoxicating scent of her musky perfume, Dan recapped, "Your parents are wonderful people."

She sighed. "I can see we need to find a place to talk that isn't so distracting."

"The moon is quite lovely tonight." Katherine appeared out of nowhere to point to a small alcove. "That little area has a wonderful view. It's also a quiet place to talk or gather one's thoughts."

"Thanks, Katherine." Katie Ruth offered Eliza's cousin a smile, then turned back to him. "How about we talk there and check out the moon at the same time?"

"Sounds good." Dan stepped aside just in time to let a breathless and laughing Cassie Lohmeier and Krew Slattery rush past them.

Dan smiled, as their joy filled the air.

If anyone had struggled to find her place in the world, it was Cassie. She seemed to have found that place with Krew, and that made Dan happy.

There was a small table and two chairs in the alcove, but instead of sitting, Katie Ruth moved to the window, bracing both hands on the sill.

Outside, a large yellow moon beamed brightly in the inky

darkness. Katie Ruth lifted her face, and moonlight bathed her skin as she talked, her back to him.

"My parents have been married for thirty-five years. While not churchgoers, when they lived in Good Hope they were active in the community and helped with Giving Tree fundraisers."

"It's a worthy cause," Dan agreed, thinking of the fund set up specifically to help those who were struggling. Not a charity, but a neighbors-helping-neighbors program.

"They were good parents to me and to my brother, Nick. The funeral home they ran was known not only for its excellent service, but for the caring and compassion they offered to those who grieved."

Though Dan couldn't figure out why she was telling him all this, he didn't cut her off.

Listening and providing wise counsel was all part of the job. Even if it wasn't, he wanted Katie Ruth to get whatever was troubling her off her chest so, hopefully, she'd be able to enjoy the rest of the party.

"When I was in middle school and Nick was away at college, I discovered something about my parents' personal lives. It was something I'd have preferred never to know."

Dan heard the brittle tension in her voice. Stepping to her, he rested a supportive hand on her shoulder.

She shuddered, but her gaze remained on the moon. "For as far back as I could remember, my parents went to Milwaukee the first Saturday of every month to socialize with friends."

He waited for Katie Ruth to continue, but she only sighed.

"It's good for couples to get together with friends," Dan interjected, more to fill the silence than to impart any words of wisdom. "Such actions strengthen a marriage."

"I'd met some of their friends. I liked them." Katie Ruth turned and rested her back against the sill. The moon's glow illuminated her golden hair so that it resembled a halo. "When I was in eighth grade, my parents appeared troubled the morning after they'd gone out. I asked if everything was okay. I thought maybe they'd had a fight with one of their friends."

A muscle in her jaw jumped.

When she didn't speak for several long seconds, he stepped closer. Dan kept his tone low even though they were the only ones in the small area. "You don't need to tell me if you don't want to."

"You haven't heard the rumors?"

The question caught him off guard. "Only that there was some scandal."

"No specifics?"

He shook his head.

Katie Ruth clasped her hands together and expelled a shaky breath. "My parents told me there'd been a new couple at the party the previous night. They were from Egg Harbor."

The fact seemed significant, though Dan couldn't imagine why. "Just down the road."

"Less than ten miles from Good Hope."

"My parents weren't acquainted with them. Another couple had invited them." Katie Ruth's gaze shifted over Dan's left shoulder. "Apparently, there was a misunderstanding. The couple didn't realize what type of party they were attending. When they discovered what went on, they were horrified."

Dan cocked his head, surprised at the strong word. "Horrified?"

Even as he asked the question, Dan knew there were people in his own congregation who would be, well, horrified that Eliza and Kyle were serving alcohol tonight.

He found himself wondering if it was alcohol, dancing or cards that had gotten the Egg Harbor couple up in arms. His money was on alcohol.

"Sex."

Dan blinked. That's what he got for letting his mind wander. He actually thought Katie Ruth had said *sex*. "Pardon?"

"They'd discovered this was a group for swingers."

While Dan had been told a thousand and one stories since he got out of seminary, he'd never heard a tale as strange as this one.

He cleared his throat. "Swingers."

"If you think hearing it now is awkward, try having the discussion when you're fourteen and these are your parents."

Dan chuckled, then quickly sobered. "I can't imagine."

"They told me their 'lifestyle,' which was basically their participation in these parties, would likely become public knowledge. I needed to be prepared."

Dan reached over and squeezed her clenched hands. "That had to be a difficult conversation. On both sides."

"I cried." Katie Ruth's shoulders lifted, then dropped. The look in her eyes told him the memory still brought pain, even after all these years. "I asked why they did it. Didn't they love each other anymore? I worried they were going to get a divorce."

Dan resisted the urge to fill the silence.

"They assured me they loved each other very much and had no intention of splitting up. They said swinging was something they'd been doing since college. It was what kept their relationship exciting and fun."

From a biblical perspective, there was plenty Dan could say on the matter. But her parents hadn't come to him seeking his counsel. This was Katie Ruth revealing, with grace and dignity, a painful time in her life.

"That must have been hard for a young teenager to understand."

"I still don't understand. But I love them." Katie Ruth swiped at a tear that had slipped down her cheek. "You'd love them, too, if you met them. Everyone likes Mike and Lisa."

"I take it the details about the party came out?"

"By Christmas, everyone knew my parents went to parties where they had sex with other couples. I heard every possible joke invented on the subject." Katie Ruth's eyes turned bleak for a second. "Boys jangled keys in front of me, then laughed like hyenas."

Dan felt his temper surge. "They should have been reported."

"To who? To Miss Briggs, my holier-than-thou school counselor, who was as horrified as that couple from Egg Harbor? To Pastor Schmidt, who condemned my parents' actions from the pulpit? The only other possibility was the police, and teasing and taunting aren't crimes."

Not for the first time, Dan realized how lucky he was to have been spared such trauma when he was a child. Still, her experiences at that tender age were probably part of the reason Katie Ruth was so good with kids. Especially the ones in middle school. She understood their struggles.

"I'm surprised your parents stayed in Good Hope then. I'd have thought they'd relocate to a place where no one knew them."

"My mom and dad, they're strong people. They weren't embarrassed or ashamed. They were only sorry for how the news affected me. Besides, it wasn't that easy to pick up and move. They had a thriving business here." Katie Ruth's eyes took on a faraway look. "They ran the only funeral home on the peninsula, which meant people had to deal with them."

"But they eventually left." Dan wasn't sure exactly when that move happened.

"Eventually," Katie Ruth agreed. "Once I was out of high school, they got an amazing deal on a funeral home that was struggling. They sold their business here and moved."

"Where is the new one?"

"Not far. It's in one of the Chicago suburbs."

Dan tilted his head. "My parents live in Lincolnshire."

"My parents are just down the road in Highland Park." Katie Ruth flashed a smile that didn't reach her eyes. "They're practically neighbors."

"It's a small world." Dan chuckled and shook his head. "If your parents ever invite mine to a party, I'll be sure to tell them to decline."

Even before Katie Ruth's lips pressed together, Dan regretted his pathetic attempt at humor.

"I'm sorry, Katie Ruth. That was out of line."

She brushed off the apology with a flick of her fingers. "It isn't anything I haven't heard before."

"You shouldn't have to hear it from your pastor." He took each of her hands in his and gazed straight into her eyes. "Or from your friend."

Katie Ruth offered him a grateful smile.

"I understand how difficult families can be." Dan kept his voice even and his eyes on hers. "I have a sister who's often gotten into trouble. It's not the same as your parents, but Oaklee is always doing or saying something that makes the family cringe."

"I'm sorry."

"There's no reason to be sorry." He offered her a reassuring smile. "Just like there's no reason for you to feel any guilt over your parents' choices. You're a good, honest person who is a credit to the community."

Ever since she became the volunteer youth director at the church last year, Dan had worked closely with this woman. He knew her dedication, her caring nature. What he couldn't figure out was, how had he never noticed before that she was so beautiful?

Of course, during much of that time, he'd been dating and then engaged to Lindsay Lohmeier. That relationship had ended last summer.

Dan gave her hands a squeeze, then released them. "I'm happy to have you in the congregation. I want you to know that I consider you a friend."

"Thank you." Emotion thickened Katie Ruth's voice, and her eyes held a sheen.

As Dan stared into her cornflower-blue eyes, he realized that *friend* wasn't the correct word for Katie Ruth and the feelings she engendered in him.

Blame it on the scent of roses in the air or the romantic classical music playing softly in the background. Perhaps it was her shiny red lips or the sweetness of the perfume teasing his nostrils.

Something had prompted the change. Did the cause really matter? All Dan knew was he'd never look at Katie Ruth the same way ever again.

～

Behind the colonnade, Gladys kept her voice low, her words for her two friends' ears only. "They don't have a clue we're watching."

She'd been a stage actress for more decades than most people in this town had been alive. Gladys knew all about vocal variation and how to project—and not project—her voice.

"He's holding her hands." Ruby, the most excitable of the three women, would have clapped her hands, but knew Gladys would slap them down.

"They're talking." Katherine, the sensible one, gave the couple a sharp and assessing gaze. "Still, they're standing closer than I'd expect two friends to stand."

"Yes, indeed." Gladys couldn't help but smile. There was nothing she liked more than matchmaking. Bringing couples together beat endless games of dominos, cards and bunco.

"Now that Cassie and Krew are happily together, it's time for our next love match." Gladys didn't like to be proven wrong, and the failed match between the minister and Lindsay Lohmeier last year still stuck in her craw. The ring had been on her finger and Lindsay had even picked out her wedding dress when she'd rabbited.

Of course, Lindsay and Owen Vaughn had been her next project, and that match had been a rousing success. The two were married now and blissfully happy, with a baby due at the end of next month.

Katherine tapped a finger against her lips. "Are you confident Katie Ruth and Dan are a good match?"

The doubt Gladys saw in Katherine's eyes rattled her confidence.

"You predict problems?" Gladys kept her tone offhand. She had her reputation as the wisest sage to preserve.

"I'm concerned that Katie Ruth showed up tonight with Dexter," Katherine admitted. "But my observations indicate the man is—oh, what is that term—no more into her than she is into him."

Gladys felt herself relax.

"Katie Ruth has spent more time this evening speaking with the preacher than she did with Dexter." Ruby's eyes grew soft as she watched the couple. "We need to get them on a date. They can't fall in love if they don't spend quality time together."

"What about the pancake supper at the church?" Gladys had planned to skip the event and attend the Wii bowling tournament at the Living Center instead.

"I love pancakes." Ruby gave a trill of laughter, her hands moving as fast as hummingbird wings as she spoke. "Especially with a lot of butter and syrup."

"Forget the food." Gladys narrowed her gaze. "We know Dan will be there. Katie Ruth is the wild card."

"She usually attends church functions," Katherine reminded them.

"Usually isn't good enough." No way was Gladys missing the tournament on a maybe. She pointed to Ruby. "You need to make sure Katie Ruth shows. Katherine and I will take care of the rest."

Katherine arched a brow. "We will?"

"We will." Gladys gave a decisive nod, then narrowed her gaze when Ruby chewed on her lower lip.

"Is there a problem, Ruby?" Katherine asked.

Ruby offered an apologetic smile. "I'm not sure I'll be able to convince Katie Ruth to attend. What if she's already got plans with Dexter? Or maybe she won't be in the mood for pancakes. What then?"

Katherine exchanged a pointed glance with Gladys.

Gladys kept her tone pleasant, though irritation chafed like an unpleasant itch. "All I ask is that you do your best."

Ruby hesitated. "I'll try."

Gladys met Ruby's gaze with a confident one of her own. "My father used to say, 'Don't try. Make it happen.'"

For a second, Ruby looked confused. Then she nodded. "I'll try really hard."

Gladys expelled a breath. Whoever said matchmaking was a breeze had never met Ruby Rakes.

This appeared to be one task Gladys would have to take care of herself.

By the time the clock chimed midnight, signaling the end of the party, Katie Ruth had danced with Dan under the mirror ball in the shape of a heart and eaten way too many lovebug marsh-mallow cookies.

She'd also laughed more tonight than she could remember laughing in the last month. If Dan's relaxed posture and easy smile were any indication, she wasn't the only one who'd enjoyed the evening.

It wasn't until everyone started leaving that Katie Ruth real-ized the man she was with wasn't the one who'd brought her. She glanced around the front parlor for Dexter and came up empty.

"Will you come with me while I look for Dexter?" Katie Ruth

asked Dan, snagging two red-and-black lovebug cookies on their way past the dessert table.

Keeping one for herself, she handed the other to Dan.

"Sure." He popped the cookie into his mouth.

She'd noticed he liked them as much as she did. One more thing they had in common.

Dan didn't take her hand or her arm as they walked through the rooms. Katie Ruth knew that would be wrong, considering she'd come to the party with another man. But, oh, how she wished she could link her fingers with his so she could enjoy the warmth of his skin against hers.

How long had it been since she'd held a man's hand or wrapped her arms around a strong male body? It certainly had been way too long since she'd kissed anyone.

Her gaze drifted to Dan's firm, sculpted lips. Katie Ruth's mouth began to tingle. What would it be like to kiss him? To press her mouth against his? To open to the sweep of his tongue and feel the heat?

"I don't see him anywhere on this level." Dan frowned. "The upstairs is off-limits."

Katie Ruth nodded absently as she inhaled the tangy citrus scent of Dan's cologne. She was glad he hadn't worn a suit and tie this evening. Dressed casually, he looked more approachable. Less like a minister and more like a man.

"Why don't you try calling or texting him?" Dan suggested.

"Good idea." Katie Ruth pulled her phone from her tiny beaded bag and texted. In seconds, she had her answer. "He went with Ethan, Clay and Ryder to play poker at the Ding-A-Ling bar."

Dan frowned at the mention of the rickety shack on the edge of town. "That dump?"

Katie Ruth chuckled. "Though I haven't been out that way in years, I've heard it's becoming somewhat of a trendy spot."

"If you say so."

She smiled. "He assumed you'd take me home, but says he'll come back if I need a ride."

Dan gave her arm a reassuring squeeze. "Tell him not to bother. I'm happy to escort you home."

Katie Ruth's heart sighed, knowing he meant every word. "Thanks."

"I'm sorry he left you. I know what it's like to have your girlfriend spend time with another man."

Katie Ruth knew he was thinking of Lindsay. That had been a totally different situation. "This isn't the same. I'm not Dexter's girlfriend. I brought him to the party so he could reconnect with old friends. Mission accomplished. Besides, I'm glad he left."

Dan's brows pulled together.

Gripping her inner boldness, Katie Ruth smiled. "Otherwise, I wouldn't have had the chance to spend the evening with you."

# CHAPTER THREE

This, Dan thought, was turning out to be a stellar evening. His original plan had been to swing by, give his regards to Kyle and Eliza, then leave. Instead, he and Katie Ruth closed down the party.

Dan smiled. He hadn't stayed until the end of a party since his college days.

"Why the smile?" Katie Ruth asked, her face upturned to his.

"I was thinking how long it's been since I closed down a party."

She laughed. "It's been a long time for me, as well."

The teenage girl in charge of distributing the coats was someone Dan didn't recognize, but Katie Ruth gave her a hug. "Astrid. It's good to see you."

The girl flashed a smile, showing a mouthful of metal braces, and handed the coat-check tickets to another girl to retrieve the garments.

"Happy Valentine's Day." Astrid studied Dan. "Is this your boyfriend?"

To her credit, Katie Ruth didn't miss a beat. She rested a hand on Dan's arm. "This is Pastor Marshall. I believe I mentioned that

I'm now handling the youth programs at First Christian. I'd love for you to stop by sometime. We have serious fun on Sunday mornings."

"I'm still thinking about it."

Astrid sent a wary look in his direction, and Dan decided it was best to let Katie Ruth handle the conversation.

"Well, I personally coordinate your age group. We meet in the church basement at ten every Sunday. You don't need to dress up. Come comfortable. There are pastries from Blooms Bake Shop, fresh orange juice and even lattes available. No charge."

Dan wasn't sure if it was the pastries or the lattes that caught Astrid's attention, but the girl looked interested.

"I might stop by."

Katie Ruth flashed a brilliant smile. "I hope you do."

Dan helped Katie Ruth on with her black coat, then slipped on his.

"I don't believe I've ever met Astrid." Dan stepped out onto the porch, still trying to place the girl. He prided himself on his memory of names and faces.

"She's not a member of First Christian. She played softball on one of the summer Y teams I coached last summer." Katie Ruth continued down the steps beside him to the sidewalk, where she paused. "Her parents divorced about this time last year. It's just her and her mom now. Her mother works a lot of hours."

"Sounds like you did church outreach in addition to coaching."

"I think Astrid would really like youth group. I believe it'd be good for her, give her a port in the storm, so to speak. From what Astrid told me, the family went to Sunday services in the past, but they don't have a church home now."

"If there's anything I can do—"

"I believe she'd like you, once she got to know you. But—"

"But…" Dan prompted when Katie Ruth hesitated.

"Astrid's dad was abusive. She tends to keep all adult males at a distance."

"Understandable."

"She's a strong young woman." Admiration ran through Katie Ruth's voice like a silver thread. "She'll get through this, but could use help. There's a program I've been wanting to implement that could help our teens. We should talk about it sometime soon."

"I'd like that."

"Well," she gave a decisive nod and flashed that bright smile once more, "it's been fun."

He stared at her outstretched hand. Instead of taking it, he pointed to his 2008 Hyundai Sonata parked across the street. "It's not fancy, but you can trust it—and me—to get you home safely."

She gestured with one hand down Main Street. "I only live a few blocks from here. I can walk."

"I'd rather you didn't." Even though Good Hope was a safe town, the thought of her walking alone, even down a well-traveled street, didn't sit well. "My car has heated seats."

"Well, then, how can I refuse?" She laughed and surprised him by looping her arm through his.

Probably, he told himself, in case she slipped. Of course, because of warmer-than-normal temperatures this week, there was no possible way her heels would find an icy patch.

He didn't care about the reason. He liked having her hand on his arm as they crossed the street.

The drive to the tiny cottage she called home, on the other side of the business district, took a matter of minutes.

The porch light was on, but Dan didn't consider waiting in the car. His father was old-fashioned, and Dan had been taught to walk a woman to her door.

"Thank you for letting me monopolize your evening." He paused on the porch, reluctant to leave.

She tilted her head back, and he caught a whiff of her light, flowery fragrance. He loved the way she smelled, like a meadow in full bloom. The enticing scent gave him a subtle, pleasurable jolt.

"It wasn't much of a hardship," she murmured.

"I'm glad." His gaze dropped to her mouth. Dan wondered if her lips would taste like sweet cherry candy.

The air around them pulsed with electricity, and his heartbeat hitched.

His control nearly shattered when she ran a tongue over her lips. She didn't smile. Shadows played in her eyes, making them unreadable.

Time seemed to stretch and extend.

Dan kept his hands at his sides and resisted the urge to reach for her.

When Dan finally found his voice, it sounded rough, choked, foreign to his ears. "Happy Valentine's Day, Katie Ruth."

She studied him for a long moment. Though her eyes remained unreadable, she smiled. "Back atcha."

Once she stepped inside and he heard the lock click, Dan did what he should have done the second his shoes hit the porch. He turned and quickly strode back to the safety of his car.

The following morning, Dan dressed quickly, eager for his daily thirty-minute run. He finished stretching and was reaching for his jacket when the phone rang.

After frowning at the readout, he pressed the phone to his ear. "Morning, Dad. You're up early."

John Marshall, a successful stockbroker, lived a well-disciplined life. The one day each week that he allowed himself to sleep in was Saturday. That was, unless he had a date to play eighteen holes with a business associate.

Since the Chicago area had been hit with another snowstorm yesterday, Dan doubted a morning of golf was on today's agenda.

"I couldn't sleep. Your mother was worried, and her constant tossing and turning kept me up half the night." His dad blew out a breath.

"What's wrong?" Dan's breath hitched. "Is Mom sick?"

"Your mother is healthy." John's gruff voice filled the phone. "It's Oaklee."

"Oaklee is sick?"

"No. No. No. Three semesters left, and your sister chucks it all." His father's censure was laced with confusion. "That girl has no sense."

Oaklee had been attending a small university in Illinois. Dan had thought she was relatively happy there. "Why did she quit? I thought she'd finally found the right major."

His father snorted. "If you can call communication studies a major."

"She seemed happy enough."

"I was just happy she was getting a degree," his father conceded. "This fall, she complained about having 'issues' with one of the professors."

Dan couldn't stop the frown. Oaklee hadn't mentioned any professor problem to him. "What kind of issues?"

"She was convinced the man had it out for her."

Dan's fingers tightened around the phone. In his experience, most people liked Oaklee. His sister might be ditzy at times, but she was caring and kind. She'd do anything for a friend. Heck, even for a stranger. "What did he do? Did she say?"

"I don't know, Daniel." Resignation rang heavy in his father's voice. "You know Oaklee. She's so sensitive. If I had to guess, I'd say it was probably something as simple as coming down on her for a late assignment. What I do know is, until she gets her act together and goes back to school, she's not setting foot in my house."

"I realize she had trouble deciding on a major, but—"

"Trouble? The girl has changed her major four times. *Four*

times." John huffed out a breath. "You know what that means. Electives that no longer count. More classes needed to satisfy prerequisites. Money wasted."

Dan forced a conciliatory tone. "It takes time for some people to find themselves."

"The girl has been nothing but trouble since the day she learned to talk."

"C'mon, Dad. You don't mean that." It had to be frustration talking. His father loved Oaklee. The man just had difficulty understanding and accepting that not everyone followed a prescribed course in life.

Oaklee might be scattered and impulsive, but she had a good heart.

Silence filled the line for several long heartbeats.

"I meant every word I said to her." The condemnation and disappointment he heard reminded Dan of his father's reaction when he'd told him he was switching from engineering to theology.

"What does 'getting her act together' mean?"

"Back to school with a solid plan for the future."

In other words, a solid plan meeting John Marshall's approval. That didn't have to be said to be understood.

"Where is Oaklee now?"

The silence had Dan's heart skittering.

John cleared his throat. "Your mother thought, hoped, you'd know."

"I haven't heard from her." Dan gripped the phone. "If she shows up here, I won't turn her away."

She was his sister. He loved her. If Oaklee needed him, Dan would be there for her.

"Daniel, you need to be careful. Think of yourself. You can't risk Oaklee ruining your reputation if you hope to advance in your career. The girl needs to own her mistakes. You need to think of your future. It's time you seriously think about where—"

"Back to Oaklee." Dan had been on the receiving end of his father's career advice too many times to count. For now, they needed to focus on his sister. "When was the last time either of you heard from her?"

"Last week. She was staying with friends downtown. But when your mother reached out to one of them when Oaklee didn't answer her phone, they said she hadn't been there in three or four days. Your mother is frantic."

Dan was feeling a little panicked himself. Where could his free-spirited sister have gone? Despite being nearly twenty-one, Oaklee was naïve and trusting. "Have you thought about calling the police?"

"No." No explanation, just no.

Dan raked a hand through his hair. "I'm serious about checking with the police. We should call—"

"And tell them what? That my adult daughter has taken off on another crazy adventure and could they pretty please track her down for us?" His father's laugh had a rough edge. "I'll tell your mother you'll call if Oaklee contacts you."

"I will." Even as he promised, Dan wondered who he could reach out to who might know where his sister was staying. It hit him that he didn't know any of her friends. "Tell Mom I'll be praying for Oaklee's safety."

"If you speak with your sister, tell her to stop acting like a spoiled brat."

"I'll let her know you're worried." But the words were spoken into silence as Dan realized his father had already disconnected the call.

Dan called his sister's number right away. He frowned as the call went straight to voice mail Dan closed his eyes.

*Dear Lord, please let Oaklee know she's loved and bring her safely home. Amen.*

Before church tomorrow, he'd see if his mother had heard

from Oaklee. If she hadn't, he'd call the police himself and see if anything could be done to find his sister.

He did a few more stretches, then headed to the sidewalk. A killer playlist had his blood stirring and his feet on autopilot by the time he left his block.

Dan's normal route, a path that took him through Peninsula State Park, held little appeal. Ignoring the turnoff onto Shore Road, he veered in the opposite direction onto Wrigley Lane.

The sidewalk soon ended. Paved roads gave way to dirt and gravel. Scattered houses, in various states of disrepair, sat back from the road. A German shepherd, staked out in a yard that was more dirt than grass, pulled at the chain and barked furiously as Dan ran past.

He'd been down this road before when he'd visited an ailing congregation member. The woman, who'd been the same age as his mother, had passed away from cancer a few weeks later.

Dan thought of his mother. He'd check in with her this evening and see how she was holding up. Though she got frustrated with her daughter, Sandra Marshall had a soft heart. But in their household, what his father said went, and she wouldn't go against his wishes.

Which meant, unless—or until—his father changed his mind, Oaklee didn't have a home.

The houses soon yielded to rolling fields as Dan continued his steady pace, planning to go until the road dead-ended. He knew he was close when the Ding-A-Ling bar came into view. The two-story wooden structure sat alone, its large plate-glass windows gleaming in the morning sun.

With nothing around it for miles, it was as if a tornado had plucked up the building and set it down in the middle of nowhere.

As Dan drew close, he realized changes had been made since the last time he'd seen the structure. The sagging porch had been shored up, the peeling siding sanded and a fresh coat of red paint applied. A plastic sign, tied between two posts, advertised White Fish Wednesdays in bold black letters.

Jogging in place in front of the currently closed establishment, Dan lifted his gaze to the second-floor windows. Shortly after he'd first arrived in Good Hope, he'd been to a small wedding reception held in the "ballroom." Was that where Katie Ruth's date had played poker?

Dan didn't know Dexter Woodard, but at the moment he was having difficulty liking the man. Even if escorting Katie Ruth didn't qualify as a "real" date in Dexter's mind, he shouldn't have left her. As if deserting her wasn't bad enough, he'd made that hurtful crack about switching partners...

A muscle in Dan's jaw jumped. Katie Ruth might have laughed it off, but Dan had seen hurt in her eyes.

He didn't know any woman who exemplified Christian goodness more than Katie Ruth. She radiated kindness, love and compassion.

Dan would have been honored to escort her to Eliza's party. Why hadn't he asked her to go with him? They were, after all, both single and unattached.

After stretching again, Dan started back the way he'd come, the thought of dating Katie Ruth circling in his head. Three words pulsed in time to the music from his playlist.

*Ask her out. Ask her out.*

He pictured them arriving together at the pancake feed tonight. Saw them having lunch after Sunday services. Heard them laughing over a pizza at Bayside. Imagined them splitting a piece of pie at Muddy Boots.

Friends of hers were friends of his. Dating her made so much sense.

Except...

He'd been engaged just last summer. Would his congregation think he was moving too fast? He dismissed the thought as he reached the main road and turned left. Lindsay was married now. She'd be having a baby soon.

Only one obstacle remained. Katie Ruth worked for the church. While it wasn't in a paid capacity, she was in charge of the youth programs, and she volunteered at Mindy's Closet most Fridays. If things went south between them, it could make things awkward.

His shoes beat a rhythm against the gravel, matching the beat of his heart. Last night, he'd wanted to kiss her. If she'd given him the slightest bit of encouragement, he'd have wrapped his arms around her and pressed his mouth to—

Dan forced the image out of his head. He would call Katie Ruth and speak with her about last night. Not to ask her out—no, he wouldn't take that step, not yet—but to apologize for any awkwardness.

Simply thinking of hearing her voice brought a smile to his lips. A cheerful smile that lasted all the way home. Until he reached his house and saw his sister on his front porch.

CHAPTER FOUR

Dan's heart lodged in his throat. Oaklee scrambled to her feet and raised a hand in greeting. Pink hair shimmered in the rays of the morning sun.

Relief washed over him with the force of a tidal wave. He sprinted the last fifty feet. His baby sister was safe.

He'd been ten when Oaklee was born. His parents had tried for years to have a second child, and they'd been overjoyed when Oaklee made her appearance.

By the time the little girl reached kindergarten, his parents had begun to joke about a mix-up at the hospital. The flamboyant daughter of two conservatives, Oaklee loved fairy wings and belting out tunes from her favorite movies at the top of her voice. She craved the center stage spotlight.

Having such a loud, noisy, free-spirited child astonished John and Sandra Marshall. It was no different now that she was an adult. From her pink hair to the tat on her ankle, Oaklee continued to march to the beat of her own drum. It was something Dan admired about her.

Dan opened his arms. "I'm happy to see you."

Oaklee squealed—there really was no other word for the

sound—and dived into his arms. She smelled of strawberry shampoo and sunshine. He hugged her tight.

After a moment, she took a step back. Only then did Dan notice the shadows. Her smile might be bright, but fatigue edged her eyes.

His gaze searched her face

The siblings shared a smile.

She paused, perhaps waiting for him to mention the university. Maybe ask why she'd chucked it all when she was so close to graduating. Those were his father's worries, not his. Dan cared only that Oaklee was safe, that she was here, with him.

He would never turn her away. "Are you hungry?"

A familiar sparkle danced in her baby blues. "I could eat."

"Come inside. I'll change and then take you to Muddy Boots for a late breakfast." He pushed open the door and stepped aside to let her enter.

Surprise skittered across her face. "You didn't lock up?"

Dan shrugged. "I went for a quick run. It didn't seem necessary."

"Dad wouldn't approve." She waggled a finger at him. A smile tugged at the corners of her lips even as she tried to mimic his father's stern expression. "Someone could have opened the door and walked right in and stolen everything of value. You'd have only yourself to blame."

"True," Dan admitted. "But this way you could have walked in and made yourself at home."

"You're living on the edge, Pastor Marshall."

Dan chuckled, finding reassurance in the sisterly teasing. "I'd make something for you here, but I'm low on everything."

"It's Mom and Dad who enjoy dining at home." Oaklee wrinkled her nose. "Not me."

"Speaking of Mom and Dad." Dan slipped his phone from his jacket pocket and laid it carefully on the side table. "They're worried about you."

A shutter dropped, and the light left his sister's eyes. "Mom, maybe. Dad, not so much."

How to answer that honestly without being hurtful? Dan searched for the right words. "They love you, Oaklee. Both of them."

A shrug was her only response.

"I'd appreciate it if you'd give Mom a quick call while I change. Let her know you're okay and you're with me."

"For how long?" Oaklee asked.

Dan cocked his head.

"How long can I stay?"

He met her questioning gaze with a firm one of his own. "As long as you want."

～

"You kissed the minister?"

Too late, Katie Ruth realized she should have stuck to the reason for the lunch—discussing possible youth program changes at First Christian. Valentine's Day should have stayed off the table.

"Would you please stop referring to Dan as 'the minister'?" Izzie's insistence on all the deets, once Katie Ruth had mentioned the party, had caused Katie Ruth to say more than she planned. "And no one kissed anyone. I simply said for one brief crazy second on the porch, I *thought* about kissing him."

And, Katie Ruth admitted, he might have wanted to kiss her.

Izzie impatiently pushed back the corkscrew piece of hair that had come loose and now hung in her face. The rest of her unruly mass of brown curls had been pulled back and secured with a leather tie. "Thinking about doing something isn't nearly as exciting as doing it."

Katie Ruth only shrugged.

The hand the local artist held up had long, artistic fingers with nails cut short. "Let me see if I've got this straight. You and *Dan* have this physical attraction thing going, but you haven't acted on it."

Hearing that didn't sit right either. "The attraction may have been only on my part. I probably got caught up in the romance of the evening. Yes, I'm sure that's what happened. I misread the signals."

Izzie rolled her eyes. "Yeah, that's what happened."

"Seriously. The full moon. The citrusy scent of his cologne. I imagined the chemistry." Katie Ruth pushed the breakfast burrito aside, remembering how her insides had quivered when she'd stood beside him on her porch.

"He wants you." When Katie Ruth began shaking her head, Izzie gestured with one hand. "Look at you. What man wouldn't be interested?"

"Dexter, for one." Katie Ruth gazed down at her plate once again, but still couldn't summon an appetite. "He found a game of poker more appealing than me."

"Some men are stupid." Izzie's tone brooked no argument. "And blind."

Katie Ruth let her gaze drift to the mural of a girl in a raincoat kicking up rain. Izzie had painted the scene shortly after she'd arrived in town several years back.

"You and the minister are a perfect match." Izzie's tone turned contemplative as she continued, swirling a fry through a mound of ketchup. "Which is why I think you messed up."

"Pardon me?"

"You shouldn't have waited for him to make the first move. If you wanted to kiss him, you should have done it."

"What? No."

"Think about it. If you had, you wouldn't be sitting here wondering if he likes you." Izzie lifted the ketchup-soaked fry and grinned. "You'd know."

~

After Oaklee finished calling their mother, Dan suggested they walk to the café, rather than drive. It wasn't far, and he hoped the exercise would burn off some of Oaklee's tension.

They started down the sidewalk, and he braced for the chatter that was sure to come. When Oaklee remained silent—a first for her—Dan picked up the conversation reins. "Mom said she hadn't heard from you. Why hadn't you called her?"

Oaklee knew as well as he did that their mother was the worrier in the family.

"I stepped on my phone last week." Oaklee lifted her shoulders, let them drop. "It's dead. Gone to heaven and not coming back."

Dan smiled. "I'm glad you could reassure her that you're okay."

"Yeah, she seemed glad to hear from me." Oaklee's voice held puzzlement.

"Why does that surprise you? You know she worries about you."

"She's been different since the protest last fall."

Dan hadn't made it home for either Thanksgiving or Christmas this year, but he'd spoken with his parents numerous times. Neither his mom nor his dad had mentioned Oaklee and a recent protest. "What happened?"

"The event was in the Shedd Aquarium parking lot."

"That location practically guaranteed prime news coverage." Dan hated to ask, but he had to know. "Were you naked?"

It had been Oaklee's part in a PETA wool protest two years earlier that his parents couldn't seem to forget, or forgive.

"Not this time. I had on this beautiful green mermaid suit." Oaklee smiled. "I was hung several feet off the ground with hooks through my mermaid skin."

What did it say that he could easily picture the scene? "What were you protesting?"

Oaklee was actively involved with a number of organizations, all good causes in Dan's opinion, although the actions of a few of the groups could be a bit extreme.

"It was a PETA event. We were urging the public not to eat aquatic animals." Oaklee appeared truly perplexed. "I still don't understand why Mom got so bent out of shape."

It was puzzling to Dan as well. "They never mentioned anything about it to me."

Oaklee sighed. "It was the topic du jour over the holiday."

"The only thing Dad mentioned was something about you having problems with a professor."

Oaklee's expression went blank. For a young woman so expressive, it was a red flag.

"I'm not going back to college," Oaklee finally responded when the silence stretched. "I won't have to deal with him again. Problem solved."

Dan frowned. "Was getting away from him the reason you quit school?"

Oaklee waved an airy hand, the rings that bedecked every finger catching the light. "I decided not to return for many reasons. Oh, look, we're here. You were right. It wasn't far." Relief flashed across Oaklee's face at the sight of the crisp blue awning with the trademark red boots.

"Beck had the inside of Muddy Boots totally updated a couple years ago," Dan informed his sister as he reached around her to open the door to the café.

The second Dan stepped inside, he saw Katie Ruth. Seated in a booth with Izzie Deshler, she looked up as the bells over the door jingled.

Dan smiled and lifted a hand in greeting.

Katie Ruth offered a return smile before refocusing on the woman across from her.

When Dan turned back to his sister, he caught her curious stare.

"Who's she?"

Dan waited until they were seated at a table to answer. "Two women from church. The one with the curly hair is Izzie Deshler. She's a local artist. In fact, she's the one who painted the mural."

Dan gestured toward the wall where a girl holding an umbrella kicked up water.

"She's talented."

Oaklee nodded, appeared impressed. "And the blonde?"

"Katie Ruth Crewes. Katie Ruth is my volunteer youth director at First Christian."

Dan was spared the need to say more when Helen, an older woman with hair as orange as her lipstick, shuffled over. She passed out menus and took their drink orders.

For the next few minutes, Dan kept his eyes on the menu and off Katie Ruth. When Helen returned, they ordered.

Helen paused, her pencil poised above the notepad, and studied Oaklee. "Let me make sure I've got this. You want whipped cream with your fries?"

Oaklee nodded and flashed the woman a sunny smile. "Is that a problem?"

"No problem." Helen scribbled, then shoved the nub of a pencil behind her ear. "Shouldn't take long."

"This is an interesting place." Oaklee cast an admiring glance at a nearby wall. "I'm guessing these splashes of blue paint on the white walls are rain."

"That was the intent, I believe." Dan took a sip of coffee, conscious of Oaklee's assessing gaze.

"You're happy here." His sister smiled softly.

"I am," Dan agreed. "For now, anyway."

Oaklee shook her head. "Dad has gotten to you, hasn't he? I can hear him now. 'Daniel, you are not living up to your potential.'"

He had to admit she did a darned good imitation of their father's imperious tone.

"Dad feels that now that I have several years of experience, I need to be actively seeking a transfer to a larger congregation. One that would allow me to soar with my strengths."

"Is that what you want?"

"There's nothing keeping me in Good Hope." Dan resisted the sudden urge to glance in Katie Ruth's direction.

He might have dismissed his father's advice if it didn't make so much sense.

Oaklee lifted the plastic glass and gulped soda, her gaze never leaving his face.

The intensity in her gaze made Dan want to squirm.

"You almost had a wife. I never even got a chance to meet her." The accusation in her tone stung because it was justified.

Even as the wedding had drawn close, Dan hadn't taken Lindsay home to Illinois. He'd also made excuses why it wasn't a good time for his family to visit. He wondered if he'd kept them apart because he'd had doubts about Lindsay and their upcoming nuptials.

He realized now just how much his actions had hurt his sister and his parents.

"I'm sure Lindsay and her husband will be at the pancake supper at church tonight." Dan gestured with his coffee cup. "You can meet her then."

Oaklee partially removed the wrapper from her straw. "I'd love to meet the Jezebel who captured my brother's heart then broke it."

It hadn't been like that, Dan wanted to say, but swallowed the words. He liked Lindsay, respected her, but she hadn't totally captured his heart. And in the week after the breakup, he'd realized what he felt was more relief than heartbreak.

Without warning, Oaklee blew on the straw and shot the paper across the table.

Dan jerked back when it struck him in the cheek.

His sister laughed like a loon.

He crushed the paper between his fingers, picturing Oaklee's reaction when she caught sight of Lindsay. If he didn't prepare Oaklee, his sister might do—or say—something to embarrass everyone.

Dan waited while Helen set down their food and moved away.

"You know Lindsay is married." Dan kept his tone easy. "You should also know she's pregnant. She and her husband are expecting a baby girl at the end of next month."

"A baby?" Oaklee cocked her head, obviously intrigued. "Is it yours?"

"No."

"How can you be sure?"

For a second, Dan wondered what universe he was in that over burgers and fries and, yes, whipped cream, he was discussing his sex life—or lack therein—at a café table with his sister. "Lindsay and I were never...intimate."

"Get out of here." Oaklee gave a belly laugh so loud it drew the attention of a couple at a nearby table.

"Oaklee." Dan spoke sharply and realized in that moment he sounded like his father.

His sister lowered her voice and appeared contrite. "Well, I suppose the no-sex thing worked out. Though I wonder how much you really liked her if you could date her all that time and not do the deed."

For one crazy second, Dan thought about asking his sister if she'd ever "done the deed." He decided he didn't want to know. He couldn't change Oaklee's past choices, but he hoped to influence future ones.

"I'm a minister," Dan reminded his sister. "I preach abstinence before marriage."

"Rock and a hard place. I guess—" Oaklee stopped midsentence. "Hey, they're leaving. Oops, not so quickly."

Dan slanted a quick glance and saw Katie Ruth and Izzie at the register, speaking with Beck.

Dressed in a formfitting black sweater and a pair of psychedelic paisley pants, Izzie fit the artist's look to a t.

Katie Ruth's long-sleeved shirt that zipped up the front, coupled with leggings and running shoes, had him wondering where she was headed.

Dan frowned when Dexter and his parents passed by on their way to a table. Instead of continuing on with his mom and dad, Dexter motioned them forward and paused by Katie Ruth.

Whatever the man said to her had her taking a few steps to the side to speak with him. They spoke for less than a minute—with him doing most of the talking—before he joined his parents.

What had Dexter said to her? Dan narrowed his gaze. Katie Ruth didn't appear upset as she returned to Izzie and Beck.

She laughed at something Beck said, and though her lips held no cherry gloss, Dan found his gaze drawn to her mouth.

"Your youth director is smokin' hot and stylin' in those skin pants."

Dan jerked his gaze back to his sister.

Oaklee's smile turned sly, and a blind man couldn't have missed the speculative gleam. "If she'd been your fiancée, I bet you wouldn't have been able to keep your hands off her."

"Oaklee." He growled the warning.

She smirked.

"Our lives are filled with temptation. It's not a sin to be tempted," Dan explained. "The sin is to yield to temptation."

"Spoken like a minister." Oaklee rolled her eyes. "You like her. You should ask her out."

"Katie Ruth is a wonderful woman." Dan absently picked up a fry and dipped it into the bowl of whipped cream. "She's very active in the church."

To his surprise, Oaklee's expression turned serious. "You're concerned you might mess up that church relationship if you date her."

"I am."

"It's a valid concern." Oaklee swiped a fry through the whipped cream. "I still think you should do it." His sister laughed at her own joke. "Date her, I mean. Not have sex with her. Unless, of course—"

"It wouldn't be a smart move."

"Katie Ruth may be a fixture at the church, but you're not her boss. And she's not yours." Oaklee leaned forward, looking more like a grown-up than a child. "You're both adults with free will. Playing it safe is boring. Ask her out. See where it goes. Besides—"

Oaklee took a noisy sip of soda through the straw.

"Besides…" he prompted.

"You've already gone through one messy public breakup." Oaklee smiled. "No way could this be worse."

CHAPTER FIVE

While Katie Ruth worked out at the Y, she went back and forth on whether to attend the pancake supper at the church that evening. She was still wavering when she ran into Gladys. The older woman strolled inside while Katie Ruth was on her way out.

"I didn't expect to see you here." Though there were plenty of programs for seniors at the Y, Katie Ruth knew Gladys usually preferred classes at the Living Center's fitness center.

"Several of us community theater veterans are starting a theater arts for kids program." Gladys patted a bulging canvas bag the color of a ripe eggplant. "Stage Makeup 101 starts this afternoon."

"The class sounds interesting. What ages are you targeting?"

"Anywhere from—" From somewhere deep in Gladys's purse came a tone that Katie Ruth recognized as the *Iron Man* theme.

Katie Ruth lifted a brow.

Gladys chuckled. "My warning ring. Fifteen minutes to show time."

Katie Ruth stepped to the side as a group of giggling teens hurried past. "Well, I won't keep you. Good luck with the class."

"Thank you." Gladys waved her free hand. "I'll tell you all about it tonight."

Katie Ruth's confusion must have shown, because Gladys added, "The pancake feed?"

"Oh, I wasn't planning to go." Something in Gladys's piercing gaze had Katie Ruth stumbling to explain. "It's been one of those crazy days. I was up late last night, and I've been going nonstop since early this morning."

When Gladys remained silent, Katie Ruth emitted a nervous-sounding laugh. "I still need to do some editing on the Open Door newsletter before it goes out tomorrow morning."

Gladys's gaze narrowed. "You're not going to the pancake supper?"

Katie Ruth blinked. Wasn't that what she'd just said? "There will be so many people there, I doubt anyone will miss me."

"Social events that promote fellowship are more enjoyable with close friends." Gladys placed a gentle hand on Katie Ruth's arm. "Dan will miss you if you don't come."

*Would he?* Katie Ruth thought of the pink-haired woman he'd been with at Muddy Boots. Even from a distance, she'd sensed a connection between the two and found herself fighting a twinge of jealousy.

Would the mystery woman be with him at the pancake supper? She supposed there was only one way to find out. "You make a good point."

"Plus, what about all the teens from the youth group? Won't they expect to see you there? How will they feel if their leader didn't think spending time with them was important?

Katie Ruth knew she didn't stand a chance against such logic. She nodded. "I'll be there."

～

That evening, Katie Ruth made the mistake of waving a little too wildly and rushing to greet Dan the instant she spotted him. She skidded to a stop when she saw the pink-haired young woman step to his side.

Schooling her features, Katie Ruth extended a hand. "I don't believe we've met. I'm Katie Ruth Crewes."

Now that she was closer, Katie Ruth noticed the stone in the girl's nose matched the pink in her hair.

"I'm Dan's sister, Oaklee." The girl, more girl than woman, smiled brightly. "I've heard all about you from my brother."

*Sister.* Katie Ruth expelled the breath she hadn't realized she'd been holding. She slanted a quick glance in Dan's direction.

"We nearly met at the café," Oaklee continued before her brother could speak. "You and your friend scurried out like your toes were on fire. Why didn't you come over to our table and say hello?"

Though Dan said nothing, Katie Ruth watched him shift from one foot to the other.

Katie Ruth met Oaklee's gaze with an equally direct one of her own. "Izzie and I didn't want to interrupt your meal."

"I suppose that's a good enough excuse." With an ease Katie Ruth envied, Oaklee shifted gears. "You're seriously cute. Blond hair, big blue eyes and a killer figure. Are you currently dating anyone? I saw that hot guy approach you in the café. Are you interested in him?"

"Oaklee." Dan's warning had his sister grinning.

"Wow." His sister lifted her hands. "You should have told me there's a rule against asking a few simple questions."

"No rules." Katie Ruth liked Dan's brash sister. Something about the girl reminded her of Gladys. "I don't have a boyfriend. The guy in the café is just an old friend from high school. And no, I'm not interested in dating him."

When Oaklee opened her mouth, Katie Ruth rushed on. She much preferred to be the one doing the interrogating than the one on the hot seat. "I had a friend in college with hair your color. It's very pretty. The tats are interesting."

In addition to one on the girl's ankle, Katie Ruth spotted another on her arm. "Do *you* have a boyfriend?"

Oaklee's smile vanished. "No." Her voice had gone flat.

There was a story here, Katie Ruth thought, but she didn't press. She shifted her gaze to Dan. "You didn't tell me your sister would be visiting."

Once again, Oaklee didn't give him a chance to comment.

"He didn't know. I showed up on his doorstep." The smile remained on Oaklee's lips, but the light in her eyes dimmed. "I'm not visiting, I'm staying. My parents kicked me out."

This was a minefield. Katie Ruth went with as neutral a reply as she could muster. "You came to a good place."

Dan slung an arm around his sister's shoulders. "I'm looking forward to having her here with me."

He sounded sincere, but Katie Ruth knew having a sister living with him would be an adjustment. Dan lived and breathed the ministry. Being willing to take on the additional responsibility of a college-age sister spoke to his character.

"You're going to love Good Hope." Katie Ruth hoped that would be the case. Though she couldn't imagine living anywhere else, whether life on the peninsula would be a good fit for Oaklee remained to be seen.

"I'm super excited to get acquainted." Oaklee met Katie Ruth's cheery smile with a sly one of her own. "I'd like us to be friends."

"I'd like that, too." Out of the corner of her eye, Katie Ruth saw Dan's ex-fiancée and her husband strolling their way, fingers linked.

She tried to think of a way to warn Lindsay and Owen, but they were too busy gazing into each other's eyes to notice the shark-infested waters ahead.

"Owen. Lindsay." Dan's voice might have been a little too

hearty, but it sounded genuine and welcoming. "I'd like you to meet my sister."

"OMG, you're the former fiancée." Oaklee stared, her mouth gaping open at the sight of Lindsay's big belly. "You really are pregnant."

Lindsay made a great show of glancing down. Her eyes went wide. "Why, yes, I guess I am."

Owen's gaze seemed fixed on Oaklee's cotton-candy-colored hair.

Lindsay extended her hand. "I'm Lindsay Vaughn. This is my husband, Owen."

Oaklee shook Lindsay's hand. "Oaklee Marshall."

"I'm pleased to meet you, Oaklee."

Oaklee's gaze turned speculative as it lingered on Owen.

It was, Katie Ruth thought, a bit like seeing a train wreck coming, but being unable to look away.

"You're the guy who knocked up my brother's fiancée."

"Oaklee."

Katie Ruth wasn't certain if the name and horrified hiss came from Dan or from her.

"That's me." Owen's hand settled possessively on his wife's protruding belly.

Oaklee's gaze shifted from Owen to Lindsay. "You're happy about the baby?"

"Deliriously happy." Lindsay responded, and she exchanged a smile with her husband.

"Good." Oaklee appeared to be deliberately avoiding looking in her brother's direction. "That's how it should be."

When Oaklee tapped a finger against her lips, Katie Ruth realized with sudden horror that the train still had some track to cover.

"I think the fact that you and Lindsay couldn't keep your hands off each other bodes well for your marriage."

Lindsay laughed as if having a young woman—someone she'd just met—comment on her sex life was an everyday occurrence.

It was Owen who steered the train down another track.

"My daughter was crazy about all things pink." Owen's lips curved. "She'd have loved your hair."

"Your daughter has great taste." Oaklee glanced around as if looking for a girl in pink. "Is she here? I'd like to meet her."

Dan's and Katie Ruth's gazes locked.

Owen cleared his throat. "Mindy passed away last year."

"She's dead?" Tears filled Oaklee's eyes. "How horrible. What happened? How did she—?"

Dan grabbed his sister's arm and called over his shoulder as he pulled Oaklee away, "Great seeing you both."

Katie Ruth nodded to Owen and Lindsay, before hurrying after Dan and his sister.

Once they were out of earshot, Dan came to an abrupt stop. "What the…what was that about?"

He ground the words out between clenched teeth, his eyes sharply focused on his sister.

If Oaklee thought her wide-eyed look was going to fool her brother, she didn't know him well at all.

"Don't give me that innocent look. You know very well what I'm talking about." Dan closed his eyes briefly as he fought for control.

"I-I didn't know his daughter died." Oaklee held up her hands as if in supplication. "How could I know?"

Dan blew out a breath. "I'm not talking about Mindy."

Katie Ruth couldn't recall the last time she'd seen Dan this upset.

"I live here, Oaklee. I work here. Not just any job. I'm the pastor." Hurt mingled with the controlled anger in his voice. "What are you trying to do to me?"

"Nothing." Oaklee touched his arm and appeared genuinely puzzled. "I was making conversation."

"Making conversation would be asking about their jobs or the baby." A muscle in Dan's jaw jumped. "Casual conversation is not bringing up a couple's sex life when you've just met them."

Katie Ruth sensed Oaklee still wasn't grasping the significance. She hadn't a clue why her brother was so upset. "As Dan's sister, your actions reflect on him."

"I'm sorry." Oaklee reached out and clasped her brother's hand. "The last thing I want to do is tank your chances for a promotion. I want you to be able to move to that bigger congregation, if that's what you really want."

Katie Ruth tried not to let her shock show. This was the first she'd heard Dan might be considering a move.

It shouldn't have surprised her. He was an excellent preacher and had stellar administrative and people skills. Still, she'd thought he was content in Good Hope.

"This isn't about me." Dan's gaze never left his sister's face. "Your questions—your comments—put Lindsay and Owen on the spot."

"I'll apologize. I'll track them down and tell them I'm so, so sorry. I'll throw myself at their feet and beg for forgiveness."

Katie Ruth assumed the girl was speaking figuratively about throwing herself at their feet, but from what she'd seen so far of Oaklee, she couldn't be sure.

Oaklee whirled and would have sprinted off, but Dan grabbed her arm.

"They're visiting with friends. Enjoying pancakes." His tone remained low and tightly controlled. "Please don't make things worse by interrupting."

Oaklee hung her head.

At that moment, Katie Ruth realized she didn't belong here. This was a private matter between Dan and his sister.

Over Dan's left shoulder, she spotted Kyle and Eliza at the refreshment table. "It was nice meeting you, Oaklee. I'm sure I'll see you around. Right now, I'm off to do some mingling."

"Can I go with you?" Oaklee was at Katie Ruth's side in a heartbeat. Her smile wavered, and her eyes pleaded. "I think my brother could use a break."

"Oaklee, you don't invite—"

"It's okay." Katie Ruth waved aside Dan's protest. He'd rescued her at the Valentine's party. She'd return the favor. "I'm happy to introduce her around."

Oaklee shot a triumphant look at her brother before linking her arm with Katie Ruth's. "Who shall we target first?"

"Remember what I said," Dan warned.

The jaunty wave she gave her brother seemed to do little to relieve his worry. His brows were still furrowed when Katie Ruth, with Oaklee now glued to her side, stepped away.

"We can start by saying hello to Eliza and Kyle Kendrick." Katie Ruth gestured to where the dark-haired beauty and her husband stood getting more coffee.

"She looks like she could be a mean one." Oaklee galloped— really it was the only word to describe the loping gait—toward the couple.

"Eliza is extremely smart." The fact that the business owner and executive director of the Women's Events League— commonly known as the Cherries—could sometimes be, well, *stern,* was an impression Katie Ruth kept to herself.

"Eliza. Kyle," Katie Ruth called out over the din of conversation.

Other than the burnt-orange scarf looped stylishly around her neck, Eliza wore all black. It suited her fair complexion and dark hair.

"I wanted to thank you for the marvelous Valentine's party the other night. The food and the atmosphere were amazing." Katie Ruth realized she was gushing and pulled back. "I appreciated being invited."

"I'm glad you and Dan enjoyed yourselves." Kyle slung an arm around his wife.

Katie Ruth caught the startled look Oaklee shot her, but ignored it. She didn't correct Kyle. After all, she'd spent nearly the entire evening with Dan. Most people probably assumed they'd come together.

Eliza settled cool gray eyes on the girl at Katie Ruth's side. "Who is this with you?"

"Oaklee Marshall." The girl extended her hand. "Dan's sister."

"I didn't realize the pastor had a sister." Eliza's gaze took in the pink hair, the tattoo and the nose stud. "You're very different from your brother."

Oaklee flashed a smile. "I'm a limited edition."

Eliza arched a brow. "Pardon?"

"I like to say I'm a Froot Loop in a bowl of Cheerios. Being unique makes life more interesting, don't you think?" Not waiting for Eliza to respond, Oaklee continued. "It'd be boring if we were all alike."

Kyle chuckled. "Very true. My sister and I are very different."

Oaklee glanced around as if trying to spot the woman. "Is your sister here?"

"Lolo doesn't live in Good Hope. She's back in Kentucky with my parents."

"Lolo." Oaklee rolled the name around on her tongue. "I like her already. I believe if your sister lived here, we'd be friends."

Kyle smiled. "A good possibility. Lolo is very artistic."

Oaklee cocked her head. "You and your wife are solidly mainstream. That doesn't mean we can't be friends. We're all unique and beautiful in our own way."

"You're forthright." Eliza studied the girl as if she were an interesting specimen under a microscope. "You say what you think. I admire that quality."

Oaklee brushed a strand of pink hair back from her face. "My dad says I lack a filter."

"I've been told that, too, by my own father." Eliza smiled

briefly. "In my situation, I don't believe it was meant as a compliment."

Oaklee grinned.

Katie Ruth could tell Eliza had taken a huge jump in the girl's estimation.

"Tell me what you think of Katie Ruth." Oaklee gestured with one hand toward her. "No filter."

Katie Ruth stiffened.

"You want to know what I think." Eliza slanted a glance in Katie Ruth's direction. "In what regard?"

"I'm thinking she'd make a good friend. Can you vouch for her character?"

"Why would you take my word?" Eliza's expression turned cool. "Wouldn't it be easier to simply ask your brother?"

"He's a minister. He says good things about everyone. Back to Katie Ruth." Oaklee gestured impatiently. "Thumbs up or down?"

"Thumbs up." Eliza frowned. "I don't believe this conversation is appropriate, considering the person we're discussing is standing right here."

"Better than talking behind her back." Oaklee shrugged. "Besides, odds are you wouldn't have invited her to your Valentine's party if you didn't like her."

"Dan." Relief skittered across Kyle's face at the sight of the minister.

"We've been having the most delightful conversation with your sister." Eliza cast a pointed look at Oaklee.

"Really?" Dan looked cautiously pleased.

"Eliza gave Katie Ruth the thumbs-up," Oaklee informed him.

Dan's gaze shot to Katie Ruth.

"Don't ask." Katie Ruth held up her hands. "Seriously, it's all good."

"There's Lindsay and Owen. They're finally alone." Oaklee's eyes lit up like a kid seeing presents under the tree on Christmas morning. "It's apology time."

"Oaklee. Wait. No." As Dan started after his sister, Katie Ruth had to chuckle.

She might have spoken too soon. *All good?*

Something told Katie Ruth that his pink-haired sister was about to turn Dan's life upside down.

# CHAPTER SIX

Though Oaklee seemed to have disappeared, Dan tried not to worry. He told himself his sister was here...somewhere.

He didn't look for her, knowing she couldn't go far without a car. The truth was, Dan was glad for the breathing room.

He ate pancakes and bacon. He chatted with members of the community and those from his congregation. Once he was through eating, he assisted the volunteers in charge of clearing the long rectangular tables of discarded plates and cups.

He hadn't caught her before she reached Owen and Lindsay. Thankfully, the two had taken her heartfelt apology, awkward as it was, in the spirit in which it was offered. He was grateful she hadn't thrown herself at their feet, although for an instant that seemed a distinct possibility.

"How's my favorite minister?"

A smile formed on his lips at the sound of Katie Ruth's voice. He turned and leaned back against the table he'd just cleared. "We've had an amazing turnout. Not just members of the congregation, but quite a few from the community. When we put this event together, outreach was one of our top goals. Hopefully, some of those who don't have a church home will now give First Christian a try."

Dan realized he was rambling. She'd asked a simple question, and he'd given her a dissertation.

He hadn't spoken with Katie Ruth since Oaklee had sprinted toward Owen and Lindsay with him in hot pursuit. Each time he looked for her, she'd been in deep conversation with someone. The last time it had been with Gladys. As he passed by the two women, he'd caught a few words. Kids. Theater. Trash.

"How's your evening going?" Dan asked, forcing a casual tone.

"I'm enjoying the fellowship." An elusive dimple he hadn't known Katie Ruth possessed flashed in her left cheek. "I introduced Oaklee to Gladys. I think the two are headed down the Yellow Brick BFF Road."

Dan pretended to shiver. "I can only imagine the schemes they'll concoct."

Katie Ruth laughed and thrust out a hand. "I thought you might like a cup of coffee."

For the first time, Dan saw she held a white Styrofoam cup in each hand. He took the one she held out. "Thank you very much."

That enticing dimple made a return appearance. "You're welcome very much."

Dan gestured with the cup, determined not to ramble. "This is nice."

At her questioning look, he continued. "You and me. Together. I enjoyed spending time with you last night at the party."

She smiled. "I enjoyed it, too."

A companionable silence descended as they sipped their coffee. They stood close enough to touch, but not touching. Still, as Dan inhaled the sweet floral scent of her perfume, he remembered last night and how much he'd wanted to kiss her.

"Did you really have no idea Oaklee was arriving today?"

Hearing his sister's name was like a splash of cold water. The tension that had eased from Dan's shoulders returned with a vengeance. He took another sip of the coffee he no longer wanted. "Her appearance on my doorstep was a total surprise."

As he spoke, he scanned the room. He thought he spotted his sister's pink hair near the pancake station. He wondered if she was troubling the volunteers, then reminded himself—again— that Oaklee wasn't a child he had to supervise.

"Do you have a minute to talk?"

She smiled. "For you, I have lots of minutes."

Dan pulled out a metal chair and motioned for Katie Ruth to take a seat. When she did, he dropped into the chair beside her. "Oaklee might be turning twenty-one soon, but she still has a lot of growing up to do. She doesn't seem to have a clue what she wants to do with her life."

Something that looked like empathy filled Katie Ruth's eyes. "Lots of kids don't at that age."

"Since starting college, she's changed her major *four* times." Dan set down his cup and raked a hand through his hair. "Now, with only three semesters left, she's refusing to go back and finish."

Instead of automatically condemning the decision as a stupid move, the way his father had, Katie Ruth hesitated for several heartbeats before responding.

"Since I work a lot with kids, I've done some reading on this particular age group. The time between ages eighteen and twenty-two is when young people start to build a sense of self. Oaklee is searching for her identity. She's discovering who she is, deep down." Katie Ruth's voice held no judgment. "She may act out, may even go down a wrong path or two, until she figures out the right road for her. All completely normal."

Dan admired Katie Ruth's generosity of spirit. He knew she was trying to be supportive of his sister's struggles, and he appreciated her giving Oaklee a pass for her bad behavior earlier.

Katie Ruth cocked her head and studied him for several seconds. "Did you always know you wanted to be a minister?"

"Hardly." Dan chuckled. "I was a chemical engineering major through my junior year."

It suddenly struck him that he'd been the same age as Oaklee when he'd stepped back and taken a good look at what was really important to him. Not to his parents. But to *him*.

A smile tugged at the corners of Katie Ruth's lips.

"What?"

She lifted a shoulder, let it drop, as the smile blossomed. "I'm having difficulty picturing you as an engineer."

"I enjoy math and science."

"I'm sure you're good at any number of things, but you're too much of a people person for engineering." She patted his arm. "You made the right choice. I truly believe the ministry is where you were meant to be."

Emotion squeezed his heart. It took Dan several seconds to find his voice. His parents tolerated what they called his "career choice," but he knew they thought he could do so much better. "Thank you."

"It may take time, but I believe your sister will also find her rightful place in the world."

"I hope so."

Katie Ruth gazed over his shoulder and offered an apologetic smile. "You'll have to excuse me. Gladys assigned me trash duty. By the way she's pointing at the garbage cans then at me, it's clear she wants me to do my job."

He frowned. "Who's helping you?"

"It's really a one-person job."

A one-*man* job, Dan thought, but didn't say.

He couldn't believe Gladys expected Katie Ruth to carry bulging sacks of refuse outside to the dumpsters at night. By herself. "I'll take care of it."

Katie Ruth shook her head, her chin lifting in a stubborn tilt.

"It's my responsibility."

She held up a hand when he opened his mouth. "That isn't to say I wouldn't accept help if a kind gentleman offered."

Gladys smiled brightly when Katie Ruth and Dan approached. Her pale eyes gleamed when Dan grabbed two sacks of trash, leaving only one for Katie Ruth. "I see you picked up a partner."

"Dan insisted on helping." Katie Ruth shot him a wink and impulsively gave him a hip bump.

He grinned. "You're going to make me drop one of these sacks.

"Just as I thought," the older woman murmured before she turned to Cory White, a local teacher who was manning the griddle. "Keep those pancakes coming."

"Just as you thought?" Katie Ruth asked, not sure if the older woman had been speaking to her or Cory.

Gladys ignored the question and draped an arm around Katie Ruth's shoulders. "There is absolutely no need to rush back. Take all the time you need. I've got things under control here."

By the time they reached the stairs, Dan swore he heard Oaklee's laughter mingle with Gladys's unmistakable cackle.

He and Katie Ruth took their time, talking about pancakes and orange versus grapefruit juice as they lugged sacks to the main floor. Once outside, they made quick work of disposing of the trash, with Dan insisting on hefting the bags into the dumpster.

The cold breeze had them heading back inside. As they made their way down the hall, Dan slowed his steps, wanting to prolong his time with Katie Ruth. And to be completely honest, he wasn't in any hurry to return to his sister. While he understood what Katie Ruth had said about Oaklee just needing time to find herself, her attitude continued to gnaw at him.

Katie Ruth was halfway to the steps leading downstairs when she appeared to realize he was no longer beside her. She turned back, puzzlement blanketing her face.

Dan motioned to her. He valued Katie Ruth's opinion. If he was off base, she'd tell him. "If you have a minute, I'd like to ask you something."

She offered a cautious smile as she approached him. "Sure. What is it?"

Dan jammed his hands into his pockets and blew out a breath. "I know Oaklee's behavior is natural, but I'm so frustrated with her. I know she's a smart girl and a thoughtful person. I just wish she could see how her actions can affect others, often hurtfully.

"It's a weakness we all share to some degree." Katie Ruth's lips lifted in a rueful smile. "My parents are very astute, but I don't think they ever fully realized how much their scandal impacted me."

"This is different. You were a child and not responsible for your parents' bad decisions." Fearing he'd been too blunt, Dan gentled his tone. "To be fair, it sounded like your parents did think about you, which is why they didn't have parties with people from Good Hope."

"Perhaps."

"Oaklee is making, has made, reckless decisions without considering how those decisions impact her future." Dan tried, but failed, to keep the disappointment from his voice. "As a minister and her big brother, I won't turn her away, but I can't just ignore her bad behavior."

"Remember, she may look like an adult, but she's still grow-ing, still learning." Katie Ruth expelled a breath. "Most of us make mistakes on our journey to adulthood."

"I can't imagine you ever doing any of the crazy things Oaklee has done." He shook his head. "She took off all her clothes for a PETA protest against wool and ran naked through Grant Park. Who does that?"

"Apparently, your sister." Katie Ruth's light tone belied the serious look in her eyes. "Like I said, we all make mistakes and do things we regret. I have regrets. Lots of them."

She took a breath. "When I was her age, I—"

Dan stopped her attempt to make him feel better about her sister by closing his hands around hers. "I admire you, Katie Ruth. Not just for all the good work you do in the community and for the church, but for the person you are. You're kind and honest. And you're incredibly beautiful."

"I like being with you, Dan. I think we're good for each other." Her husky voice, or maybe it was the admission, stirred something in him.

Dan let his gaze drop to her generous mouth, to the lips shiny with gloss.

Still, he jolted when he felt her arms slide around his neck.

She gazed up at him, her eyes dark and swirling with emotion. "Last night on my porch, I wanted you to kiss me. I was disappointed when you didn't."

He'd wanted to, but had held back. Concerned he was moving too fast. Concerned about propriety. Concerned about so many things that, at the moment, no longer seemed important.

Katie Ruth was right. Everyone made mistakes. He wouldn't make the mistake of overthinking again.

When Katie Ruth had talked about it with Izzie, she'd nearly convinced herself she'd blown the connection she shared with Dan out of proportion.

Seeing him tonight confirmed that the flame of attraction that flickered the night of the Valentine's party burned as hot as ever. She tried to not think about the disapproval in his eyes when he'd talked about his sister's reckless behavior.

Katie Ruth reminded herself that her own crazy behavior was in the past. Back then, she'd been desperately searching for who she was and what she wanted out of life. It hadn't taken her long to realize being a party girl wasn't for her. She knew now that—

Dan's mouth closed over hers, stilling the regrets and fanning the flames.

In seconds, the smoldering fire burned out of control. Katie Ruth grasped his shirt in her fingers. She wanted to be closer, wanted to feel his skin against hers, to—

Dan turned his head from her mouth, his breath coming in harsh pants. "We have to stop." He took her shoulders and stepped back. "There's this crazy electricity between us." The finger that he trailed down her cheek wasn't quite steady. "A powerful magnetic pull. Do you feel it?"

"I do." Katie Ruth suddenly recalled Oaklee's words to Lindsay.

Though she knew one could have lust without love or caring, she had to side with Dan's sister on this one. To make a relationship work long term, there had to be sizzle.

Dan had never spoken in any detail about what went wrong with him and Lindsay, but Katie Ruth had never seen any visible spark between the two. Still, he *had* cared enough about the woman to ask her to marry him.

He held out a hand to her. "We should get back."

Katie Ruth ignored it. She didn't want to ask, but she needed to know.

"What's this," she gestured from herself to him, "about?"

Katie Ruth was reassured when he took her hand and brought it to his lips, pressing a kiss on her knuckles.

"I'd like to date you." Dan cleared his throat. "If you're interested, we could start slowly. Maybe catch a movie or go out for dinner?"

Katie Ruth found his hesitant smile endearing.

"You could come to my house one night. I'll make dinner." Katie Ruth loved spending time in the kitchen, but cooking for one wasn't much fun.

Dan blew out a breath. "Ah, that probably isn't a good idea."

"Why not?"

"Because of the perception." When she didn't say anything, he continued. "As a minister, I'm held to a higher standard. Being alone with you in your home might lead to speculation of impropriety."

She resisted the urge to laugh. "Seriously?"

He nodded. "Except..."

He tapped two fingers against one thigh, his expression turning thoughtful.

"Except..." she prompted.

"Oaklee living with me, being in my home, may give us some leeway." His gaze met hers. "If you don't mind making that meal at my house, I'll gladly provide the ingredients."

Katie Ruth connected the dots. "If I'm at your house, we'll have a chaperone."

"Yes." Dan spoke without apology.

"She'll be there to make sure we keep our clothes on." The words popped out. Katie Ruth wondered if Oaklee's bluntness was catching.

Dan chuckled and squeezed her hand. "You surprise me, Katie Ruth."

While Dan's laughter eased her embarrassment, Katie Ruth told herself she needed to remember that Dan was a minister.

One with high standards. When despair threatened, she shoved it down. He was also a reasonable man. Hadn't he been understanding when she'd told him about her parents' lifestyle? Then again, their sexual proclivities weren't hers.

"Is something wrong?" The concern in Dan's voice broke through her thoughts.

Katie Ruth found reassurance in his warm brown eyes. He liked her. He wanted to date her. He'd made that clear.

*A perfect match.* Izzie's words filled her with hope.

Yet, Katie Ruth couldn't help but wonder if Dan would still like her, still want to date her, if he knew *all* her secrets.

# CHAPTER SEVEN

Katie Ruth banged her knuckles against Dan's front door. She let out a breath as anticipation flooded her. Tonight, she'd be alone with Dan for the first time since last Saturday. Alone, that was, if you didn't count Oaklee the Chaperone.

Five days had passed since the pancake supper, and their first official date had yet to happen. It wasn't from lack of trying. Dan had had church obligations four out of those five nights. The one night he'd been free, she'd had Ami's baby shower.

Katie Ruth was here now only because this meeting had been set two weeks ago. She and Dan would discuss the changes she hoped to make to the youth program at First Christian.

While here, she would also interview Oaklee for an upcoming feature in the Open Door newsletter.

Katie Ruth rapped again on the door and rang the bell. While she waited, she shoved her hands into her coat pockets. Too late she realized she should have brought gloves.

She considered punching the bell again when the door flew open.

"Sorry. I was in the kitchen." The cold air that slapped Oaklee in the face had her eyes going wide. "OMG, talk about a blast of arctic chill. Get inside before we both turn to ice."

It might not be *arctic* weather, but Katie Ruth slipped past Oaklee, grateful to be out of the wind. The pleasant scent of applewood assailed her nostrils and drew her gaze to the great room. "You've got a fire going."

"I told Dan that bad boy is blazing anytime the temp slips below forty." Oaklee held out a hand for Katie Ruth's parka, then hung it on the coat tree. "I love your top. So bright and colorful."

"Thanks. It's new." After her workday at the Y had ended, Katie Ruth had stopped home to freshen up and change. She didn't want to look overly dressy, but jeans seemed too casual for a business meeting.

Oh, who was she kidding? She wanted to look her best for Dan. She'd settled on the tunic top in a geometric pattern, leggings and boots.

"You curled your hair." Oaklee touched one of the gentle waves that fell around Katie Ruth's shoulders. "You look adorable."

"Thanks, Oaklee. You're looking pretty cute yourself."

Oaklee glanced down. "I dressed up for our interview."

"You didn't have to—"

"Just kidding." The laugh Oaklee emitted came deep from the belly.

Katie Ruth chuckled. The girl was a mini-Gladys, from the top of her sequined mermaid headband to the tips of her purple Chucks. "You got me."

"You're an easy target." Oaklee softened the words with a wink, then gestured toward the sofa. "Let's hunker down in front of the fire. Trust me, you'll want the extra warmth. My brother insists on keeping the heat at sixty-five."

Katie Ruth didn't comment as she took a seat. What would Oaklee think if she confessed that her thermostat at home was set even lower? "I take it Dan isn't home yet."

"Not yet." Oaklee dropped down on the other end of the over-stuffed sofa and heaved a sigh. "My brother is a workaholic. We can do my interview first, if you want. Get it out of the way."

"Works for me." Katie Ruth retrieved a notepad and pencil from her bag and set them on her lap. "How are you liking life in Good Hope?"

Oaklee placed a dramatic hand against her forehead. "This question is obviously a blatant attempt to get me to lower my guard and reveal something you can sensationalize for your newspaper exposé."

The comment was so ridiculous, Katie Ruth choked out a laugh. "I don't sensationalize, and this article won't be in any newspaper. It's set to run in the Open Door."

Oaklee propped her high-tops on a leather hassock. "What's the difference?"

"The *Gazette* is the weekly newspaper. Open Door is an e-newsletter I put out every day."

The girl tapped a finger against cherry-red lips. "You're both editor and reporter?"

"Jane of all trades, that's me."

"I thought you worked at the Y."

"That job pays the bills. The newsletter is a labor of love."

Oaklee grabbed a handful of grapes from a bowl on the coffee table. She jiggled them in one hand and motioned for Katie Ruth to help herself. "Dan says you volunteer at the church. A lot."

"Working with the youth, watching them grow in their faith, is a privilege." Katie Ruth took a couple of grapes, then sank back into the sofa cushions.

"When you were my age, is this what you thought your future would look like?" Oaklee's intense blue eyes bore into her. "A job at the Y, a newsletter editor and a church volunteer?"

"I'm happy with my life."

Oaklee wagged a finger. "Not what I asked."

Because her response seemed important to the girl, Katie

Ruth took a second to think back. "When I started college, I didn't know what I wanted to do. I majored in journalism because I liked to write. I participated in a lot of intramural sports because, well, I like sports. Back then, I wasn't sure if any of it would translate into a career." Katie Ruth shrugged. "But God had a plan for my life. I believe I'm right where I was meant to be."

It struck Katie Ruth that this interview had gone off the rails. Oaklee should be answering these types of questions, not her.

"Your turn." Katie Ruth lifted her notepad. "Before I begin, let me assure you that you'll be given a draft of the article to approve. Nothing will go out without your approval."

"Cool." Oaklee grabbed more grapes. "Fire away."

"Let's keep it general for now. Why don't you start by telling me a bit about yourself?"

"I come from a family that values high achievement. Youngest child. Biggest disappointment." Shadows played in Oaklee's eyes, making them unreadable. "I'm the one they use as an example of what not to do."

Katie Ruth offered a sympathetic smile. "What were you studying in college?"

"The most recent was communications with a minor in theater." Oaklee popped another grape into her mouth, chewed.

*That's right*, Katie Ruth thought. Dan had mentioned his sister had changed majors several times. "I can see those studies being an excellent fit for someone with your outgoing personality."

"My parents didn't think so, but then, my dad wants me to be a doctor, a lawyer or a CPA." Oaklee gave a humorless chuckle. "Can you see me being happy in any of those professions?"

"Not really."

Oaklee blew out a breath. "Not following their prescribed path means I'm a disappointment with a capital D. According to him, I lack focus and make one wrong decision after another."

"Ouch."

"My parents and I don't see eye to eye on anything." Oaklee's eyes blazed. "They think my protests on behalf of PETA are stupid. They told me that to my face. I don't expect them to protest at my side, but why can't they accept that righting wrongs being done to animals is important to me?"

"Perhaps—"

"I've made mistakes. I admit that. Who doesn't? My parents judge me because I've made mistakes." Despair laced Oaklee's words. "Why can't they judge me on how honest and kind I am?"

"It'd certainly be a better world." Thanks to Oaklee's openness, Katie Ruth was getting a good picture of an idealistic young woman still searching for her place in the world. Only one part of the story puzzled her. "What I don't understand is, if communications and theater were such a good fit, why did you drop out?"

"It's...complicated."

The pain that flashed in Oaklee's eyes had Katie Ruth raising her hands. "We don't need to go there. We can—"

"I want to tell you." Oaklee's voice faltered. "But it has to be off the record."

Katie Ruth nodded. "You have my word."

"You won't tell my brother."

"I won't tell anyone."

Oaklee grabbed a few more grapes, but made no effort to eat them. Just when Katie Ruth was starting to think Oaklee had changed her mind, she squared her shoulders.

"A year ago, I became involved with one of my professors. Julian is smart, funny and really hot. He made me feel really special and...loved." A bleakness filled Oaklee's eyes. In that moment, she looked much younger than her twenty years. "He taught most of the courses in my minor and directed all the stage productions. When I broke up with him last September, he didn't take it well."

Oaklee had dated a professor? Katie Ruth was pretty sure that was unethical, even at the university level, but kept her tone conversational. "What did he do when you told him it was over?"

"First, he sent flowers. When that didn't achieve the desired result, he got pissed." Oaklee expelled a shuddering breath. "He started screwing with my grades, and I didn't get a part in the fall musical that should have been mine."

For several heartbeats, neither of them said a word.

Oaklee's gaze remained focused on the flickering flames. "With it being such a small school, I couldn't avoid him. Especially if I continued in theater. Halfway through the semester, I dropped the courses he taught and changed my minor."

"I'm sorry you had to go to such extremes."

"He wasn't finished with me." Oaklee rubbed her forehead as if a headache threatened. "Rumors about me began circulating. Nothing I could pin on originating from him, but I knew he was behind the lies. By the time the semester ended, my reputation was toast."

Oaklee didn't give details, and Katie Ruth didn't ask. The misery on the girl's face told Katie Ruth that whatever Julian had done, whatever lies he'd spread, had hurt her deeply.

"Do you have any idea why he'd go to such lengths to get back at you?"

"I honestly don't know. I didn't think he was that kind of guy." Oaklee appeared genuinely perplexed. "I assumed once I told him it was over, that would be it."

Once again, Katie Ruth thought back to her own youthful indiscretions. Vegas. The bachelorette party. Judd. At least she'd been lucky he was a nice guy. When she ended it, he just accepted it was for the best and moved on.

"When I thought about going back to campus second semester, I had a panic attack." Oaklee attempted a spooky shudder, but just looked miserable. "It was scary."

"Oh, sweetie. I'm so sorry."

"He was married. Julian told me he and his wife were separated, and I believed him. When I found out in September they were still together, I broke it off. I loved him, but I couldn't be with him." Oaklee's gaze dropped to her hands.

"Don't blame yourself. You were a student. The man preyed on you."

Oaklee shook her head. "He flirted with me, sure. I flirted right back. I wanted to date him, and sleeping with him was my choice."

"He was older and in a position of power," Katie Ruth insisted. "The man is a predator and should be reported."

"I can't do it, Katie Ruth. I *won't* do it. Julian is popular and well-respected by students and faculty." Oaklee shifted her gaze to the fire for several seconds. "When I was home over holiday break, I mentioned to my parents that a professor had it out for me. They didn't believe me. If your own parents won't believe you, no one else will."

"*I* believe you, Oaklee."

Oaklee reached over and grasped Katie Ruth's hand, gave it a squeeze. "Gladys is right. You are a sweetheart."

The odd compliment had Katie Ruth blinking for a second. She refocused. "Maybe if you told your parents why—"

"Tell them I slept with a married professor?" Oaklee snorted. "They'd see it as another major screw-up. This time, they'd be right."

Katie Ruth thought of her own major screw-up. She'd never told her parents what had occurred during that Vegas weekend. For a second, she considered sharing the story with Oaklee. At the very least, it would show the girl that you didn't have to let a past mistake define you.

But remembering that Oaklee was Dan's sister and a woman with no filter had Katie Ruth swallowing the impulse.

"My dad made it clear that unless I returned to finish my degree, I wasn't welcome in his house. But I can't go back." Oaklee's voice broke, then steadied. "I probably shouldn't have come here either. Dad is angry with Dan for taking me in."

"I believe you being here will be good for both you and Dan." Katie Ruth offered a reassuring smile. "Your brother doesn't take enough time out for fun. You can show him there's more to life than work."

"I can try, but Dan is a tough nut to crack." Oaklee sighed. "You know he'll pressure me to go back."

Katie Ruth hesitated. "He wouldn't if he knew the full story. He—"

"You can't tell him, Katie Ruth." Oaklee's tone took on an urgency.

"Tell me what?"

For a second, Katie Ruth froze. She turned, and her heart flip-flopped. Dan stood in the foyer, still wearing his coat.

She wondered how much he'd heard, then decided it couldn't be much or he wouldn't have asked the question.

"I was thinking of making an excuse to leave once you got here, but Katie Ruth made it clear I'm your chaperone." Oaklee stood and stretched. "Did you pick up the pizzas?"

Dan gestured to where two boxes sat on a side table. "I set them down so I could take off my coat."

"Pizza?" Katie Ruth slowly pulled to her feet. She hadn't considered she'd be interrupting their dinner.

"You don't think I'd schedule a meeting at this time of day and not feed you." Dan's smile slipped slightly. "Unless you already have supper plans?"

"Nope. No plans."

Relief washed across Dan's face. Removing his jacket, he hung it next to Katie Ruth's on the coat tree. "That's good news."

Oaklee punched her brother's arm on her way to the pizza boxes. "I'll take these to the kitchen. You entertain Katie Ruth."

Dan's eyes danced with amusement. He lowered his voice in a conspiratorial whisper, though Oaklee had already disappeared from sight. "I suspect this is my sister's way of giving us a few minutes of alone time."

Katie Ruth smiled and crossed to him. "I like Oaklee."

Dan reached out to touch one of her curls. "I like these."

"Oaklee said you would. She knows everything."

He closed the small distance between them. "Then she knows how much I've missed you this week."

"I've missed you, too." The admission came out in a rush as the enticing scent of his cologne wrapped around her like a lover's caress.

With a gentleness that had her heart swelling, Dan enfolded her in his arms. When she laid her cheek against his chest, he tightened his hold and rested his chin against the top of her head. "We'll find a time for a real date. Soon. I promise."

"I'm holding you to that promise." She lifted her head, and when their eyes locked, Katie Ruth saw her own desire reflected in his warm brown depths.

Giving in to need, she brushed her lips against his mouth.

Dan's lips curved before he kissed her back with a slow thoroughness that left her weak and trembling.

Katie Ruth's voice wasn't quite steady when she spoke. "I guess it's time to get down to business."

"Not yet." He took her hand and gently locked their fingers together. "Food first."

"I know pizza is the main course." Katie Ruth gazed up at Dan through lowered lashes. "What's for dessert?"

His gaze dropped to her still-tingling mouth. When his eyes darkened, she resisted the urge to do a happy dance.

She settled for squeezing his fingers. "Excellent choice."

CHAPTER EIGHT

"I'm amazed you made it home before six." Oaklee glanced up from the pizza boxes she was opening as Dan strode into the room with Katie Ruth. "Anyone tell you that you work too much?"

Dan ignored the remark, but the jab hit its mark.

Lindsay had once told him he didn't need a wife. He was already married...to his ministry.

He'd apologized for neglecting her, admitted he'd been distracted and promised to do better. But until he'd tried to find a night free this week to take Katie Ruth on a date, he hadn't realized just how little time he had available.

This week, his nights had been filled with everything from a weekly men's Bible study to visiting Dexter's mother and other hospitalized members of the congregation. Even tonight's meeting, arranged weeks ago, revolved around the youth ministry.

Katie Ruth studied the kitchen table, then stepped to pick up a quilted place mat shaped like a flower. "These are so bright and cheerful. The raised tulip reminds me spring is just around the corner."

Dan gestured to his sister. "Oaklee made them."

"You did?" The admiration in Katie Ruth's voice had a smile blooming on his sister's face.

"There's a sewing machine at the Living Center. I whipped these up after work yesterday." Oaklee's tone remained nonchalant, even as her fingers stroked the stem of the red flower.

"I have no talent in this area." Katie Ruth offered a self-deprecating smile. "I can barely sew on a button, while you—"

"Save the gushing." Oaklee pointed to a chair. "I already decided to give you a couple slices of pizza."

Katie Ruth laughed. "What can I do to help?"

"Sit down." Oaklee shifted her gaze to Dan. "You, too, Daniel."

Katie Ruth's brows lifted. "Daniel?"

Dan winced.

"That's what Dad calls him." Oaklee shot her brother a smug look. "Dan is too ordinary a name for his precious son."

"What does your dad call you?" Katie Ruth asked, curious.

"Trouble." Oaklee chuckled when Katie Ruth groaned. "You walked right into that one."

The pizza was barely on the table when Oaklee asked Dan about his day. She seemed genuinely interested, so it didn't hit him immediately that the conversation was focused on him.

Once the realization hit, Dan cut his answer short and smiled at Oaklee. "How's your job at the Living Center going? Remind me again what it is that you do there."

Out of the corner of his eye, he caught Katie Ruth's smile of approval.

"Well…" Oaklee set down her slice of cheese pizza. No animal protein for his little sister. "I'm really a glorified gofer. Though most of the residents are independent, they still like having someone available to run errands or drive them to appointments. Yesterday, a couple of ladies who didn't want to brave the cold gave me a list, and I went to the market for them. I also do some phone and computer troubleshooting."

Several times this week, Oaklee had mentioned the residents

of the Good Hope Living Center were "a hoot," but she hadn't gone into detail. Dan had been so focused on his own concerns he hadn't asked any questions.

"They appreciate what I do for them." Oaklee touched a pink strand of hair. "I thought they might be turned off by my appearance, but I was wrong. I've even got Gladys and her friends thinking about getting matching tats."

"You know Gladys has had quite an illustrious career on the community theater stage." Katie Ruth bit into a slice of pizza covered in pepperoni.

"She told me all about being a celebrated actress and now a director." Oaklee appeared suitably impressed. "This fall, she'll be directing a production of *Pump Boys and Dinettes*. When I mentioned I played Prudie in a high school production, she had me sing for her. She wants me to try out. She thinks I have a good shot at getting the role."

"Oaklee, that's wonderful." Katie Ruth gave his sister a high five.

*Not so wonderful*, Dan thought. If his sister stayed in Good Hope for the production, she wouldn't be returning to college in the fall.

"I hope you try out." Katie Ruth's voice turned persuasive. "If you get the part, I'll be in the front row for every performance."

"Seriously?"

"Seriously."

Despite his reservations, he was touched by the generosity of Katie Ruth's offer.

While they ate, both he and Katie Ruth kept Oaklee talking by asking questions. The young woman responding with enthusiasm and passion was a stranger to Dan.

He saw Katie Ruth watching him. Most women would have been upset that tonight's dinner conversation revolved around his sister's new job.

Katie Ruth didn't appear upset. She seemed happy to see him reconnecting with his sister.

He would not take such generosity for granted.

Dan thought again of all the mistakes he'd made with Lindsay. He hadn't even known she was dissatisfied with her position as a floral designer at the Enchanted Florist. Yet, she'd been unhappy enough to quit, without having another job in the wings, shortly after their engagement ended.

As he relocated to the living room with Oaklee and Katie Ruth, Dan vowed it would be different with Katie Ruth.

*He* would be different.

This time, it wouldn't be all about him.

"You don't need me here," Oaklee protested when Katie Ruth motioned for her to take a seat.

"We do. We're reviewing the game Katie Ruth is proposing to have middle schoolers play during youth group." Dan pointed to his sister. "You bring a fresh, young perspective."

"If any part of this involves memorizing Bible verses, I'm warning you now, I'm outta here." Oaklee swiped a thumb through the air.

Dan grinned. "Understood."

"The lack of anything biblical is actually what concerns your brother about what I'm proposing." Katie Ruth kept her tone matter-of-fact.

Katie Ruth glanced at Dan, who only took a sip of the soda he'd brought with him to the living room.

"What did you say when he voiced those concerns?" Oaklee leaned forward, clearly intrigued by the controversy.

"I asked that he reserve judgment until we could discuss it in more detail. Being a fair and reasonable man, he agreed, and we set this meeting." Katie Ruth's fingers shook slightly as she pulled out the cards. "A little background might help you understand why this project means so much to me. I had some difficult high school years."

Oaklee's brows pulled together. "Why?"

"It doesn't matter why," Dan began, obviously hoping to spare her the need to explain. "It—"

"It's okay, Dan. Oaklee and I are friends." Katie Ruth met Oaklee's gaze, and an understanding passed between the two women. "My parents were swingers. They had a group they met with once a month in another city and…"

Katie Ruth kept the explanation simple and factual. There were plenty of opportunities for Oaklee to crack a joke, but the girl's expression remained solemn. By the time Katie Ruth finished, sympathy darkened Oaklee's blue eyes.

"I felt all alone." Katie Ruth's breath caught, then she began again. "My brother, Nick, was away at college. Other than my parents, there were no relatives to turn to in Good Hope."

"What about your pastor?" Oaklee asked.

"Pastor Schmidt condemned my parents from the pulpit."

Oaklee gasped. "No way."

"Way." A lump formed in Katie Ruth's throat. She cleared it. "His actions served to alienate me from God at a time I needed Him most."

"But you're active in the church now." Oaklee's gaze grew puzzled. "What happened?"

"Pastor Schmidt retired and moved away. A minister named Dan Marshall took his position." Katie Ruth turned to Dan, and this time her smile came easily. "I realized that Pastor Schmidt's words and actions did not reflect God's grace and mercy."

Tears filled Oaklee's eyes. "I'm sorry, Katie Ruth."

"I believe everything that's happened to me in my life—good and bad—helped mold me into the person I am today." Katie Ruth hoped Oaklee's experience with the professor would end up being a positive force for change in her life, as well.

"Thanks for sharing what I know was a difficult period in your life." Dan reached over and placed a hand over the ones Katie Ruth had clenched in her lap.

"Now I really want to hear what you're proposing," Oaklee blurted, and they all laughed.

"I've done quite a bit of research on what works with kids this age." As Katie Ruth continued, she felt herself relax. "The general consensus seems to be that starting each session with icebreaker questions works best. These questions may seem silly, but they're innocuous and don't cross any boundaries."

Katie Ruth paused and glanced at her notes. "Some examples are, 'What song do you play the most on your phone?' Or, 'What's your favorite sundae topping?'"

Oaklee thought for a second, nodded. "I'd answer those."

Katie Ruth glanced at Dan.

"Go on."

"Each week, we'd also touch on one way to show interest and build friendships."

Katie Ruth pulled out three sheets of paper. She handed Dan and Oaklee one each and kept one for herself. "Listening carefully may seem basic, but these are kids, so we can't assume they know these things."

"I see something I don't always do." Oaklee looked up and met Katie Ruth's eyes. "This says once you ask a question, you should let the person responding talk uninterrupted."

"That's a difficult one for us all," Dan agreed.

Katie Ruth's gaze dropped to the paper in her hands. "I like this part, how spending time with someone, especially while engaging in outdoor activities, often gives you a good indication of their temperament."

"This silent-observer one is good, too." Oaklee studied the page. "Body language and a person's actions speak more loudly than words. Sort of the old, 'If a person shows you who they are, believe them.'"

"This sounds interesting, Katie Ruth." Dan steepled his fingers. "But where does God come in?"

"You and I have discussed the importance of creating a welcoming environment where the kids can be themselves and build friendships." Katie Ruth's eyes locked with Dan's. "We'll start each week with prayer and the discussions will focus on how God works in our lives."

Dan settled back in his seat and seemed to consider her words.

When he nodded, Katie Ruth let out the breath she hadn't realized she'd been holding.

"It hurts me to think of all that kids face on their journey to adulthood." Dan shook his head. "I want to do more to help."

"You've done so much." Katie Ruth took his hand. "Since you took over as pastor, attendance is up across all the programs. Kids and adults alike know you truly care."

Dan laced his fingers with hers. As if forgetting that Oaklee was in the room, he brought their joined hands to his mouth and kissed them. "Thank you for that."

Katie Ruth caught Oaklee's wink. A second later, the girl yawned. "I'm going to video-chat with some friends on the new phone my brother bought me. Then I'm heading to bed."

Dan glanced at the clock on the mantel. "At this time?"

"Get a clue, Daniel." Oaklee lifted her hands and cupped them around her mouth like a megaphone. "The chaperone is leaving the living room."

Katie Ruth choked back a laugh even as her mind swirled with possibilities.

Dan relaxed against the back of the sofa. "I know why Oaklee really made a quick exit."

Katie Ruth's gaze turned mischievous as she slid closer to him. "To give us a chance to be alone?"

"That's part of it."

"What's the other part?"

"She knows I still need to put the finishing touches on my sermon for this week." He chuckled. "I believe she feared I might ask for her help."

"Oh, Dan. I'm sorry." In a single fluid motion, Katie Ruth was on her feet. "I didn't even ask if you had things to do once we finished with our meeting."

"Please don't go." He grabbed her hand and tugged her back onto the sofa. "Not yet."

"You have work to do."

"You could help me." Dan offered what he hoped was an enticing smile. "It could be fun."

"You really think I could be of help?"

She appeared stunned by the thought.

"Of course." There was no doubt in his mind. "It shouldn't take long. The sermon is done and would be fine delivered the way it's written. But it feels as if there's something missing. I think I'm too close to it."

"I'd be honored to help."

"I appreciate it." He pushed up from the sofa and retrieved his sermon notes from his briefcase.

Instead of reading the sermon, he hit the highlights. "You can see I went back to the beginning, to Adam and Eve. Anything jump out at you?"

Katie Ruth paused, appearing to give the question careful consideration. "I like that you're starting the Lenten series with Adam and Eve."

When she didn't continue, Dan found his fingers tightening around the notes. "But…"

"It's all good."

"But…" he prompted again when she didn't continue.

"You may be missing an opportunity. Perhaps you might consider hitting a little harder the temptation we all face." Katie Ruth spoke quickly, as if wanting to make sure she got the words out. "Everyone can relate to being tempted. Or to having a friend who encourages you to do stuff you know is wrong."

Her expression darkened, and he found himself wondering if she had such a friend.

"Of course, ultimately it's our responsibility to say no. That's what you might stress." Katie Ruth lifted a shoulder and let it drop. "Maybe it's because we were talking about kids earlier. We both know it isn't just middle schoolers who face temptation."

Dan started writing, realizing that emphasizing this thread would take the sermon to a different level.

When he looked up several long seconds later, he found Katie Ruth staring, wide-eyed.

"It helps? What I said?"

He held up his hand for a high five. "Spot-on."

"Well, maybe if I helped you, you could help me."

"Anything." Dan found he couldn't pull his eyes from her face.

"It might be good to carry the temptation theme into youth group." She chewed on her lower lip. "Have one question after the icebreaker that deals with temptations kids face. What do you think?"

Dan grinned. "I think you and I make a great team."

CHAPTER NINE

Oaklee glanced at Gladys as they strolled down the street. When she'd shown up at the Living Center and received her assignment from the front desk, her entire afternoon had been blocked off with "shopping companion to Gladys Bertholf."

Gladys was a queen bee with plenty of drones, er, friends buzzing around. Oaklee was surprised she needed her. Unless... the older woman simply wanted someone under the age of eighty to carry her purchases. That was fine with Oaklee. She'd spent the entire morning inside, so being outdoors on this unusually warm and sunny day was a treat.

"Where are we headed?" Oaklee glanced around as they walked at a surprisingly fast clip. There were any number of businesses on this stretch of road. It didn't matter to her where they went, but she was curious.

"The Daily Grind." Gladys slanted a sideways glance at her. "How does a mocha latte sound?"

"Sounds delish."

"Have you had a kouign amann since you've been in town?"

"I don't even know what that is," Oaklee admitted.

"Oh, my dear, you are in for a treat." Gladys cackled. "They're a pastry so sweet and rich, they're positively sinful."

"Are you leading me into temptation?"

For a second, Gladys appeared puzzled. Then she cackled again. "Good one."

Oaklee hurried to open the door to the Daily Grind, and Gladys swept inside, her brightly colored caftan swirling around her lean frame.

After following her to the counter, Oaklee hung back, knowing Gladys liked to run the show.

Oaklee understood the need. She was the same way.

"Cassie." Gladys flung out her arms as if greeting someone she hadn't seen in years.

"Gladys. Hello." Cassie, Oaklee decided, was a pretty woman who would be stunning with more makeup. Still, the woman had some really fine highlights.

Pink, Oaklee had quickly discovered, was a difficult color to maintain. She wondered how she'd look as a blonde, or maybe a brunette with caramel highlights.

"When's the wedding?" Gladys asked.

"We've settled on May." A blush traveled up Cassie's neck. "Krew wants me—us—to have a nice ceremony."

"He's a good man."

*High praise, coming from Gladys*, Oaklee thought.

"Yes, he is." Cassie's gaze settled on Oaklee.

Gladys gestured. "This is Dan Marshall's sister, Oaklee. She's helping me run errands today."

Oaklee spoke in a conspiratorial whisper as she said, "Gladys is going to introduce me to sin."

Cassie's eyes widened.

Gladys laughed. "I love this girl. She's never had a kouign amann. That ends today."

"Oh, you are in for a treat." Cassie glanced at Gladys as if knowing she was the decision-maker. "Two or one?"

"Two. I'm not sharing." Gladys grabbed her wallet. "While you're at it, rustle us up each a mocha latte."

"You *are* living dangerously," Cassie teased as she plated the pastries, then turned to make the drinks.

"I'm not going to get out of this life alive, so I might as well enjoy every minute."

Oaklee grinned. Five minutes with the older woman and she'd already decided she wanted to be Gladys when she grew up.

Gladys brushed away Oaklee's attempt to pay, the older woman's attention firmly back on Cassie.

The way Gladys studied the ring and the woman wearing it told Oaklee that the pastries and drinks weren't why they were here.

"I'm very happy for you and Krew." Gladys's eyes softened. "I know you'll be happy together."

"I have the family and the man I've always wanted."

"The man you deserve. Will Clint be a problem?"

"Clint signed away his rights to Axl," was all Cassie said on that. "Krew plans to adopt the three boys."

"Wonderful news." Gladys reached across the counter and patted Cassie's hand. "Now if you can manage to keep that mother of yours from taking over the wedding, you'll be set."

"I'm hoping she and Len will get engaged and she'll be too busy planning her own."

"Your mouth, God's ear." Gladys turned and surveyed the dining area. After a second, she pointed. "That one, by the window."

Taking the cue, Oaklee picked up the tray holding their order and headed for the table. It was a good spot, bright and sunny.

Once they were seated and Oaklee had taken a bite of the flaky pastry, she looked up at Gladys, wide-eyed. "OMG."

"Told you so." Gladys sat back in her chair and studied Oaklee with a smug smile that quickly turned speculative. "Is your brother dating anyone?"

As Oaklee had just bitten into the kouign amann, she took her time answering.

Gladys tapped the top of the table with a long nail painted bright purple. She beat a staccato beat with her nail while Oaklee savored the buttery goodness, then washed it down with a long drink of her latte.

Oaklee inclined her head. "Dating?"

"Do I need to define the term?"

Oaklee grinned. "I'm jacking with you."

Gladys raised a jet-black brow. "I like your spunk."

"I'm not sure how many actual dates he and Katie Ruth have been on, but he seems stuck on her. From what I observe, the feeling is mutual."

"Excellent." A pleased look filled Gladys's eyes as she lifted the latte to her lips.

"What's this about?" Oaklee jerked her head in Cassie's direction. "Are you some kind of town matchmaker?"

The eyes that met hers were wide with astonishment. "I'm not sure what you mean."

"Now who's jacking with who?" Oaklee popped another bit of the caramelized pastry into her mouth. "You know exactly what I mean. You came here specifically to find out how Cassie and her guy are doing. Now, you're asking me about my brother's dating status."

"You're perceptive."

Oaklee shrugged.

"I'm interested in people." Gladys spoke carefully. "In their relationships. In what's going on with their lives."

"Bull."

Gladys's eyebrows winged up. "Pardon me?"

Oaklee studied her for a long moment. It hit her suddenly, and she couldn't help but grin. She pointed. "You *are* a matchmaker."

The expression of confusion Gladys feigned might have

worked on someone less savvy, but Oaklee had a talent for seeing through bullshit.

"The hand to your throat is a nice touch," she told the older woman. "Maybe you could suck in air, you know, like you're really shocked."

The smile that spread over Gladys's face started slowly. "I'm not going to be able to fool you, am I?"

"Nope." Oaklee finished off the last of the kouign amann.

"Then," Gladys nodded as if making a decision, "I guess you'll have to join us."

~

Katie Ruth read through the interview Oaklee had approved, then hit send. Today's version of the Open Door newsletter was now on its way to countless homes in the area.

She'd been the editor for five years. It was one more thing on an already overflowing plate, but Katie Ruth enjoyed the work. Because she kept it short, a few newsy articles, an occasional spotlight on a local business or a person new to the area, along with a few sentences of local gossip, it wasn't a burden.

The gossip section was the most popular feature. Katie Ruth tried to include only what she could substantiate and never anything mean-spirited.

The section today included news that the search continued for Roy Davis's heir. Roy, a local cherry grower and longtime Good Hope resident, had died recently after a fire swept through his home. On a lighter note, Katie Ruth added news that Good Hope's baby boom showed no signs of slowing down. This time, it was the mayor and his wife looking forward to a baby this spring.

*A baby.*

There had been a time when Katie Ruth hadn't been sure she wanted children. Heck, there had been a time when she'd thought she hadn't wanted a husband. Or even a steady boyfriend. Then she'd gone to Vegas for the bachelorette party…

It was strange how, lately, memories of that weekend kept stealing into her consciousness at the oddest times.

Her phone dinged, and she picked it up, noting someone had contacted her on Messenger. Odd, since most of her friends preferred to text.

Her blood went cold when she saw the message was from Judd Stevens.

*Katie Ruth. Need to talk with you asap.*

"Speak of the devil," Katie Ruth muttered under her breath. What could Judd possibly have to say to her after all these years?

She was curious, but not curious enough.

Before she could change her mind, Katie Ruth blocked him.

Everyone made mistakes, and Judd was one of her biggest. She'd moved on and assumed he had, too.

Why did he want to talk to her now? And why make it sound urgent?

*Not my problem*, she told herself as she dropped her phone back in her bag. She was a different person now than she'd been when she'd known Judd. The last thing she needed was someone from her past screwing up her present.

Judd was history. That's where he needed to stay.

Oaklee scrutinized Dan from her perch at the edge of the sofa. "The pants are okay, although brown chinos aren't a fave of mine. But you absolutely are not leaving this house wearing that shirt."

Dan glanced down at the black polo he'd put on for his date with Katie Ruth. "What's wrong with it? This is one of my favorites."

"I know it is, because I've seen it at every family gathering." Oaklee closed her eyes briefly as if gathering strength.

"It's stylish."

"Look at the collar, Daniel. Maybe it was stylin' in a long-ago decade before I was born, but not in any of the worlds humans currently inhabit." Oaklee pointed to the hall in the direction of the bedrooms. "Put on the maroon plaid that Mom gave you for Christmas. I helped pick it out."

Dan returned wearing the cotton button-up shirt. He had to admit it fit well.

Oaklee studied him for a long moment, gave a nod. "Did you splash on some of the cologne I got you for your last birthday?"

"Yes, Mother." Dan's droll tone made his sister laugh. He hadn't planned to consult her on clothing—she'd just inserted herself—but there was an area where he could use her guidance. "I need your honest opinion about something."

Oaklee straightened, TV remote in hand. "This sounds interesting. You have my total attention."

"Dinner." Dan held up two hands, pressing one forward and then the other. "Muddy Boots. Bayside Pizza."

"Isn't the pizza place where you proposed to Lindsay?"

"Yes, but Katie Ruth loves their goat cheese salads."

"Doesn't matter. It's out. At least for tonight."

"I guess Muddy Boots gets the nod."

"You're not taking her there either." Oaklee shook her head vigorously. "The entire town will be there, buzzing around your table. Another couple—or two or three—will probably ask to join you."

That wasn't far from the realm of possibility. "But—"

"Don't worry. I took the liberty of making a reservation for two at Sombreros in Egg Harbor. Gladys told me they have the best Mexican food."

"I know Katie Ruth likes the food at Muddy Boots." Dan puffed out his cheeks. "What if she doesn't like Mexican food?"

"Of course she likes Mexican food. What kind of person doesn't like Mexican food?" Oaklee shot back. "If Katie Ruth doesn't like Mexican food, you should just go ahead and dump her. You need a woman who enjoys a little spice."

Dan only smiled. "I appreciate the clothing advice. I promise to do you proud tonight."

"You are such a dork."

"I'll take that as a compliment, from one dork to another." When Oaklee's laughter mixed with his, Dan realized just how much he was enjoying getting to know his sister. "And I appreciate you making the reservations at Sombreros. I don't know why I didn't think of it myself. I've been there before, and Gladys is right, the food is fabulous. Muddy Boots could have been a problem."

Looking very much like Gladys at her regal best, Oaklee made a rolling gesture with one hand. "So you bow before my wisdom."

"On everything except dumping Katie Ruth." Dan grinned. "Even if the woman doesn't like Mexican, I'm not giving her up."

## CHAPTER TEN

In the past two weeks, Katie Ruth spent time with Dan at a variety of church functions, but actual *dates* had been in short supply. Though they'd gone together to deliver a baby gift to Beck and Ami last week. James Thomas "JT" Cross had arrived the last day of February.

The baby, with his strawberry-blond tufts of hair and chubby cheeks, had everyone in the family mesmerized.

Katie Ruth and Dan hadn't stayed long. Beck's parents had been visiting from Georgia, and Dan had to get to his men's Bible study.

Tonight, well, tonight, it would be just her and Dan. Katie Ruth dipped a chip into the salsa on her plate and smiled, feeling completely and utterly relaxed.

Sombreros, a popular Mexican cantina in Egg Harbor, was just far enough down the road to ensure some alone time. "How did you know I like Mexican?"

"Wild guess." Dan smiled slowly, and she felt her insides go to jelly. He lifted his tumbler of iced tea in a mock toast. "To an enjoyable evening."

"I'm sorry you have to skip the alcohol."

Since he was the designated driver, Katie Ruth had ordered the pomegranate margarita she'd been craving.

"It isn't a sacrifice. I'm not much of a drinker, anyway."

Katie Ruth clinked her glass against the tumbler and took a sip. The margarita hit the spot. She let her gaze linger on Dan. He looked positively yummy this evening. "Is that a new shirt?"

Surprise widened his eyes. "Relatively new. Do you like it?"

"Very much." There was something about the colors in the plaid that made his eyes look like pools of milk chocolate. Her heart stumbled. "It's very stylish."

"That's what—" The sound of raised voices had both of them turning their heads.

At a nearby table, the servers sang *Happy Birthday* at the tops of their voices to a boy wearing an oversize sombrero.

Katie Ruth picked up her margarita glass. "This is nice."

"It's a great restaurant," Dan agreed.

"Well, yes, it is, but that isn't what I meant."

He inclined his head.

"I love all the places to eat in Good Hope." Katie Ruth searched for the right words. "With you being the minister and me living there my entire life, we know so many people. It's impossible to eat anywhere in town without someone stopping by the table."

"The increased privacy is one reason some ministers prefer larger cities." Dan smiled and thanked the server who'd brought their food—enchiladas for her and a chimi for him.

Katie Ruth forked off a bite of enchilada. "More privacy and more opportunity, right? Is that how your parents see it? If you were in a big city, you would have more opportunities for success?"

Dan nodded and swallowed his food. "Yes, that's how they see it."

Katie Ruth pushed a bit of enchilada around on her plate. "So then, are you considering a move?"

His eyes widened as if the question surprised him.

It seemed fairly straightforward to Katie Ruth. To keep from filling the sudden silence, she grabbed a couple of chips and stuffed them in her mouth.

"I'm happy in Good Hope." Dan attacked the chimi that had been fried to golden perfection. "Though my dad's arguments in favor of making a move make sense."

The fork in Katie Ruth's hand stilled halfway to her mouth.

"Of course, Dad views the ministry through the same lens as any corporate gig." Dan chuckled. "The larger the congregation, the more the salary and higher the prestige."

A sick feeling filled the pit of Katie Ruth's stomach. "How do you see it?"

"I have a passion for ministry. I want to go where I can best serve." Dan's eyes blazed with conviction. "When a call comes—if one does—I'm praying that it will be clear where I can best serve. Whether that's in Good Hope or in Lincolnshire or someplace else."

Katie Ruth washed a piece of enchilada stuck in her throat down with a gulp of margarita. "Lincolnshire?"

"The same suburb where my parents live. A church near their house is looking for an associate pastor. On the surface, it looks like a good fit."

Katie Ruth nodded as if him moving to Illinois made perfect sense. "You're seriously considering the position?"

Dan set down his fork. "I haven't been through a formal interview yet, but yes, I'm open to the idea." Two tiny lines formed between Dan's brows. "It seems that a large congregation would offer more opportunities for me to fully use my talents. As well as give me a more balanced home life."

"Maybe." Katie Ruth washed the chips down with the rest of her margarita.

"You sound skeptical."

He'd opened the door, so she walked through it. "I think it all depends on church politics. If you're hired as a senior pastor, you may be given more leeway. If not, you'll likely be forced to follow the direction envisioned by the senior pastor and the board."

Dan's brow remained furrowed. "Are you saying you don't think I should explore the option?"

"That isn't at all what I'm saying." Katie Ruth signaled the waitress for another margarita. "Your life. Your choice."

"There are perks to living in a bigger city." Dan's tone remained easy, but his eyes had turned watchful.

"Like I said, it's your choice to make. What I think, what your father thinks, doesn't matter."

"You talk about how hard it is for us to have dinner without being interrupted. That wouldn't be an issue in a larger community." Dan's eyes took on a distant gleam. "Lindsay also hated the constant interruptions. Then again, she had trouble seeing herself as a minister's wife. It's not an easy road."

"The road would be easier if you love the man behind the pulpit." Katie Ruth liked Lindsay and considered her a friend. She didn't, for one second, approve of how she'd treated Dan. "Lindsay never loved you."

"I realize that now." His fingers curved around the tumbler of tea. "I also accept I never loved her. Not the way a man should love a woman he pledged to marry."

"I need to clarify one thing." Katie Ruth smiled her thanks when the server handed her the margarita.

Dan's gaze remained fixed on her.

"When I said it was nice to be here because odds are we won't be interrupted, I didn't mean I hate it when people stop by to talk. I actually enjoy visiting with friends. But just for tonight, I want to be alone with you."

"I appreciate the clarification." He reached over and squeezed her hand.

For some reason, the sweet gesture had her blinking back tears. She was done with this subject. Katie Ruth forced a smile. "Is Oaklee still enjoying her job?"

"She loves it. I believe it's taken her by surprise how much she enjoys being around an older generation." He chuckled. "Oh, and Gladys Bertholf is Oaklee's new best friend."

"Told you." Katie Ruth laughed aloud, grateful to have something to focus on besides the possibility of Dan leaving Good Hope. "Your sister is a Gladys-in-training."

Dan winced.

"Oh, c'mon. Gladys is a wonderful woman. There are worse role models your sister could latch on to."

"You're right. It's just—"

Recalling the discussion last week about listening skills, Katie Ruth resisted the urge to interrupt. Though her appetite had fled, she stabbed another bite of enchilada.

"Oaklee has started quoting the woman. Worse, you know how Gladys can be. Oaklee has begun 'suggesting,'" Dan made air quotes, "how I can better live my life."

Now he'd lost her. "What kind of suggestions?"

"For example, taking you out tonight. She—"

"What?" Katie Ruth's heart slammed against her chest wall. "Are you telling me the reason you made time in your schedule was because your *sister* suggested it?" Katie Ruth felt her temper inch upward. "Did she suggest kissing me the other night? Perhaps she's given you instructions for how to behave tonight when you take me—"

"Stop," Dan ordered in a commanding tone she'd rarely heard him use.

Katie Ruth blinked.

"My sister has nothing to do with tonight."

"You said she suggested you take me out tonight."

"That isn't what I said."

At her skeptical glance, he held up a hand. "I admit it may have sounded that way. The truth is, Oaklee has talked a lot about me not living my life to the fullest."

"You're a busy man." Despite her hurt, Katie Ruth automatically rose to his defense. "I don't know anyone in Good Hope who works harder than you."

"That's what I thought when she first said it. It was knee-jerk. But instead of protesting and listing the reasons why what she said wasn't true, I kept my mouth shut and listened." Dan's smile turned rueful. "While it's true I lead a busy life, I'm beginning to see I don't have a balanced one. I rarely take time out for fun."

Katie Ruth relaxed her death grip on her drink. "So tonight is about fun?"

"There isn't anyone whose company I enjoy more." Dan scooped up salsa with a chip. "When I'm not with you, I find myself thinking about you. I hope this is just the beginning for us."

Katie Ruth's heart swelled with emotion. She met his gaze. The time for playing it cool was over. "I'd like that, too."

Dan took her hand then, his fingers playing with hers. In the dim light of the restaurant, Katie Ruth found herself falling a little more in love with him.

"Well, isn't this a cozy scene?" Acid dripped from the woman's tone.

Katie Ruth jerked her hand free of Dan's with such force the back of it whacked her margarita glass.

Only Dan's quick reflexes saved it from spilling.

Edna Peabody and her husband, Ronald, stood tableside. A hostess, clutching menus, paused several feet away.

Dan pushed to his feet and shook Ron's hand. "It's good to see you both."

Disapproval rolled off Edna in waves as her sharp gaze narrowed on Katie Ruth. Scrawny with a long neck, Edna reminded Katie Ruth of the turkey vultures commonly seen in Devil's Lake State Park. Even her hair had silver streaking the dark sides like wings.

"I believe you both know Katie Ruth." Dan gestured to her, his voice pleasant.

Katie Ruth forced a smile. "Edna. Ron."

"We're not personally acquainted," Edna clarified as Ron remained silent. "We know her by *reputation*."

Dan appeared to be momentarily struck speechless by the woman's rudeness.

Katie Ruth had more experience in such "polite" slights. "Wow, thanks, Edna. I've gotten quite a few compliments about my work with the youth group, but coming from you, that means a lot."

When Edna's eyes narrowed, Katie Ruth let her smile widen.

The older woman finally shifted her gaze to Dan. "I didn't realize the two of you were involved."

For a second, Katie Ruth wasn't sure how Dan would respond. She tried to tell herself she would understand if he explained away this dinner.

When he reached across the table and took her hand, Katie Ruth nearly jumped.

"Katie Ruth and I are dating." He gave her hand a squeeze, then released it.

"You know her parents…" Edna began, shaking her husband's hand from her arm.

"I'm sure you're familiar with the words 'judge not.'" Dan didn't need to say more.

Edna's thin lips pressed together.

"Why are you standing there?" Edna said to her husband, jerking her head in the direction of the hostess. "Can't you see the woman is waiting to seat us?"

Without another word, Edna whirled and strode off.

"Good to see you, Preacher." Ron shifted his attention to Katie Ruth. "Sorry about that."

The hostess, as if sensing distance was best in this situation, seated the two at the far end of the dining room.

Though seconds earlier Katie Ruth had been nearly positive she'd opt for dessert, she felt that a pall now hung over the table.

"I don't want to cause trouble for you." Hot tears stung the backs of her lids, but Katie Ruth blinked them away. In a matter of minutes, her hopes of a future with Dan had been dashed. "I know we just said we want this to be our beginning, but maybe…" She took a deep breath and forced herself to get out the words. "Maybe we shouldn't be starting something. I don't want your association with me to damage your reputation."

He stared at her for a long time, searching her face. "Is that what you want?"

"This isn't about what I want." Her voice rose, then broke. She took another steadying breath. "You're destined for bigger and better. Anyone can see that. The congregation, your father, and I can see that, too. I don't want to stand in your way."

"I don't want you to stand in my way either."

Katie Ruth looked up and saw a small smile soften Dan's otherwise serious expression.

"I much rather have you standing by my side. Katie Ruth, your parents' actions are not yours." Dan's gaze remained steady. "I'm proud to be with you. That isn't going to change."

Katie Ruth thought of the message from Judd. She told herself that had been one weekend, so far in the past it barely counted. It had nothing to do with now. Nothing to do with the woman she was now.

"I was going to suggest we leave." Katie Ruth spoke slowly and felt a smile lift her lips.

As if picking up on the past tense, he smiled. "Now?"

"Want to split some fried ice cream?"

~

"I came up with more questions for the youth group." Katie Ruth scooped up the last bite of ice cream.

Dan supposed it was inevitable the talk would turn to business. They were both so involved in the ministry at First Christian it was difficult to keep from bringing up related topics.

He didn't mind, but the memory of Lindsay's long-suffering expression whenever he'd brought up church business had kept him from mentioning anything tonight.

The coffee he and Katie Ruth had ordered with dessert had been refilled. Dan sipped the rich Colombian blend, and contentment washed over him. "Do you recall any of them?"

"I have them with me." She pulled her bag to her lap and began rummaging through the contents. Heaving an exasperated breath, she set her phone, a slim wallet and a deck of cards on the table while continuing to search.

"Are these it?" Dan picked up the cards.

Katie Ruth lifted her gaze from the bowels of her purse and shook her head. "Cassie gave those to me. I was working on my list at the Daily Grind, and she asked what I was doing. When I told her that I was trying to come up with a list of questions, she hurried off and said that reminded her of something she needed to get rid of. She came back and dropped these in my bag."

Dan began to flip through the deck.

Katie Ruth huffed out a frustrated sound. "I can't find my list."

"That's okay." Dan lifted the hand holding the cards. "We could see if any of these questions work."

Katie Ruth's expression turned doubtful. "I don't think we'll find anything appropriate for middle schoolers. Cassie mentioned these were for couples. When I tried to tell her my questions were intended for the youth group, she just waved me off and said I had to take them off her hands. She made it sound as if the deck had been passed all around Good Hope."

Dan cocked his head. This was sounding familiar. He swore someone had mentioned the cards to him. "You can't pass them along until you've answered three questions."

Katie Ruth's eyes widened. "You've heard about them?"

"I can't remember from who, but yes, they're rather notorious." Dan studied her. "Apparently, some of the questions are mild, and others are," he searched for the right word, "racy."

Katie Ruth laughed. "Better not show this deck to Edna."

"Good point." He glanced at the cards. "If you're feeling adventurous, I can pull one from the deck."

She wrinkled her nose, and her tone turned teasing. "As long as I reserve the right not to answer."

"Absolutely." Dan set the deck on the table, then pulled a card from the middle and read aloud. "When you and your partner argue about an issue, what do you say to resolve it?"

"If we change the word 'partner' to 'friend,' we could use a question like this with the youth group." Katie Ruth's brows drew together. "Maybe have it read, 'When you and your friend disagree about an issue, how do you resolve it?'"

Dan nodded. "That would foster discussion. Such as if your friend is suggesting something that is clearly wrong, you need to state your opinion firmly and stand your ground."

"Or," Katie Ruth said, "if it's not clear who is right or wrong, you may have to agree to disagree."

"Someone could also take the question as if you've disagreed and you know you're wrong, what do you do? I think some teens, or adults, prefer to just pretend it didn't happen and move forward."

"Instead of just apologizing to someone, first admit that you know you wronged them and ask for forgiveness."

"I like the question." Dan tapped the table with his hand. "It'd be a good one for adult Bible study, too."

"I agree. I'll make a note of it." Katie Ruth's gaze slid to the deck. An impish gleam filled those baby blues. "What do you say?

Shall we stop now while we're ahead? Or try another and take our chances?"

# CHAPTER ELEVEN

Dan didn't immediately answer as Edna and Ron chose that moment to sail by the table on their way out the door.

Katie Ruth glanced briefly in their direction. Dan offered a nod and a smile, but the couple's eyes remained firmly on the exit.

When Dan returned his attention to her, Katie Ruth didn't mention the couple. Instead, she let her fingers hover over the deck. "One more?"

Dan grinned. "Let's do it."

She took the top card, flipped it over. "How do you feel about your partner's exes?"

"It seems to me that question is designed to ferret out jealousy."

Katie Ruth found it interesting that Dan analyzed the question rather than answering it. That was okay with her. She didn't have any exes of any importance. Even Judd had been a momentary blip.

"Jealousy and envy are common at that age, so this would also be a good one to use." Katie Ruth chewed on her lower lip. "The discussion leader could make the topic more broad, not just talking about past relationships but about sibling rivalry and possessions."

"It amazes me how relevant these questions are and how they really can cause a person to look deep in many different ways." Dan studied her. "How do you feel about my exes?"

"Are there others besides Lindsay?" Katie Ruth could have bitten off her tongue. Asking him about his past left the door open to him asking about hers. She held up a hand. "Sorry. Not my business."

Dan smiled. "No take-backs."

Surprise must have skittered across her face at the terminology, because he laughed. "It seems I've been spending too much time with my sister."

"I don't want to pry—"

"You're not prying. We're getting to know each other." The warmth in his voice had the protest dying on her lips. "I've really only had two serious relationships. The first was with Sharla. We met in college and dated for nearly two years. My family loved her."

"She met your parents." Since he hadn't gone to college in his hometown, he must have taken her home. "That does qualify as serious."

"We'd tossed around the idea of getting married once we graduated." He shook his head. "It seems so long ago now."

Katie Ruth told herself to let it go. The more questions she asked, the more he'd feel free to ask her in return. Still, she wanted to know why they'd split. "What happened?"

"She was shocked when I told her I'd decided to go into full-time ministry."

Katie Ruth knew he had to be leaving something out. "Why was she surprised? Surely she knew you were considering it."

Dan flushed. "Actually, I thought of it as my decision to make. I didn't want to involve her until I knew for certain it was what *I* wanted. Does that make sense?"

The nod Katie Ruth offered came grudgingly. "I understand you wanted to be certain of your own feelings. But you'd dated her for two years and talked about marriage."

"You think I should have said something to her before."

"I do." Katie Ruth wasn't about to sugarcoat her feelings. "Putting myself in her shoes, I'd have felt betrayed that you'd kept something so important to yourself."

"That's pretty much word for word what she told me." Dan expelled a breath. When he met her gaze, she saw the regret. "I apologized, but it was too late."

"Why too late?"

He was quiet for a long moment. "She had no interest in being a minister's wife."

Katie Ruth now understood. "It was the ministry that was the problem."

He nodded.

"I bet that's why you didn't bring it up."

Dan raised a brow.

"You knew she'd try to talk you out of it."

"She did try."

"But by that time, you already knew it was the right decision for you."

He lifted his hands. "I can't imagine doing anything else with my life."

"If she couldn't understand that, if she couldn't see herself as a minister's wife, then it's best you broke up."

"My dad sure didn't see it that way."

"Parents don't always know best." Katie Ruth chuckled. "Mine thought I should be a funeral director."

Dan's mouth dropped open. "Seriously?"

"To be fair, I helped out a lot at Amigone in high school. I was good with clients." Katie Ruth shrugged. "Being able to comfort and support those who'd lost a loved one was the part I liked the best. The other stuff not so much."

"Do they still hold that choice against you?"

The way he asked the question told her that his parents still did.

Katie Ruth smiled. "That is one upside to having parents who subscribe to an...alternative lifestyle. Generally speaking, they aren't big on being judgmental. At least, mine aren't. They accept that I'm right where I'm meant to be." Katie Ruth smiled. "Like I said, they're great parents."

"You're lucky."

Katie Ruth thought back to those middle school and high school days. Back then, she never could have said this, but she meant every word. "I am. Very lucky."

Dan glanced down at the card, then back at her.

Katie Ruth's heart skittered as she fought for something that would distract him from—

"What about your exes?" A thoughtful look crossed his face. "Since I've been in Good Hope, I don't recall you dating anyone steadily."

Katie Ruth seized on his words. "I've never dated anyone steadily."

"Never?"

"Never." It was true. They were talking about dating *steadily*, so Judd didn't qualify. "I'm the type of woman magazine articles tell you to be wary of."

Confusion furrowed Dan's brow. "Why?"

"The thought is, if you reached the ancient age of thirty without having been in a serious relationship, it indicates you have commitment issues."

Dan cocked his head. "Do you?"

"Do I what?"

"Have commitment issues?"

Instead of tossing out a quick "no," Katie Ruth took a few seconds to consider. "I don't believe I do. Back in high school, I was scared to let any guy get too close because I worried he'd think I was like my parents."

"In college?"

"My longest relationship was four months." Katie Ruth gave a laugh. "I was too busy with activities."

"What about after college?"

Katie Ruth lifted her hands and let them drop. "Too busy working, and no one has interested me."

Her eyes locked with his.

*Until you.*

Dan whistled as he unlocked the front door of his house and flicked on the hall light. Taking Katie Ruth to Egg Harbor had been the smart move. They'd been able to laugh and talk without interruption. Other than running into Ron and Edna, it had been smooth sailing.

When his gaze had locked with hers, he'd realized Katie Ruth was falling for him the same way he was falling for her. It was still hard for him to believe that such a lovely, accomplished, wonderful woman wasn't married.

His time with Sharla had taught him—and then Lindsay had reinforced—that not every woman would be happy being a minister's wife.

Then Katie Ruth had come into his life.

He smiled.

"How was the date?"

Dan flipped on the living room lights and found Oaklee on the sofa. "What are you doing sitting in the dark?"

Oaklee motioned to a chair, and Dan dropped into it.

"There's light from the moon." Oaklee relaxed against the sofa cushion. "I was practicing 'mindfulness meditation.' Being still in the quiet and darkness is a good way to clear your mind of clutter."

"I'll have to try it sometime." Dan studied his sister's face. "Are you sure you're okay?"

"Peachy keen." She made a come-ahead motion. "Tell me about your date."

"Well, *Mom*." He paused and saw a smile chase away the sadness he'd seen seconds earlier. "I had a nice time. The food was good, and Katie Ruth is amazing."

"What did you talk about?"

"You want a blow-by-blow?"

"Yes, please."

He laughed. "I never got this level of interrogation from Mom or Dad."

"Consider yourself lucky." Oaklee sighed. "I swear if Dad could have gotten his hands on a lie detector machine, he'd have hooked me up after every date."

"He wants the best for you."

"They were freaked I'd get pregnant and they'd be stuck with me and a baby."

"I'm sure—"

"I heard them say it."

"To you?"

"No, to each other." Oaklee cupped both ears. "I hear everything."

"I'll keep that in mind." Dan kept his tone light. "The reason I'm so late is Katie Ruth and I went through more questions for middle schoolers."

Oaklee's moan sounded like a dying buffalo.

"What's the matter?"

"Tell me you didn't spend the entire night talking church business."

"It was interesting and very enjoyable."

"For you maybe." Exasperation colored Oaklee's words. "But for Katie Ruth—"

"She enjoyed it, too," Dan insisted.

His sister's skeptical look had him continuing. "She was as excited as I was to discuss the questions. It's like we're a team."

That seemed to mollify Oaklee somewhat, but he could tell she wasn't entirely convinced.

"You're telling me you talked church stuff the whole night."

"No. We didn't talk church stuff the entire night."

"Hallelujah!" Oaklee jumped up, threw her hands in the air and did a little boogie. At his startled look, she chuckled. "Being a minister, you've already got one strike against you. If you can't even show her a good time when you go out, this isn't going to work."

"It's not like that." For some reason, it was important to Dan that he convince his sister the night hadn't been a bust.

The time at the restaurant had been enjoyable, not only for him but for Katie Ruth. He was sure of it, or pretty sure of it. When he'd walked Katie Ruth to her front door, where they'd shared several kisses, he'd been positive.

But Oaklee's skepticism was doing a number on his self-confidence.

"We discussed past relationships."

Oaklee straightened on the sofa. "That sounds promising. Has she had many? What were they like?"

"She hasn't dated anyone for more than a few months."

"Problems with commitment?" At the look he shot her, Oaklee pursed her lips. "She's old."

"She's my age."

"Like I said, she's old. She should have had at least one serious relationship by now."

"Well, she said she hasn't."

"You believe her?"

Dan didn't appreciate Oaklee questioning Katie Ruth's veracity. "Katie Ruth is one of the most honest people I know."

"When are you seeing her again?"

"Sunday in church."

"What is the matter with you? Don't you know anything about women?"

Dan raked a hand through his hair, suddenly weary. "Enlighten me, oh wise one."

If Oaklee caught the sarcasm, she ignored it. "While it's nice that you invited her out for dinner, this is a Thursday night. Friday and Saturday are *date* nights."

"It doesn't ma—"

"It does matter," Oaklee insisted with a vehemence that startled him. "When my, ah, my previous boyfriend took me out, it was always early in the week."

Dan shot her a questioning look.

"I wasn't important to him." Oaklee expelled a breath. "I see that now. Katie Ruth *is* important to you."

He slowly nodded.

"There's a music festival tomorrow night in the barn at Rakes Farm. Money from the ten-dollar admission goes to the Giving Tree."

Dan recalled seeing a poster of the event. He hadn't been into live music since his college days. "Do you want to attend?"

"I already have plans to go with someone." Oaklee tapped a finger against her lips. "What about you? Who do you want to take?"

"Point made. I'll call Katie Ruth in the morning and see if she's interested."

"Call her now. I bet she's still up."

Dan didn't need to look at the clock to know it was close to eleven. Unless it was an emergency, he'd made it a practice to never make calls after nine.

"You wouldn't want her to accept an offer to go with someone else." Oaklee crossed her arms and tapped her foot, an expectant look on her face.

Dan pulled out his phone.

Katie Ruth answered on the first ring. "Dan. Hi. Is everything okay? Did you get home safely?"

The fact that she didn't sound sleepy was a good thing. Conscious of Oaklee's eyes—and those ears—on him, he left the room.

"I'm home, and everything is fine." He kept his voice low until he reached the kitchen. "I enjoyed being with you this evening."

"I had fun, too."

For a second, Dan was seized by the childish urge to put Katie Ruth on speaker and have her repeat the words for his doubting-Thomas sister.

"I don't know if you heard about the music festival at Rakes Farm tomorrow night." He paused, giving her time to say if she already had plans.

"I did hear about it."

Well, that was totally unhelpful.

"I wondered if you'd like to go." He pushed out the words, feeling as awkward as a sixteen-year-old asking out a girl for the first time. "With me."

He couldn't believe he'd added that last bit. He waited for her to laugh.

"I'd love to go with you. Let me pull up the events calendar and see what time it starts."

He waited and listened to her murmuring to herself.

"Good. It starts at seven." She hesitated. "I assume you want to be there when it starts?"

"Whatever works for you."

"You're being mighty accommodating," she teased.

"I'm looking forward to seeing you again," he said. "The festival is an excuse."

Was that a happy sigh or only his overeager imagination?

"I'm working at the Y tomorrow, but I'm off at six. Pick me up at six thirty?"

"I'll be there." Dan tightened his grip on the phone, and his voice became a husky rasp. "Good night, Katie Ruth."

"Good night, Dan." He heard the smile in her voice. "Until tomorrow."

When she clicked off, Dan stood with his hands braced on the counter. He would see Katie Ruth tomorrow.

Sometimes, he decided, little sisters really did know best.

# CHAPTER TWELVE

While Dan paid the suggested admission to the festival, Katie Ruth studied the barn's Welcome to Spring decor.

She recognized Lindsay's touch in the huge vases of tulips and daffodils. Colorful fairy lights shone overhead, and the linens on round tables boasted a variety of spring colors.

The two cash bars were doing a booming business, but there was still an abundance of people at the refreshment tables that offered tea, lemonade and water.

According to the circular she'd been handed, three bands would each play for forty-five minutes with fifteen-minute breaks in between.

"Look, Dan." Katie Ruth pointed to the sheet as he stepped to her side. "This one is a Christian rock band out of Milwaukee."

He leaned close, and her heart did a little somersault at his nearness. His brows pulled together. "I don't believe I've heard of Baggage Claim."

"They had that big hit, 'Look Up.'" She turned her head, which brought her mouth even closer to his. "I know their star is on the rise, but if they're willing, we might be able to work with the other churches and bring them back for a teen concert."

"That's a great idea."

She flushed. "That's me. Lots of ideas."

"Lots of *good* ideas."

"Hey, guys."

Katie Ruth turned, and there was Lindsay, looking even more pregnant, if that was possible.

"I'm surprised to see you here," Katie Ruth said as Owen and Dan shook hands. "Isn't your baby due any day?"

"Thirteen days to go." Lindsay squeezed her husband's hand. "You know what they say about a watched pot. Besides, I wanted to see how the flowers look."

Katie Ruth pulled her brows together in puzzlement. "You didn't see them when you set this up?"

"This time I didn't do the setup," Lindsay said while rubbing her swollen belly. "Owen, Izzie and KT took care of it this afternoon while I napped."

"They're lovely," Katie Ruth told her. "You do the best—"

"Well, isn't this an interesting group?" Oaklee flashed a smile at Owen and Lindsay.

"Play nice," Dan warned.

His sister wrinkled her nose. "I like Lindsay and Owen."

"I've been hearing a lot about how talented you are," Lindsay told Oaklee.

A startled look crossed Oaklee's face. "You have?"

"Gladys showed me some of the unusual quilted place mats you made for her and her friends." Lindsay studied the girl. "I loved the way the flowers popped out from the mats, so I showed them to Izzie and KT."

"Why?" Oaklee asked bluntly.

"We're partners. I do floral, while Izzie and KT do specialty gift items that are sold along with the flowers." Lindsay's tone turned businesslike. "Your designs are fresh and original. I believe we could sell them in our shop."

"Are you serious?"

Lindsay pulled a card from her purse. "Call me. We can talk more."

"I will." Oaklee's expression turned serious. "Thanks."

"We're going to do more walking and check out the silent-auction items." Lindsay took her husband's arm. "Lead the way."

Oaklee waited until they were out of earshot to shriek. "Did you hear that?"

"It's very exciting." Katie Ruth gave the girl a hug.

"What's the good news?" Marigold asked.

The youngest Bloom sister looked stunning and stylish in heeled boots and a tunic top. She'd recently added several streaks of violet to her tumbled mane of blond curls.

"I'm going into business with Lindsay," Oaklee announced.

Marigold cast a look at Dan, who just shrugged.

"The two of them are going to talk about carrying some of the items that Oaklee makes," Katie Ruth clarified.

"Your hair is super cool," Oaklee told Marigold in a mercurial change of topic.

"Thank you." Marigold returned the girl's smile. "Hair is my business. I love changing things up."

"I'm thinking of changing mine," Oaklee told her.

Dan cast a questioning glance in Katie Ruth's direction, but she shrugged. It appeared, like him, this was the first she'd heard of these plans.

"What are you considering?" Marigold asked.

There was no judgment in the hair stylist's voice, no disapproval of the pink that had obviously been self-applied.

"Something like Cassie's blond hair with the light blond highlights." Oaklee cocked her head. "Or maybe go back to my brown hair roots and add caramel highlights."

Marigold studied her for a long moment. "Either would work with your skin tone, as long as you don't go too dark with the brown."

"That's what I was thinking, too."

Marigold smiled. "The great thing about hair is you can change it. Pick one. Have your hair that way for a while, then do the other."

"Would you color it for me?" Oaklee held up a hand before Marigold could respond. "I need to be honest. I don't have a lot of cash, but I could make you a baby quilt."

Marigold's smile froze. "What would I do with a baby quilt?"

"Well, duh, your one sister just had a baby, and the other will be having one this spring."

"Okay." Marigold appeared unaware of her husband's hand lightly stroking her back. "Bring fabric samples with you when you come in for your appointment. I'll choose the colors for the quilt."

"Fabric samples are only the beginning." Oaklee waved a hand. "I can show you pics of different types of baby quilts."

Marigold's brows drew together. "I thought there was only one kind."

"You *are* out of the loop." Oaklee pulled out her phone and scrolled to a picture. "This is a heart rag quilt. One of my personal faves."

Katie Ruth peered over Oaklee's shoulder to catch a glimpse.

"It's lovely." Marigold lifted her gaze. "You can make one of these?"

"I can make you exactly what you want."

Marigold thrust out her hand. "We've got a deal. Call my salon on Monday. We'll find a time for you to come in."

"Will I look as beautiful as you when I walk out the door?" Oaklee asked.

"I'm a hair stylist." Marigold's blue eyes took on an impish gleam, and Katie Ruth waited for the zinger. "Not a miracle worker."

Oaklee's loud guffaw had people nearby turning to stare. "I like you, Marigold. You're cool beans."

Out of the corner of her eye, Katie Ruth noticed Baggage

Claim was getting ready to start their set. She touched Dan's arm. "I'm going to move closer to the stage. I want to see how the band members interact with the teens clustered around the stage."

"Good idea." Dan turned to the others, gestured with his head. "Katie Ruth and I are going to check out the band. Are you coming with us, Oaklee?"

Oaklee looped an arm through Marigold's. "I'm staying here with my new BFF."

A look of startled surprise crossed Marigold's face before her lips quirked up in a wry smile. "We have a way to go for BFF status."

"I grow on people," Oaklee declared. "Don't I, Katie Ruth?"

"She does indeed." Katie Ruth wiggled her fingers. "See you, guys."

Dan glanced back at the group several times on their way to the stage. "I feel as if I'm foisting my sister on any willing human."

"She's an adult." Katie Ruth kept her tone matter-of-fact. "I've known Marigold my entire life. Trust me, she's capable of taking care of herself. That includes extricating herself from your sister should the need arise."

"You're right." He gave her arm a squeeze.

Katie Ruth stopped to the left of the stage. The band members looked to be in their early to mid-twenties. They wore all black except for the band name in iridescent purple on the front of their shirts.

"They're a good-looking group of guys." Katie Ruth had to speak into Dan's ear as the group tuned up.

"They seem to agree with you." Dan pointed to the teenage girls standing in front of the stage.

Once the band started to play, Katie Ruth lost herself in the music. Song after song drew her in with the beat. She couldn't help moving to the music, and around song number five, Dan pulled her to the dance floor, where they joined other couples and singles dancing to the songs.

The music pulled her in, but the lyrics wrapped around her heart. Words about love and forgiveness, about starting over and never being alone.

Katie Ruth clapped as loudly as everyone around her when the set ended. She watched the young men interact with the girls wanting their autographs.

*Friendly*, *polite* and *respectful* were the three words that popped into her head.

"Do you want to ask them if they'd be interested in coming back to Good Hope, or should I?" While Katie Ruth knew she'd likely be coordinating the event, Dan was the pastor.

He would be the one working with other clergy in the area to garner support and a financial buy-in for the event.

"You'll be their contact person, Katie Ruth. It'll be good for them to put a face with a name."

Katie Ruth noticed the band's manager was motioning his guys along. "C'mon, men, the next band needs to set up."

Once the band was on the move and everything appeared under control, Katie Ruth approached the man and began her pitch.

～

Dan liked the way Katie Ruth communicated, gesturing wildly with her hands. Her enthusiasm and energy were contagious.

The band manager, a guy in his late thirties, appeared entranced.

"What's she doing with that guy?"

Oaklee's voice had him turning. "What'd you think of Baggage Claim?"

"I liked 'em." Oaklee gestured with her head. "Why is Katie Ruth cozying up to their manager?"

"She's not cozying up. We're considering booking them for a concert in the fall." Dan's eyes followed the two where they took a seat at a table far from the stage. "This is the initial contact. Katie Ruth will handle the coordination, which is why she's speaking with the manager."

"She's kind of your perfect match, huh?"

Dan focused on his sister.

"Don't give me that 'what are you talking about now?' look." Oaklee rolled her eyes. "Crazy about church activities plus crazy about you equals Dan Marshall's perfect match."

"You think she's crazy about me?"

Oaklee laughed. "She looks at you as if you're some kind of rock star, which we both know you aren't."

Dan couldn't help but grin at Oaklee's observation.

"You look at her as if—"

When his sister didn't continue, Dan inclined his head. "How do I look at her?"

"As if you love her. That's how you look at her."

*As if you love her.*

His sister's words circled in his brain as Katie Ruth rejoined him. Her mood was upbeat and infectious. Apparently, the manager had been interested in her proposal.

"Once we get buy-in from the other churches in the area, we'll need to figure out a date and secure the venue." Katie Ruth's flushed cheeks and bright eyes had Dan wanting to pull her into his arms. "I'm thinking the fall would be the perfect time. Perhaps September, maybe in conjunction with the Harvest Festival. We could do an outdoor concert as long as we can come up with a date that isn't too late in the year."

She paused and gazed up at him. He knew she was waiting for his reply, but he couldn't seem to pull his gaze from her mouth.

"Dan?"

When he looked up, he saw in her eyes that she knew exactly where his mind had strayed.

"Sounds like a good plan." He cocked his head. "Are you ready to leave?"

The last band was halfway through their set, and then there would be the last-minute rush to bid on the silent-auction items. Perhaps Katie Ruth would want to stay.

Dan had seen the band he wanted to check out. He'd socialized and mingled with members of his congregation, but now he was ready for alone time...with Katie Ruth.

"I am ready." She glanced around the large room. "What about Oaklee?"

"She came with Gladys and her friends." He shrugged. "I assume they'll drop her off."

"There's no one better than Gladys." Katie Ruth's lips curved. "Like your sister, she might be bold and in-your-face, but she's got a heart of gold."

"I realize you've had a long day." Dan stopped when they reached his car, placing one hand on the roof. "But I'm not ready for the evening to end."

She gazed up at him with those clear blue eyes. "What do you have in mind?"

"We could grab coffee at the Grind, or we could sit out on the deck of the Flying Crane and have a drink? It'll be cool by the water, but they should have the heat lamps on."

Unless they drove into Sturgeon Bay, there weren't a lot of late-night options in Good Hope during the off-season. He supposed he could have mentioned the hotel or Bayside Pizza, but they'd already eaten, and taking a woman to a hotel didn't seem wise, even if they would only be grabbing a drink in the bar.

"I'd kind of like to sit out on the deck, but—" She chewed on her lower lip. "Are you sure going to a bar isn't a problem for your congregation?"

"If I was going there and getting drunk, that would be a problem." He opened the door for her. "Having one drink isn't an issue."

As Dan drove them back into Good Hope, he let Oaklee's words circle in his head.

*Your perfect match.*

Only when they were on the Flying Crane's deck, gazing out over the moonlit water, cups of steaming coffee on the table, did Katie Ruth return to the topic of Baggage Claim. "I really think the kids will be able to relate to their lyrics."

Dan thought back to the various songs in the set. "Temptation, forgiveness, mercy…"

"Grace," Katie Ruth added.

"Appropriate for the struggles we all face," Dan agreed.

The scrape of a chair being pushed back had them both turning to watch Ethan toss a couple of bills onto the table. He'd spotted Eliza's brother when he first arrived. The two guys he was with were unfamiliar to Dan.

"Hope it turns out okay," one of the men at his table called out.

Ethan gave a nod as he pulled on his jacket. Worry blanketed his face as he crossed the deck.

He would have passed the table where Dan sat with Katie Ruth, but Dan stopped him with a hand on his arm. "Is everything okay?"

"I got a text from Kyle. Eliza is in labor. They're at the hospital in Sturgeon Bay." Ethan's voice was steady, but Dan saw the concern in his eyes. "The doctors are thinking about shipping my sister to Froedtert in Milwaukee. She's having some trouble with the delivery. Kyle said I didn't need to come, but he sounded relieved when I said I was on my way."

Dan pushed back his chair and stood. "I'd like to be there, too, if you don't think I'd be in the way."

"That'd be good." Ethan glanced at the door. "Prayers certainly can't hurt."

Katie Ruth scrambled to her feet, but Ethan had already disappeared from sight.

"We should hurry, too." Dan dropped a ten-dollar bill on the table. He headed for the parking lot, with Katie Ruth at his side. The taillights of Ethan's car were barely in view when Dan took the wheel and Katie Ruth slid into the passenger seat.

"I want to get there as soon as possible." Dan slanted a glance in her direction. "Do you mind riding along? It would take more time to drop you off."

"No. Go." Katie Ruth's brows pulled together. "I believe Eliza just turned thirty-five weeks. Initially, they thought she was due around the second of May, but the ultrasounds have indicated she's further along. They moved up her due date to around the twentieth of April."

Katie Ruth paused for a breath. "I'm sorry. I'm rambling."

Dan nodded, his eyes fixed on the road. A light rain had begun to fall. At this time of year, he supposed he should be grateful it wasn't snow.

"I know you need to stay focused on your driving, but I was wondering if we could say a little prayer on the way?"

Dan found himself touched by Katie Ruth's suggestion. "Why don't you start, and I'll chime in?"

"Dear Lord," Katie Ruth began.

Dan listened to her prayer. Her faith was so apparent, so pure, that for a second when she paused—apparently waiting for him to add his words to hers—he was at a loss.

Then he thought of Kyle and Eliza and the baby girl they'd been waiting for, and the words flowed.

"Amen." Katie Ruth's voice echoed his word. She expelled a breath. "I feel better putting this in His hands."

*Perfect for you.*

The words stayed in Dan's head as they reached the hospital and hurried inside.

# CHAPTER THIRTEEN

Katie Ruth kept pace with Dan as their shoes slapped against the shiny linoleum on their way to the hospital's maternity wing.

She'd expected Ethan to be alone, but he sat with Lindsay and Owen in the waiting area. The three jumped to their feet.

Katie Ruth inwardly shuddered when she saw the fear on their faces.

Dan stepped to them. "How's Eliza and the baby?"

"The medication they gave her to stop the labor didn't work. They gave her a steroid shot to help the baby's lungs." Lindsay's voice began to shake, and she brought a hand to her mouth.

Ethan remained silent.

Owen tugged his wife close. "She'll be fine. You'll see."

"Yes, but what about the baby?" Lindsay's voice was thick with unshed tears. "She wasn't due to be born for weeks."

"The baby will be fine, too." Though fear remained in Owen's eyes, his confident words appeared to soothe the worst of his wife's fears.

"Is Jeremy coming?" Katie Ruth didn't ask about Eliza's or Kyle's parents, knowing both lived out of state. But Jeremy was

Kyle's half brother and the closest thing to family he had in the area.

"On his way," Owen confirmed.

"How did you get here so fast?" Dan asked Lindsay. Like Owen's, his voice remained calm and steady.

"We stopped over to see Eliza and Kyle after the festival, and we were there when the contractions started." Lindsay wrung her hands.

"Does Ami know?" Like everyone else in Good Hope, Katie Ruth knew Ami and Lindsay were Eliza's closest friends.

"I'm keeping her updated." Regret crossed Lindsay's face. "JT is so little she didn't want to leave him. It's killing her not to be here."

Ethan glanced at the closed set of doors leading to the labor and delivery area. "It's been a while since Kyle came out."

"I hope that means—" Lindsay began.

"Everything is okay," Owen said so firmly that Katie Ruth wasn't sure who he was trying to convince.

Footsteps echoed in the hallway. Seconds later, Jeremy burst into the room. Katie Ruth hadn't thought Fin would come—she and Eliza weren't particularly close—but Fin was at her husband's side.

Jeremy skidded to a stop. "What's the latest?"

Lindsay gave him and Fin the same report she'd given Katie Ruth and Dan moments before.

"Who can we speak with to get an update?" Clearly used to being in charge, Jeremy glanced around, but there was no one in sight.

"I wish we could do something to help." Lindsay began to pace, her husband's worried eyes following her every step.

"We could pray." When all eyes shifted to Katie Ruth, she felt oddly embarrassed.

"Good idea," Fin agreed.

Lindsay settled her gaze on Dan.

Katie Ruth wondered if it was only her, or did it seem like Dan's deep voice and heartfelt words reached all the way to the heavens when he asked God to place His healing hand on Eliza and the baby?

"Dear Father," Dan said in closing, "help Eliza and Kyle to feel your presence and gain comfort from the knowledge that you are with them. Let them draw strength from you and give them peace in this uncertain time. Amen."

The door to the labor and delivery area flew open. Kyle stood in blue scrubs, wearing the expression of someone who'd been hit in the chest with a two-by-four.

Katie Ruth hung back as the others rushed forward.

"How's my sister?" Ethan demanded.

Lindsay clutched Kyle's arm as tears slipped down her cheeks. "Are they going to transfer Eliza to Milwaukee?"

"There's no need." Kyle collapsed in a nearby chair. "Our little girl is like her mother. She decided today was the day, and by God, no one was going to stop her."

Ethan expelled a ragged breath. "And Eliza?"

Kyle grinned. "Happy. So very happy."

"Ava is here?" Jeremy dropped down next to his brother. "Already?"

*Ava.*

Katie Ruth smiled. She hadn't known the couple had settled on a name.

"Both Eliza and the baby are doing well. I could tell she was feeling better when she started ordering around the nurses. Our daughter is perfect." Kyle's grin held a mixture of relief and elation. "Eighteen inches long and five pounds six ounces. Breathing on her own. Screaming on her own is more accurate."

"Congratulations." Dan extended a hand.

Kyle took Dan's hand, and their gazes locked. "I heard the end of the prayer. Thank you for that."

Reassured that everything was under control, Katie Ruth and Dan said their good-byes.

On the drive home, Katie Ruth leaned her head against the back of the seat.

"Tired?" Dan asked.

"Exhausted." Katie Ruth opened her eyes. "I was worried about Eliza and the baby."

"I'm happy it all worked out."

"Me, too."

"I'm glad you were with me tonight."

Katie Ruth understood. Though Sturgeon wasn't far from Good Hope, the drive could be a boring one, especially at night. "I'm happy I could keep you company on the drive."

"That isn't what I meant." With his eyes on the road, Dan reached over and took her hand. "We worked together like a team tonight. It felt good."

"I didn't do anything." Katie Ruth wanted to wave her hand, but she liked the feel of his around hers too much. "I just asked a couple questions."

"You have a soothing way about you. It's calming to others." He smiled. "And to me."

"Well, if I was of any help, I'm glad." She gazed into the darkness. "Most of all, I'm glad there was a happy ending. I envy Eliza."

Dan remained silent, obviously concentrating on the road. The earlier rain had ended, but fog now settled over the highway, dropping visibility to several car lengths.

Katie Ruth didn't mind the silence. With Dan, the silence wasn't awkward or tense, but comfortable. The slight chill in the outside air was dispelled by the car's heated seats.

"What is it about her life that you envy?"

Lost in her thoughts, Katie Ruth blinked. "Pardon?"

"You said you envy Eliza. What is it about her life that you envy?"

"She found someone who's her perfect match in every way." Katie Ruth sighed, remembering the drama when Eliza and Kyle had first met. Thankfully, like tonight, there was a happy ending. "Now they're married and have a daughter."

When Dan didn't immediately respond, Katie Ruth felt her cheeks grow hot.

"It isn't like I'm on a search for Prince Charming or anything." Katie Ruth spoke quickly, not wanting him to think she was a hopeless romantic.

She was thirty, not sixteen. There were no stars in her eyes.

"If by Prince Charming you mean someone who loves and respects you, someone who will support you in achieving your goals, I say why not search for that person?"

Katie Ruth gave a noncommittal shrug, though she wasn't sure Dan could see the movement in the dim light.

"Sometimes, that person doesn't ride up on a white horse, or have a million dollars in the bank." Dan's tone remained easy and conversational. "Sometimes, the man could be, say, a minister."

Katie Ruth froze for a second, wondering if she'd heard correctly. The air of watchful waiting permeating the interior told her she had.

She shifted in her seat toward him as much as the safety belt would allow. Her heart had butterfly wings brushing against her throat. It took several swallows to find her voice. "What are you saying, Dan?"

"I'm saying that I'd like for you to give me a chance to win your heart." This time, it was his turn to clear his throat. "What do you say, Katie Ruth? Is there a chance I could be your Prince Charming?"

∾

Katie Ruth shut her front door and collapsed against it, her heart hammering. Though Dan's kisses had seemed extra sweet, it'd been the look in his eyes that had her swooning.

When she'd told him that yes, there was a good chance he could be her Prince Charming, his relieved grin had touched her heart. They'd continue to date...and see where it went from there.

The thing was, Katie Ruth didn't need more dates or kisses to know Dan was the man for her. How could any woman not fall for such a man? Dan Marshall was good and kind and so sexy he sent her heart racing each time he looked in her direction.

Still smiling, Katie Ruth dropped onto the sofa and heaved a happy sigh. It had been such a wonderful day. Not only had she gotten so many ideas for the youth concert, but Eliza and her baby girl were healthy, and she and Dan were growing closer by the second.

Though it was late, Katie Ruth was too wired to sleep. After jotting a couple of items on her to-do list for tomorrow, she scrolled through her Facebook and Instagram accounts before moving on to her texts.

There was one from a number she didn't recognize.

*Katie Ruth, I have to speak with you asap. Call me. Judd*

He had her phone number.

Gooseflesh dotted her arms. How could Judd have gotten her cell number? Katie Ruth wrapped her arms around herself to stop the chill, but they had no effect.

Why was he reaching out to her after all these years?

The problem was, Katie Ruth wasn't still friends with any of the women she'd known back then. After that weekend, she'd put her partying life behind her.

She'd been out of control during that trip, her recklessness fueled by an invitation from a guy she'd dated casually before she left for Vegas to "swing" with him.

That conversation had been her first indication that her

parents' unorthodox behavior had somehow become public knowledge among her eclectic circle of college friends. She'd thought she'd shrugged off the question, but her behavior once she reached Vegas said differently.

Katie Ruth stared down at her phone. Should she text Judd and tell him to leave her alone? Remind him they had nothing to say to each other?

If this was a spam message, she wouldn't respond. A return text would let the person know this was a working number, a number connected to someone who would respond.

Just as she would with any other spammer, Katie Ruth blocked his number.

She had a good life in Good Hope. The girl she'd been when she ran into Judd on that dance floor in Vegas no longer existed. The last thing Katie Ruth wanted was for her past—especially an episode of such short duration—to interfere with the present.

Which meant she was keeping Judd Stevens firmly in the past.

~

"She's a gorgeous baby." Katie Ruth gave one last glance at the dark-haired baby wrapped in a pink blanket festooned with frolicking lambs.

"Ava is definitely a keeper." Eliza gently stroked the fine hair of her daughter. "Kyle and I argue constantly over whose turn it is to hold her."

"You should have seen when my parents and Lolo were here." Kyle shook his head. "Everyone wanted a turn."

"Ed and Cheryl are coming tomorrow," Eliza said, referring to Kyle's biological father and his wife. "I'm sure it'll be the same thing all over again."

"A baby can't have too much love." Dan's gaze dropped from Kyle and Eliza to the baby. "You're blessed."

"We are." Kyle looked at Dan. "Thanks again for coming to the hospital. And for the prayers."

"Yes," Eliza added. "Thank you."

Katie Ruth noticed as they finished saying their good-byes that no one had mentioned Eliza's parents. Eliza had mentioned that her brother had been over several times to see his new niece, but she hadn't said anything about her parents.

"I wonder if Eliza's parents are planning to come by." Katie Ruth took Dan's arm as they strolled down the sidewalk toward the business district and her cottage.

Instead of driving the short distance to Eliza and Kyle's large Victorian home, Dan had left his car at her place and they'd walked there hand in hand.

Dan's brows pulled together. "I wonder what's going on there."

Katie Ruth didn't have to wonder. "In Eliza's family, it's all about Ethan. Though Eliza rarely speaks of it, everyone in town knew when we were younger that there was only one child in their family, and it wasn't her."

"I sincerely hope that isn't the case." Concern filled Dan's voice. "My sister feels that way, but I know my parents love her dearly."

Katie Ruth wasn't about to get into the relationship with Oaklee and her parents. But she'd grown up in Good Hope and remembered how the Shaws doted on their son.

"You can't have forgotten how Eliza's dad sold the house right out from under her. The house that her grandmother wanted her to inherit?"

"I had forgotten." Dan hesitated. "Speaking of parents, I'm going to be driving to Chicago tomorrow to visit mine."

"Really?" Katie Ruth had spent the afternoon with Oaklee, and the girl hadn't said anything about taking a trip. "How long will you and Oaklee be gone?"

"Actually, my sister isn't going with me."

"Why not?"

"My parents, well, my dad is still insisting that until she goes back to school, she's not welcome in his house."

"I hoped he'd softened by now. Did he ask you not to bring her?"

Dan expelled a heavy breath, then gave a slow nod. "I'm going to try to talk to him about her while I'm there."

"How did she take the news?"

"She doesn't know I'm going."

Katie Ruth's feelings must have shown on her face, because he hurriedly added, "I'm telling her tonight."

"She'll be crushed." Katie Ruth thought of her own parents. Say what you wanted about their unusual lifestyle, but they would never do something like this. Not to her. Nor to Nick. "Are you going to tell her that her father still doesn't want her there?"

"Give me some credit." As if realizing he'd spoken more harshly than he'd intended, Dan softened his tone. "I'm going to be honest. I'm going for a job interview and stopping by to see our parents."

"Job interview?"

"It was one of the reasons I wanted to see you tonight." He blew out a breath. "The call to interview came this morning. With Easter on the horizon, there weren't many times open, but tomorrow afternoon worked for both me and the search committee members."

"You're speaking of the associate pastor position at the church in Lincolnshire." Katie Ruth spoke slowly, trying to corral her thoughts. "The large congregation you brought up before."

"Yes." Dan tried to contain his excitement, but Katie Ruth knew him too well to be fooled. "I'm not sure how many they plan to interview, but I know they're hoping whoever they hire will move up when the senior pastor retires in five years."

"Sounds like you're interested." Katie Ruth kept her voice and expression neutral.

"I'm interested in speaking with them." Dan took her arm, spun her to face him. "Come with me. See the facility, talk with the ministers and the staff."

"I can't go with you." Katie Ruth gave a little laugh. "What would they think?"

"They'd think you were important to me." His voice grew husky. "You *are* important to me."

"I appreciate the offer, more than you know." Katie Ruth softened the upcoming refusal with a smile. "But we're not yet at the stage where you need to consult me. This decision is between you and God."

For a second, she thought he might argue, but then he nodded and pulled her to him. They fit perfectly together. Katie Ruth wished she could hold on to this moment, and this feeling, forever.

# CHAPTER FOURTEEN

On Friday, Katie Ruth took an extended lunch hour and met Oaklee at Marigold's. From the distressed-wood sign hanging from an ornate iron holder to the vintage Capodimonte porcelain chandelier with hand-painted flowers, the interior of the shop on Main Street was on par with any high-end salon in a large city.

Oaklee's eyes widened as they stepped inside the front door. Her gaze shifted from the tin ceiling original to the building to the exposed brick wall, then finally to the gleaming hardwood floor. "This place is amazeballs."

"Wait until you see what Marigold can do with hair," Katie Ruth told the girl. "Her talent is what's amazing."

"Thanks for the compliment." Marigold stepped from the back room, her tumble of blond curls pulled up in a bun, the hair tie covered with a scarf that had a brightly colored Wonder Woman pattern. Her pants, shirt and smock were all black.

"I'm still not sure what color I should try." Oaklee reached up and touched her own hair.

Marigold's gaze shifted to Katie Ruth.

"Oaklee asked me to come."

"Katie Ruth is the sister I always wanted," Oaklee told Marigold. "My brother is great, but it's not the same."

"I can't speak to brothers, because I've never had one." Marigold gestured for Oaklee to take a seat in the chair, then swept a cape around her. "I have three sisters. While they can be infuriating at times, I wouldn't trade them for the world."

"Katie Ruth and my brother are dating."

Appearing to fight a smile, Marigold slanted a glance at Katie Ruth. "Is that right?"

"I'm hoping it gets even more serious," Oaklee confided. "Then she'd be my sister for real."

"Time will tell," Marigold murmured, studying a lock of Oaklee's pink hair. "Instead of stripping, we'd be better going over the pink with a warm caramel brown. The permanent color will pull out the pink before depositing its own color."

"I bleached my hair before putting on the pink," Oaklee told her.

Marigold nodded. "We may need to adjust the brown if it fades, but that would be from the bleached hair not holding the permanent color, rather than from the pink."

"Sounds complicated," Katie Ruth said.

"Not at all." Marigold eyed Oaklee's shoulder-length hair. "Your hair is damaged. With your round face, your current style isn't the most flattering."

"If you're talking radical change, I'm up for it." Oaklee smiled. "Mohawk? Shave it all off?"

Marigold appeared to carefully consider those options until Oaklee laughed and said, "My brother would have a heart attack. Let's take those off the table, for now anyway."

Katie Ruth could easily see Oaklee with the half-shaved, half-long style that was so popular in certain circles.

"I was thinking you'd look amazing with a short bob with side-swept bangs." Marigold lifted a strand of pink hair and let it drop as she circled the chair. "The straight short bob will add length to your face, while the side bangs will add angles that counteract the roundness."

"Sure." Oaklee shrugged. "Chop it off."

Marigold glanced at Katie Ruth.

Katie Ruth lifted her hands. "I'm merely an observer."

By the time Marigold whipped off the cape, Katie Ruth had to blink twice.

"What do you think?" Marigold gave Oaklee a hand mirror so she could check the back.

"I love it." Oaklee reached up with a trembling hand. "But I don't look like me."

Marigold studied her. "I've always believed our hair should reflect our personality, who we are inside. Is it the color or the cut? We can make changes. I want you happy."

When Marigold took a step forward, Oaklee made a cross with her fingers. "Don't touch it. I love it."

"If it doesn't reflect who—" Katie Ruth began.

"It's different. That doesn't mean I want to change it." Oaklee fluffed the strands with her fingers. "I just need time to get used to this new—even more amazing—me."

Marigold exchanged a glance with Katie Ruth.

"If you decide you want something different, I'm happy to make changes," Marigold assured her. "Just give me a call."

Katie Ruth didn't know who was more startled when Oaklee flung her arms around Marigold. "You are a hair genius. Thank you."

The three turned when the bells over the front door sounded.

Ethan strolled into the salon, smiling at the scene. "That's what I like to see. A satisfied customer."

"Hi, Ethan." Marigold gestured toward the floor. "Give me a sec to sweep up, and I'll be with you."

"What about the quilt patterns I was going to show you?" Oaklee asked.

"We'll schedule a time." Marigold reached into her pocket and handed the girl a card. "This has my cell number. Text me some times when you're free, and we'll make it happen."

Oaklee slipped the card into the pocket of her jeans and shifted her attention to Ethan.

Eliza's brother was a handsome man, with the same lean build, dark hair and gray eyes as Eliza. Katie Ruth had never understood how he'd managed to reach his late twenties without any serious entanglements.

"You should shave one side," Oaklee told him. "You know, that low-fade, comb-over look that's so popular."

Ethan studied her for a long moment. A slow smile lifted his lips. "Thanks for the suggestion. Have we been introduced?"

"This is Oaklee Marshall, Pastor Dan's sister." Katie Ruth stepped forward. "Oaklee, this is Ethan Shaw, Eliza Kendrick's brother."

"Pleased to meet you, Oaklee."

"Your sister can be scary."

Katie Ruth nearly groaned aloud at Oaklee's comment.

Ethan laughed. "True, but she's a marshmallow on the inside."

Oaklee appeared skeptical. "If you say so."

"I'm ready for you, Ethan." Marigold appeared to be fighting a smile.

"Go bold or go home," Oaklee called back as they left the salon.

"I wish I'd known you in high school." Katie Ruth slipped her arm through Oaklee's. "I think we'd have been good friends."

"I'm glad we met now." Oaklee lifted a hand to touch her shiny, sleek hair.

"Why is that?"

"Because I got through high school okay, and so did you." Oaklee met Katie Ruth's gaze. "When I really needed a friend, I met you. If you ever need a friend, I'll be there for you."

～

Dan had his plans for the day firmly in place. Once he finished with the interview at the church, he'd head to his parents' house for dinner. Tomorrow morning, he'd drive back to Good Hope and Katie Ruth.

As he waited to be ushered into the conference room where the interview would take place, Dan found himself wondering how Oaklee's hair appointment had gone. For someone who came across as brash and bold, Oaklee could be surprisingly unsure at times.

He was glad Katie Ruth was with his sister.

"Pastor Marshall." A man whom Dan recognized as the senior pastor at Lincolnshire Christian stepped out of the conference room and extended his hand. "I'm Ted Martelle."

"It's good to meet you, Pastor."

"Please call me Ted."

"Dan." He gave the man's hand a firm shake.

For the next three hours, Dan sat at an oval table with Ted and the six men who comprised the search committee, answering each question, real and theoretical, tossed his way.

They started with the theological. They felt that his beliefs would shape everything he did with the church. After a break, they moved on to his philosophy.

After a series of questions, a stern-looking man with a well-trimmed goatee leaned forward, resting his forearms on the shiny tabletop. "What are some of the most important ideas and practices that you think cultivate health in a church?"

Dan smiled. "One of my passions is building a sustainable youth ministry."

He went on to describe many of the changes he'd made at First Christian since becoming the pastor four years earlier, then followed up with the plans for more involvement from middle schoolers and even tossed in the Christian rock concert that would be done in conjunction with other area churches. "I've also done research and plan to work with our volunteer youth director on coming up with five key documents, starting with a directory of youth, volunteers and visitors; an annual events calendar; job descriptions and—"

"That's very interesting," Ted waved him silent, "but we have a very well-organized youth staff here. The youth pastor is in charge of that area. Why don't you give us ideas and practices that would be relevant to your duties as an associate pastor in a larger congregation?"

Dan answered the question easily—and, it appeared by the head nods, to their satisfaction—but it stung that he would be so far removed from the youth ministry he loved.

After another break, which had Dan realizing just how weary he was, they reconvened, fresh water and steaming coffee on the table.

Ted folded his hands on the table where he sat directly across from Dan. His sharp eyes had remained fixed throughout the interview process. If he, too, was growing weary, it didn't show.

"As I'm sure you're aware, most of the biblical qualifications for pastoral ministry relate to a person's character." Ted's expression remained serious. "Our final set of questions will be more personal."

Dan answered the questions easily, until they got to the one about family. "Although my father wanted me to be an engineer, they've been supportive of my being in the ministry. I have one younger sister, who has taken more of an interest in her faith since moving to Good Hope."

"How would your sister feel about you moving to Lincolnshire should the position be offered to you?"

The question was an easy one to answer. "The plan is for Oaklee to go back to college in September. Since my parents live in Lincolnshire, the location couldn't be more conducive to family time."

Peter, a younger man with a mop of blond hair, glanced down at the papers in front of him. "You're not married."

"No, I am not," Dan confirmed. "I've never been married."

"Are you dating anyone steadily?" Peter asked.

For the first time, Dan hesitated. What existed between him and Katie Ruth was new. He knew where he thought he wanted the relationship to go, but his experience with Lindsay had taught him that there were no guarantees.

Still, to say he wasn't dating anyone steadily would be a lie and a betrayal of what he and Katie Ruth shared.

"For the past month, I've been dating a young woman in our congregation." Dan kept his tone easy. "Katie Ruth is our volunteer youth director."

Ted nodded approvingly. "I realize it's quite early days, but do you know how she'd feel about being a pastor's wife?"

"Katie Ruth would make a wonderful pastor's wife." Dan's voice warmed the way it always did when he thought of the perky blonde with the generous, caring heart.

He took a moment to briefly describe her actions recently in the maternity waiting room. "She was a comforting presence to everyone there."

A chorus of approving nods rippled around the table.

Dan answered a few more questions. He waited for the question *Is there anything else you feel we should know?* but it never came.

When preparing for this interview, he'd carefully considered what he would say if that question was asked. Did they have the right to know about Katie Ruth's parents? It didn't seem so, considering he and Katie Ruth had been dating for only six weeks.

They weren't engaged, hadn't spoken about marriage. Yet, Dan knew that if he were to leave Good Hope, he would ask Katie Ruth to come with him, as his wife.

"I believe that's all our questions." Ted offered a warm smile. "Is there anything you would like to ask us?"

Dan had compiled a list of questions. As he could tell

everyone around the table was getting tired, he led with his top three. "How are decisions made?"

Over the past four years, Dan had enjoyed the freedom given to him by the congregation to try new programs, even to tinker with worship times.

"We've recently set up a task force in an effort to streamline our committee/church council structure." Ted gave a little laugh. "When it took months to address some simple repairs on the church structure, we realized we had a problem of too many fingers in the pie."

"We're confident the task force will come up with workable suggestions to improve our dysfunctional governance structure," Peter added.

*Dysfunctional governance structure.*

The description made Dan think of a corporation, rather than a church. He reminded himself that a large church needed an effective structure to be able to serve the members and the community.

"Thank you. I appreciate your forthrightness." Dan glanced down at his sheet of questions. "What kind of pastor do you tell your friends your church needs?"

He made notes of the answers, then ended with, "What is the best thing this church has done in the last five years?"

By the time his questions were answered, it was nearly seven. He made it to his parents' home in twenty minutes, another plus for accepting the position if it were offered.

His mother had kept dinner warm for him, and they sat around the small table in the kitchen, he with his plate of lasagna and vegetables and his parents with their decaffeinated coffee.

"You said it went well," his father reminded him once Dan had gotten in a few bites of food. "Do you think they're going to offer the position?"

"If I had to guess, I'd say yes."

His mother clasped her hands together. "That's wonderful news. Isn't it, John?"

"It'd be good to have you close," his father agreed. "Not to mention this would definitely be a step up for you."

"If I take it." Dan took a bite of garlic bread and wished he'd thought to call Katie Ruth on the drive over. In the past month, she'd become his touchstone, centering him in a way he hadn't expected.

"*If* you take it?" His father frowned. "Why wouldn't you accept the position?"

"Is it your girlfriend?" his mother asked. "Oaklee told me you're dating someone."

"That doesn't make the woman his girlfriend." John shot a sharp glance at his wife, then narrowed his gaze on his son. "Even if he did have one, if she wasn't willing to move with him to support his career, she's clearly not the right sort of woman for him."

Dan's spine stiffened. Something in his father's tone said he'd already dismissed Katie Ruth as of no consequence. "Katie Ruth is very important to me."

John inclined his head. "What does 'very important' signify?"

"I like her," Dan said simply, knowing that didn't begin to express what Katie Ruth meant to him.

"Enough to factor her thoughts into an important life decision?" The chill that wove its way through his father's words told Dan his views on the matter.

Then again, what had he expected? In his family, his father's business moves had dictated where they lived, though his mother also had a career.

Dan stabbed a piece of broccoli. "Yes. I will factor in her preferences."

"That's ridiculous."

"John, it's his—"

"Sandra." One word from his father was all it took to silence his mother.

"While I appreciate your input, this is a decision between me and God." Dan met his father's gaze with a steely one of his own. "And between me and the woman I love."

# CHAPTER FIFTEEN

Dan left his parents' home right after breakfast on Saturday. He made the four-hour trip to Good Hope in three and a half hours. On the road, he replayed the interview in his mind and considered his conversation with his parents.

By the time he stopped in front of his house, the only thing he wanted to do was see Katie Ruth. His call went straight to voice mail before he noticed she'd sent him a text.

*At Y. Playing b-ball. Join me.*

After grabbing his gym bag, Dan headed there. He used to get together regularly with several guys for a pickup game over lunch, but had gotten out of the habit.

Right now, running on a court sounded heaven-sent.

When he stepped onto the basketball court, he stopped. Katie Ruth was the only woman on the hardwood.

Dan recognized Beck, Max, Cade and Jeremy immediately. Then Clay and David Chapin. Finally, Ryder and Ethan.

They hadn't yet noticed him, so he studied the teams and listened to the G-rated trash talk. Katie Ruth appeared to be on the team with five, while the other team was making do with four.

Even in gym shorts and a Packers T-shirt, with her hair pulled up in a tail, she was beautiful.

She was also a good ball handler. He noticed the other team had chosen not to guard her. Probably none of the guys wanted to be the one to block her.

Katie Ruth ran down the court, never taking her eyes from the ball in Jeremy's control, setting herself up in a corner. When Jeremy passed the ball to her, she took the shot.

"That's three, count 'em, three points," she taunted, doing her own version of a boogie dance.

While the other team groaned, her teammates gave her high fives. Ryder slung an arm around Katie Ruth's shoulders and gave her a squeeze. Dan discovered jealousy was an unfamiliar, yet strong, emotion.

As he watched, Katie Ruth lifted his arm from her shoulders and took a step back, an easy smile on her face.

Only then did she notice him on the sidelines. A broad smile split her face as she crossed the court. When she reached him, she rose on her tiptoes to press her lips lightly to his.

"Welcome back." Her eyes searched his. "I missed you."

"I missed you, too." His hands settled on her hips. "A lot."

"Do the kissy thing later," Jeremy called out. "We have a game to win."

"Dan," Beck called out, "you're on our team."

The next half hour passed quickly, with Katie Ruth scoring another three-pointer for her team. As he dribbled the ball down the court, Dan wondered why he'd quit playing.

Not only because of the exercise, which he sorely needed, but because he genuinely liked these guys. He was nearly in position, the ball in his hands, when Katie Ruth appeared from out of nowhere to block his shot.

Jeremy scooped up the blocked shot, made his way down the court to score.

"That's game," someone called out.

Katie Ruth wrinkled her nose. "Sorry."

Dan slung an arm around her shoulders, much the way Ryder had earlier. With him, she didn't pull away. "Great block."

"Thanks." Katie Ruth glanced at the other men. "I appreciate you letting me hang on the court with you."

"Anytime, Katie Ruth." Jeremy winked. "You're our secret weapon."

"Not anymore," Ryder groused.

As the men headed for the showers, Dan and Katie Ruth crossed the court more slowly, his fingers linked with hers.

"Do you have plans for the evening?"

She smiled. "I do."

His heart dropped.

"I'm spending the evening with my boyfriend. He just got back into town."

Everything in Dan relaxed. "What are you and this boyfriend of yours going to do tonight?"

His teasing tone had her lips curving. "Since it's a nice evening, I thought we could grill out at his house. Perhaps watch a movie afterwards, or maybe play a board game."

Dan knew many contemporaries would label such activities lame or boring, but it sounded good to him. Better than good, actually. He couldn't imagine anything better than spending the evening with Katie Ruth.

Katie Ruth touched his arm. When he shifted his worried gaze to her, she smiled. It was as if she could read his mind. "Oaklee will be glad you're home."

She didn't need to say more. Oaklee would be their chaperone tonight, just like every other night.

Dan wished it could be different. He longed for alone time with her. There were so many things he wanted to tell her without his sister hearing every word.

For her part, Katie Ruth didn't appear to mind that they wouldn't be alone. At least that's the impression she gave.

Until they reached the point in the hall leading to the locker rooms where he would go right and she'd go left.

Her fingers tightened around his hand when he attempted to release hers. "Perhaps after dinner, you and I could take a walk? Just the two of us."

Dan grinned. The fact that the day suddenly seemed a whole lot brighter didn't have one thing to do with the fluorescent lights overhead.

～

On the way home, Dan stopped at the grocery store and left with a cartful of food. He was fumbling with the lock at his front door while juggling two sacks when the door abruptly opened.

"Give me one of those."

Dan blinked. The voice was familiar, but the young woman snatching a sack from his hand was a stranger.

"Oaklee?"

Already on her way to the kitchen, his sister turned. She lifted a brow. "Problem?"

"Your...your hair. It's different."

She flashed a smile. "Marigold did it. Do you like it?"

Dan studied the cut and the color. "I do. What made you decide to take the leap?"

"Not so much of a leap."

He followed his sister to the kitchen, setting his sack beside the one she'd placed on the counter. "It's very different."

"I believe you already made that clear." Her smile flashed. "This is my natural color."

"Really?" Dan frowned. He'd thought for sure his sister was a blonde.

She nodded. "It's been a long time since you've probably seen it au naturel."

"The cut suits you."

Her hand rose to touch the strands. "Marigold is a genius with hair."

That settled, they unpacked the sacks in companionable silence. It wasn't until Dan had lit the grill on the deck that Oaklee brought up their parents.

"How's Dad?"

Dan didn't want to think of his father right now. Especially not when Katie Ruth would be at the house any minute. Perhaps it was best to get this conversation out of the way. "Same."

"I bet he gave you an earful about me. After he lectured you on how you should be living your life."

Dan wished he could disagree.

"What did he say about the new position? He's all for it, isn't he?"

The doorbell rang before Dan could respond.

"That must be Katie Ruth." Oaklee whirled and was headed to the front door before Dan could take a step.

Moments later, his sister returned, Katie Ruth at her side.

Dan shut the hood of the grill, set down the spatula and drank in the sight of her. How could he miss someone he'd just seen?

"I brought a pie." Katie Ruth held out the carrier. "Homemade."

"Is it cherry?" Oaklee asked. "Cherry is my favorite."

Katie Ruth set the pie on the counter. "It's actually Dutch apple."

"That's your favorite." Oaklee pointed to her brother.

A warmth rushed through him. Dan couldn't believe Katie Ruth had remembered. On the drive back from Sombreros, they'd somehow gotten on the topic of favorite desserts, and he'd casually mentioned his fondness for Dutch apple pie.

"I hope we have ice cream to go with it." Oaklee jerked open the freezer door.

"I keep the ice cream downstairs," Dan told his sister. "If we have any, it'll be there."

"I'll check."

Oaklee had barely started down the steps when Dan wrapped his arms around Katie Ruth. "I'm glad you came."

"Thank you for inviting me."

She smiled up at him, and his heart swelled with emotion. It seemed so natural, so right, to press his lips to hers. The kiss started out slowly, as if they had all the time in the world.

Her arms wrapped around his neck, her fingers sliding into his hair as he deepened the kiss. Oh, how he'd missed this. Oh, how he'd missed her.

"There was only this carton, but it—"

Dan sprang back at the sound of his sister's voice.

"—should be..." Oaklee's voice trailed off. A knowing gleam filled her eyes. "Were you two making out?"

"We, ah..." Dan, known for his way with words, found himself stumbling to explain.

"I missed your brother, and he missed me." Katie Ruth spoke in an unapologetic tone.

"Cool." Oaklee held up the carton of vanilla. "I'll put this in the freezer up here."

"What's on the menu tonight?" Katie Ruth asked. "Other than pie and ice cream?"

Food, always a safe topic. Dan seized on it. "The burgers are on the grill. I picked up coleslaw at the market's deli counter, and there's a bag of chips in the cupboard."

"Sounds good to me." Katie Ruth glanced around. "What can I do to help?"

"I'll set the table," Oaklee said. "You make sure Dan doesn't burn the burgers."

Dan shot his sister an I-owe-you look and stepped onto the deck with Katie Ruth.

She immediately turned to him, placing her hands on his shoulders. "Where were we?"

Dan chuckled. As he slid his arms around her, he realized this was how it was supposed to be with someone you loved. The mutual need, the closeness, the feeling of coming home.

He'd never had this before, never experienced this depth of feeling before. As he lowered his mouth to hers, he knew he never wanted this feeling to end.

～

Katie Ruth wanted to hear all about Dan's interview, but she let him and Oaklee steer the conversation until dessert was on the table.

Once a slice of apple pie, topped with an obscene amount of ice cream, sat before her, she could wait no longer. "Tell me about the interview."

Dan's fork stilled on its way to his mouth.

"Thank you." Oaklee clapped her hands. "I would have brought it up myself, but I wanted to hear about the basketball game first."

"It was interesting." Dan set down his fork and leaned back in his chair. "I expected a committee, and that's what I got. Six men sitting around a conference table."

"How many women?" Katie Ruth asked.

"None." Dan pulled his brows together. "I'm embarrassed to admit that, until this second, that fact hadn't registered."

Oaklee rolled her eyes. "Tells you what they think of women."

Dan shook his head. "We don't have enough information to make that leap."

"I'm sure Dan will check that out before making a final decision."

"I will." Dan met Katie Ruth's gaze. "Keep in mind, I haven't been offered the position."

"Did everyone pummel you with questions?" Oaklee spoke around a mouthful of pie.

"Pummel me?"

"You know, like sharks going in for the kill." Oaklee's eyes brightened at the thought.

Puzzlement filled Dan's eyes. "Why would they do that?"

Katie Ruth dipped her spoon into the ice cream, intrigued by this glimpse into sibling interaction.

"To see how you react under pressure."

"No pummeling. The senior pastor, Ted Martelle, posed the majority of the questions." Dan's lips twitched. "Not a shark in sight."

"Bor-ring," Oaklee pronounced.

Katie Ruth decided it was time to step in. "What kind of questions did they ask?"

Dan shot her a grateful glance. "They started with the theological."

"What's that?" Oaklee asked.

"My beliefs. Pastor Martelle said, and I agree, that a minister's beliefs shape everything he or she does with the church."

Katie Ruth smiled. "I'm sure you wowed them."

"I was honest. My faith is a part of me and is what drew me to ministry."

"Let's move this along." Oaklee made a rolling motion with her hand.

"If this is boring you, you don't have to stay," Dan told his sister.

Oaklee's gaze slid from Dan to Katie Ruth. She grinned. "I get it. You two want to be alone to discuss 'church business.'"

Pushing back her chair, Oaklee stood. "I'll be in my room if you need me, but otherwise I won't be coming out. If you get my drift."

Dan chuckled when she sauntered out of the room. "Life was sure boring before Oaklee."

"She's a wonderful girl." Katie Ruth smiled. "I really like your sister."

Reaching across the table, Dan squeezed her hand. "I'm glad."

"After verifying that you are a man of faith, what did they want to know?"

"I won't bore you with each question…"

"Stop." She laughed, wrinkling her nose. "For the record, I think Oaklee was angling to be asked to leave. She wanted to give us this time. Like I said, she's a sweet girl."

"Sweet?"

"Yes, sweet. Don't you dare say anything different."

Dan lifted his hands in surrender. "I wouldn't think of it."

"Okay, so tell me more about the interview."

Katie Ruth listened as he talked, hearing his passion. The man had a burning desire to serve God. Those men around that conference table couldn't help but be impressed.

"Was there anything they said that hit you wrong?"

"What do you mean?"

"Anything that wasn't what you expected?"

"Well, I found out I wouldn't be involved at all in the youth ministry. I knew they had a youth minister on staff, but I thought as an associate pastor I would have some input."

"Not your purview."

He expelled a breath. "Not my purview."

"You've got so many good ideas that I'm sure that was disappointing." Katie Ruth kept her tone light. "Anything else?"

Dan began to shake his head, then stopped. "The committee/church council structure sounds unwieldy, but they are actively working to remedy it."

"That's good."

"Yes. Those were the only two areas that gave me pause. Then we moved into the personal area, character issues."

Katie Ruth couldn't hide her surprise. "Why would they even interview you if they had questions about your character?"

"Not my character, but you know, how does my family feel about my being in the ministry, stuff like that."

*Character issues.*

Katie Ruth's blood turned cold. "What did you tell them?"

"The truth. That my father wasn't keen on me being in the ministry at first, but my parents have been supportive. I told them my sister has taken more of an interest in her faith since moving to Good Hope." His brown eyes met hers. "They also asked if I was dating anyone steadily. I said I am."

She cleared her throat. "Did you?"

He nodded, reaching over to take her ice-cold fingers in his warm hand. "I bragged on you a bit. I told them you're our volunteer youth director and are very involved with the congregation. I believe they were impressed."

"I wonder if they'd have been as impressed if they knew about my parents. I assume you didn't tell them about that."

When he shifted uncomfortably in his seat, she had her answer.

"I didn't feel it was necessary to share that information."

"Because we're not engaged. Because I'm just your girlfriend."

"Partially, and because your parents' actions are not your actions." Dan paused. "I considered what I'd say if they had asked about your family."

Katie Ruth's heart skipped a beat. "What would you have said?"

"Because of the sensitive nature of the information, I would have asked to speak with Pastor Martelle privately." Dan's fingers tightened around hers. "I'd have told him about the swinging, but stressed that their actions are not yours. Their beliefs are not yours. I'd reiterate that your personal actions are above reproach."

Katie Ruth forced a smile. She deeply regretted her actions back in college. She'd asked God for forgiveness and knew she'd been forgiven.

But God was one thing.

She wasn't confident that, if her past became known, Pastor

Martelle and his godly men would deem her worthy to be a pastor's wife.

Perhaps she wasn't giving them enough credit. But she wanted only the best for Dan. If she told Dan about Judd, he'd be honest if another search committee asked about her. Which meant her secret past must remain a secret.

Forever.

# CHAPTER SIXTEEN

A week later, Katie Ruth sat with Oaklee and the three women Oaklee had dubbed her "posse."

As the five sat around a table in Blooms Bake Shop, Katie Ruth relaxed with her cup of herbal tea and listened to the women tease Oaklee about needing to find her "a nice young man."

There was something about the interior of the bake shop in the heart of the Good Hope business district that Katie Ruth found soothing. It might have been the mint-green trim around the windows and doors or the three-tiered round table holding prepackaged bags of treats. Most visitors commented on the antique chandelier, but what always drew Katie Ruth's eye was the It's Cupcake Time clock.

Katie Ruth heard the women giggle as Oaklee informed them she wanted a man as "trashy" as she was.

"You're not trashy." Katie Ruth didn't care if Oaklee was joking. She wouldn't allow the girl to put herself down.

Oaklee shifted her gaze, and Katie Ruth saw the surprise in her eyes. "I was joking."

"I don't like that kind of joking." Emotion had Katie Ruth's voice turning husky. "We've all done things we regret, things we wish we could take back. That doesn't make us bad or trashy. It makes us human."

"We all fall short of the glory of God," Ruby murmured.

"Some of us more than others." Gladys cackled, her laugh growing louder when Katie Ruth shot her the stink eye.

"Oh, lighten up." Gladys spoke good-naturedly. "Since we're forbidden to speak of Oaklee's desire for a trashy boyfriend—"

Bells over the door jingled, and Ethan strode in.

"Or rather, speaking of nice respectable young men." Gladys waved a hand in the air. "Yoo-hoo, Ethan. Over here."

"Respectable equals boring." Oaklee muttered the words, but didn't bother to lower her voice.

Ethan raised a dark brow.

"What brings you to the bakery today?" Gladys asked.

"I thought I'd take some pastries to Eliza and Kyle," he said absently, his gaze now on Oaklee. "You look different."

Katie Ruth glanced at Oaklee and realized she was wearing a dress.

"You look the same." Oaklee popped a bite of doughnut into her mouth. "Like my dad."

Ethan glanced down at his suit. "Your brother wears a suit every Sunday."

"He looks like my dad, too."

Ami stepped from the back and called out, "Oh, Ethan, I'm sorry to keep you waiting."

"Ladies." Ethan inclined his head, then strode to the counter as the bells rang again.

"Speaking of our wonderful pastor." Gladys's curious gaze settled on Katie Ruth. "How are you and—?"

"Wow. This is a motley crew."

"Oh, for goodness sake," Gladys muttered as Izzie crossed to the women, interrupting her interrogation.

Katie Ruth rose to hug her friend. Something about Izzie seemed different today. "What's the matter?"

Izzie lifted the phone in her hand. "I got a text from my sister. My mom had a small stroke."

"Oh no. Is she in the hospital?" How strange, Katie Ruth thought. She'd known Izzie for nearly four years and had no idea about her background.

"She's at home." Izzie dark eyes remained hooded. "It sounds as if she's having trouble tending to business."

"I'm sorry to hear that." Katherine spoke up, appearing genuinely concerned. "What are you going to do?"

"Is your sister able to care for her?" Ruby asked.

"My sister and her husband have two small children."

"That makes things difficult," Gladys said.

"Where does your family live?" Oaklee asked.

"Not far. In Michigan." Izzie glanced at the bake case. "I better get my scone. I'm doing a mural for the Bayshore Hotel. I've a tight deadline for completion."

"If you need anything, let us know," Gladys said, and everyone around the table nodded.

Katie Ruth realized this was what she liked best about Good Hope. People were always ready to help each other in any situation.

She wondered if Dan would miss this camaraderie and caring when he took the job in Lincolnshire. A sharp pain lanced her heart. She reminded herself that he hadn't been offered the job. Perhaps he wouldn't even take it.

If he did take it, what would that mean for her? For them?

"Earth to Katie Ruth."

Katie Ruth blinked at the sound of Oaklee's voice and found everyone at the table staring at her. "I'm sorry. What did I miss?"

"Gladys thinks we should throw Dan a birthday party." Oaklee smiled brightly at Katie Ruth. "What do you think?"

Katie Ruth realized she didn't even know the date of Dan's

birthday. "Are you thinking of a small party? I'm not sure Dan would be comfortable with something big and flashy."

"Who doesn't like big and flashy?" Gladys scoffed.

"Dan needs to get out of his own way," Oaklee asserted with the brashness of youth.

"But if he doesn't like big and—" Ruby stopped when Gladys shot her a warning look.

Katie Ruth had the feeling if she protested too much, this group would go ahead and plan something without her.

Pushing her cup aside, she leaned forward and focused her attention on Gladys. "Tell me what you have in mind."

Dan strode down the hallway of the hospital and paused outside Lindsay's room. He'd been in the middle of paperwork, never a favorite task, when the phone had rung.

Olivia Vaughn, eight pounds and change, had arrived that morning. When Owen had asked Dan if he would come to the hospital and say a blessing over the child, Dan hadn't hesitated.

After Mindy's death from cancer last year, both Lindsay and Owen had been on edge about the pregnancy. But the months had gone by without a hitch, and according to Owen, it had been a quick delivery with mom and baby doing well.

Dan rapped on the door.

"Come in."

He was surprised to find only Lindsay and the baby in the room. "Where's Owen?"

"He went down to the coffee cart in the lobby." Lindsay lowered her voice, though they were the only ones in the room. "What they serve here is awful, and he wanted the good stuff."

"This must be Miss Olivia." Dan moved to the rocker where Lindsay sat, a swaddled pink bundle in her arms. He caught a glimpse of blond hair and a rosebud mouth that moved even in sleep. "Congratulations."

"Thank you." Lindsay gestured with her free hand to a nearby chair. "Sit down. Please."

Dan sat. "I'm happy for you and Owen."

"We're lucky we found each other." Lindsay's lips lifted in a soft smile. "Now we have Olivia. Life, well, it couldn't be better."

"Don't take this the wrong way, but our breakup was the best thing that could have happened to both of us." Dan saw that now. At the time, he'd been hurt and, yes, angry. But God had been looking out for him and Lindsay.

"You understand now."

He arched a brow.

"What it's like to really love someone." Lindsay stroked the fine down fuzz atop her baby's head with one finger. "You and I never loved each other."

"No. We didn't."

"Now you have Katie Ruth." Lindsay's eyes held a twinkle. "She's a wonderful person and well-suited to being a minister's wife."

"Katie Ruth and I are enjoying getting to know each other better."

Lindsay's eyes held a mischievous gleam. "We both know you like what you see."

The door pushed open, and Owen powered into the room. "I couldn't remember if you could have coffee, but I got you a cup."

The mechanic skidded to a stop when he spotted Dan. "Wow. That didn't take long."

Dan stood. "Any excuse to get out of working on the church budget."

"We appreciate you coming." Owen crossed the room, set the cups on the bedside stand and clapped Dan on the shoulder.

"How could I miss the chance to see this little miracle?" Dan thought of Mindy. "Mindy would have loved a baby sister. Especially if she could deck her out in all pink."

For a split second, Dan wondered if he should have brought up Mindy, but realized she would always be a part of this family, of this community.

Gone but never forgotten, Mindy, with her gap-toothed smile and her love of all things pink, was woven into the fabric of Good Hope.

Though his eyes remained somber, Owen laughed. "Pink with sequins."

"We're going to tell this little one all about her wonderful big sister." Lindsay paused to clear her throat.

The family and friends would soon be descending on the hospital room, and Dan knew that Lindsay and Owen wanted this to be a private time. "Shall we pray?"

When the two lowered their heads, Dan began to speak, "Heavenly Father, thank you for the life of this child whose care you have entrusted to Owen and Lindsay. Keep her safe from harm and—"

As he continued, the words poured out. Dan's faith was as much a part of him as the air he breathed. What he'd told Ted and the committee was true. His passion was serving the Lord.

Once the prayer concluded, Dan stood by the rocker and placed one hand over the infant's head.

"Olivia Vaughn, may the Lord bless you and keep you. May…"

When Dan finished the blessing, he looked up, shifting his gaze from Lindsay, who now had tears in her eyes, to Owen, whose eyes also appeared suspiciously moist.

"I'll let you enjoy your daughter, and your coffee, before all the friends and family arrive."

"Thank you, Dan." Lindsay's gaze locked with his. In that moment, Dan realized he'd received his own kind of blessing. Any lingering hurt and heartache between them were gone.

"You're very welcome. Congratulations, again."

"I'll walk you to the elevator," Owen told him before kissing his wife. "Be back in a sec, Lin."

She smiled. "I'm not going anywhere."

Owen stepped from the room, and once the door had closed behind them, he turned to Dan. "Thanks for coming and for your kind words about Mindy."

"Your daughter was very loved." Dan rested a hand on Owen's shoulder. "Give Olivia a few years, and I'm sure she'll capture everyone's heart, too."

"Things are okay between you and Lin now."

Though spoken as a statement, Dan heard the underlying question. "Yes, we're okay. She's with the man she was meant to be with and—" Dan paused, not sure how far he wanted to take this.

"You're with the woman you're meant to be with." Owen grinned. "I'd say we're both lucky SOBs."

Dan laughed. "We certainly are."

Katie Ruth tossed the heavy ball down the lane and crossed her fingers, hoping at least a few pins would fall. She and Oaklee had met ten kids from youth group at Pin Chasers, a bowling alley in Sister Bay.

This was one of the monthly Thursday-night activities set aside for fun and team-building games. At the moment, they were engaged in a game called Spare Me.

After dividing into three teams, Katie Ruth and her teammates took turns in the same frame until all the pins were knocked down.

This game had followed several others. When they first arrived, they'd paired up in teams of two for "blind" bowling. The teammate's job was to help the blindfolded partner line up and take a straight shot without crossing the foul line.

Oaklee had been hilarious. Blindfolded or not, she couldn't escape throwing gutter balls no matter how hard she tried. Because Oaklee was clearly the worst bowler of the group, and the most good-natured, it made everyone else feel comfortable regardless of their skill level.

They were in the last frame of the final game of Spare Me. Being around kids and being physically active were in Katie Ruth's wheelhouse. Toss in that it was a church activity, and she couldn't imagine anything better.

Unless Dan had been able to come.

But he'd had the church budget to contend with, and she understood he couldn't come to every youth activity.

"Woo-hoo," Oaklee called out, then put her fingers to her lips and whistled. "WTG, Katie Ruth."

Katie Ruth turned to the alley just in time to see the last pin wobble then tumble down.

"You got a strike." Astrid, who'd unexpectedly come along, took Katie Ruth's hands and began jumping up and down. "A strike."

When the others poured into her lane to congratulate her, Katie Ruth felt a surge of satisfaction. The kids hadn't gotten caught up in winning and losing, but had worked together and cheered each other's successes.

The parents began arriving to pick up their kids, and soon only Oaklee and Katie Ruth remained.

"Do we need to pay?" Oaklee asked.

"Already taken care of." Katie Ruth sat beside Oaklee on one of the plastic chairs to remove her bowling shoes. "Are you hungry? We could—"

"I'm hungry." Dan sat down on the other side of her, looking overdressed in his tailored slacks and button-down shirt and tie. "May I join you?"

Oaklee's shoes were already in her hands and the boots back

on her feet. She stood. "Sounds like fun. You two will have to enjoy yourself without me tonight."

"I didn't realize you had plans." Katie Ruth looked up from the knot in her laces.

"I have a date," Oaklee announced.

Dan's eyes narrowed. "With who?"

"With a sewing machine." Oaklee tied the laces of her bowling shoes together. "Lindsay asked me last week if I could get together some items to sell at her booth at an upcoming craft festival. I want to get started."

"But we skipped dinner," Katie Ruth reminded her.

"There's food in the fridge. Trust me, I'm a girl who can take care of herself." Oaklee turned to Dan. "Since you're here, you can give Katie Ruth a ride home. I'll drive her car."

"I don't know if that's a—"

Katie Ruth had already reached into her pocket. "Heads up."

Oaklee caught the keys in midair. "I'll be safe."

"I know." Katie Ruth smiled. "Otherwise, I wouldn't give you the keys."

"You're really okay with her driving your car?" Dan asked, even though by this time Oaklee was out the door.

"Yes." Katie Ruth huffed out a breath, her gaze focused on her feet. "These darn laces. In a second, I'm going to cut these shoes off me."

"Let me see what I can do." He took her foot, placing it on his lap. He bent his head to study the lace, then went to work.

His dark hair glistened in the overhead lights like rich, polished walnut. The subtle scent of his cologne teased her nostrils.

Katie Ruth's breathing quickened. She resisted the urge to stroke his hair, remembering how soft it was between her fingers whenever they kissed.

"There you go." He straightened and shot her a triumphant smile.

Their eyes locked. The room around them shrank until it was just her and Dan, tethered together by an invisible force. She couldn't look away.

"Katie Ruth." His voice was hoarse as his hand reached out to cup her face.

She leaned slightly forward, her gaze never leaving his face, eager for the feel of his skin against hers.

A loud cheer erupted from the lanes in front of him.

"Three strikes in a row," a male voice called out. "You're on fire."

Dan jerked back, his hand dropping to his side. His smile turned rueful. "For a second, I forgot where we were."

Not trusting herself to speak, Katie Ruth nodded.

Dan stood, waiting while she took off the other shoe, then put on her sneakers. He didn't touch her again until they'd dropped off her shoes and were outside.

He linked his fingers with hers. "I can't seem to keep my hands off of you."

Katie Ruth could tell the thought troubled him, so she forced a light tone. "I'm simply irresistible."

He stopped at the car, and his gaze met hers. "You are to me."

She gave a soft laugh and slipped into the passenger seat. On the way to Good Hope, she gave him the highlights of the bowling activity, focusing on the team-building aspects.

"It was fun. We'll definitely have to do it again." She stopped. "I wonder if the church in Lincolnshire does these kinds of activities."

"I don't know." He slanted a glance in her direction. "That would be the youth pastor's call."

"I know," Katie Ruth responded quickly, not wanting him to think she was reminding him that he would have no say in the matter if he took the job. "I'm just interested in knowing what kinds of activities other youth leaders find beneficial."

"You're great with kids."

"Thank you."

"Have you ever thought of making youth ministry your full-time job?"

Katie Ruth cocked her head, confused. "I have a full-time job. Besides, there isn't any money in the church budget for a full-time youth director."

"You're right. Not at First Christian." Dan shifted in his seat to face her. "There are other churches, other communities."

Katie Ruth's heart slammed against her ribs. "What are you asking me, Dan?"

"If I take the position in Lincolnshire, would you consider coming with me?"

# CHAPTER SEVENTEEN

Katie Ruth waited so long to speak, Dan wasn't sure she was going to answer. He wasn't sure he wanted her to answer.

The question had popped out. Every time he thought about accepting the position in Illinois and leaving her, a knot formed in the pit of his stomach.

"What is it you're really asking me, Dan?"

The quiet words had him answering honestly.

"I don't know. I haven't been offered the position, but I can't imagine you being here." He gestured wide with his arm. "And me being there."

"I understand."

"You do?" How could she when he didn't understand himself?

"I feel the same way when I think about not seeing you every day." She chuckled, her face softening into a smile. "You're addictive, Dan Marshall."

He lifted a hand and cupped her cheek again. "You're important to me."

She leaned into his caress, and her eyes fluttered closed for a second. Then she straightened. "Nothing needs to be decided now. Once you're offered the position, we can talk."

"They may not offer." In some ways, he wished the decision could be taken out of his hands.

"They'll offer." She took his hand and brought it to her mouth, pressing a kiss in the palm. "No one measures up to you."

"I wish I had your confidence."

She winked. "That's why you keep me around."

"I wondered why." He grinned and set the car on a homeward course.

On the drive back to Good Hope, Katie Ruth gave him more anecdotes that occurred during the bowling event.

Dan listened and even made a few of what he considered insightful comments. Inside, his brain whirled, and he found himself praying for clarity.

Could you really fall in love with someone you'd dated for only six weeks? Could you really even know someone fully in six weeks? Of course, Katie Ruth hadn't been a complete stranger before. Still, he couldn't deny things were moving quickly. The practical side of him said he needed to take this slow, but one fact remained absolute.

He couldn't imagine leaving her behind.

∼

Dan's voice broke the silence. "I didn't realize you were working in the shop today."

The "shop" was Mindy's Closet, a small area connected to the church that accepted donations of children's clothing. Every Friday, people in the community could stop by and shop for free.

Katie Ruth looked up from where she was sorting donations. How could one man make her heart beat faster simply by walking into the room?

"One of the volunteers called in sick, and I had time free this afternoon. With spring in sight, everyone is thinking about lighter-weight clothes. The shop was super busy up until about ten minutes ago. Since then, nothing. Of course, we close in fifteen minutes, so that might be part of it."

She was babbling. Some of it she knew was because Dan had stepped close and her nerve endings were pinging. The other was because of their talk last night. Once he heard from the church in Lincolnshire, there would be a lot for them to discuss.

As she resumed sorting, Dan's arms came around her from behind, his breath warm on her neck.

She leaned back against his broad chest and sighed. "How can a day seem like a year?"

"That's how it seems to me, too." He brushed her hair with his lips. "Spend the rest of the evening with me."

"You've got your sermon to work on tonight," she reminded him. "And I—"

"I forgot you had plans with Izzie tonight." Dan staunched his disappointment.

"Actually, Izzie canceled."

Dan turned her in his arms. "Why?"

"Her mom had a small stroke." Katie Ruth pulled her brows together. "Izzie took a quick trip to Michigan."

"I'm sorry to hear that. I'll keep her and her mother in my prayers." Dan took a moment, then cocked his head. "Does that mean you're available tonight?"

She brought her hands up to rest on his shoulders. "As a matter of fact, I am."

"We can do whatever you want."

"Do you have your sermon ready to go?"

Dan shifted uncomfortably. "It's coming along."

When had she started to be able to read him so well? "Which means there's still work to do."

He tapped her on the nose. "You let me worry about that."

"I've got a better idea." Katie Ruth smiled at him. She couldn't help it. Just knowing she would get to spend the evening with him made her smile. "Why don't I come over? We can get a pizza from Bayside and work on your sermon."

"Sounds wonderful." His gaze narrowed as his eyes searched her face. "Are you sure you don't mind?"

She kissed him. "I'd rather spend a quiet evening at home with you."

Dan stilled and muttered something under his breath.

"Problem?" Katie Ruth arched a brow.

"Oaklee is working on something at the Living Center with Gladys tonight."

"Why is that a problem?" The second the question left her lips, Katie Ruth realized she already knew the answer. "Oh."

Dan nodded. "We can't be alone in the house."

The disappointment in his eyes had Katie Ruth swallowing what she'd been about to say. The unfairness of it didn't matter. It was important to Dan not to give even the slightest hint of impropriety.

As that was important to him, it was important to her as well.

"Okay, forget the quiet evening at home." Katie Ruth kept her tone matter-of-fact. "It's still the off-season, so restaurants won't be nearly as crowded, even on a Friday night. That said, I think we should avoid Bayside Pizza. It's always busy on weekends."

"I agree," Dan said a little too quickly.

Katie Ruth wondered if he, like she did, thought of his proposal to Lindsay every time he stepped through the doors.

"Muddy Boots will be crazy, too," Dan said. "Their fish-and-chips Friday special is extremely popular."

"We could eat at the restaurant in the hotel, but that might look weird." Katie Ruth puffed out her cheeks. "What about eating before, then getting together, say, at the Grind for coffee and to go over the sermon?"

"That isn't much of a date."

She reached down and took his hand. "Being with you is enough."

"I promise we'll have a nice meal together on my birthday." His smile, so open and trusting, tore at her heart.

Technically, Katie Ruth hadn't promised not to say anything to Dan about Gladys and Oaklee's party plans. She knew Dan was envisioning a different kind of evening to celebrate his birthday. One that didn't involve a surprise and a roomful of people.

"Come over here." Katie Ruth tugged him by the hand to two straight-backed chairs against a far wall in the small shop. "I've something to tell you."

Once he was seated, she glanced at her watch, saw the time to close the shop had passed and locked the door. Only then did she return to sit beside him.

"What's this about?" A frown worried his brow. "If you can't come tomorrow, we can postpone and celebrate my birthday another time."

"I want to celebrate with you." Katie Ruth swallowed, hoping she was making the right decision. "The thing is, Oaklee and Gladys are planning a surprise birthday party for you."

She went on to give him all the details she had, which weren't many.

"Wow." Dan raked a hand through his hair. "I thought Oaklee knew I didn't like that kind of thing. Then again, I've been gone from home since she was eight, and my parents were never into parties."

"I didn't know whether to tell you or not." Katie Ruth chewed on her lower lip. "Keeping this from you felt like I was being disloyal to you."

At his questioning glance, she continued. "If our roles were reversed, I'd want you to tell me. Not so I could stop the party, but so I could be prepared. I wouldn't be expecting a quiet evening and find myself in the middle of a party."

"Thank you for telling me." He tipped her chin up with his finger. "I *was* looking forward to a different kind of evening. Don't worry, I'll act surprised."

"Okay." Still, the doubt niggled. Had she ruined the fun? Maybe Dan would have enjoyed the surprise.

"Hey."

Dan's voice had her pulling her thoughts back to the present.

"You did the right thing." He pulled her to him and held her tight. "I'm glad there are no secrets between us. Just know you can tell me anything."

Katie Ruth rested her head against his shoulder. She squeezed her eyes shut.

Could she really tell him anything? Or was it sometimes best to keep the past in the past?

The next morning, Dan glanced at the number of bowls his sister set out on the counter. "What's with all the bowls? Are you expecting a crowd?"

Oaklee whirled. Two bright swaths of pink slashed her cheeks. "I'm trying to see what bowls we have while I plan what salads to make."

"Is that what we're having? Salad?"

Oaklee scowled. "No, that's just what I'm making, ah, right now."

"Okay." Dan gazed at the tablet that held his sermon and read through it for the final time.

He couldn't believe how enjoyable it had been to fine-tune it last night with Katie Ruth over cups of hot chocolate. Her questions and comments had prompted him to hone his message until they both felt good about it.

What would it be like to have her at his side for the rest of his life? If she was his wife, they could be alone together. Every day. Every night.

He would be there for her. She'd be there for him. He could

trust her. The fact that she'd confided the party details told him she wasn't a woman who kept secrets.

"I'm heading over to Katie Ruth's."

Dan looked up. "For a visit?"

"She's going to help me make the salads, er, salad."

"What kind are we having?"

"I, ah, haven't decided yet." Oaklee's gaze narrowed on him. "You're still planning to make shut-in calls this afternoon?"

He thought about teasing her, telling her he was spending the entire day at home. Instead, he nodded. "I'll be leaving around noon. Don't expect me back before five."

"Fab-u-licious."

At his raised brow, she flushed. "I want to get everything perfect for you and Katie Ruth this evening."

Dan's heart went out to his sister. He was suddenly ashamed of teasing her. She was going to all this work for him. "Thank you, Oaklee, for everything."

A wary look filled her gaze.

"I mean it. You've been so helpful around here, and I'm enjoying getting to know you better."

"This sounds like one of those speeches before you give someone the old heave-ho."

Dan laughed. "No heave-ho. I meant what I said when you arrived. You're welcome to stay as long as you want."

Tears sprang to Oaklee's eyes, appearing to surprise her as much as they did him. She hurriedly swiped them away. "Good to know."

Dan crossed the kitchen and placed his hands on her shoulders. He met her gaze. "You're a wonderful woman and an amazing sister. I love you, Oaklee."

She flung her arms around his neck and hugged him tight for several seconds, then stepped back. "Happy birthday, bro."

When he heard the front door shut, Dan smiled, his heart filled with love for this intelligent and caring young woman.

He fully admitted he hadn't known how he felt when Oaklee had shown up on his doorstep. Relief, certainly. But also some trepidation. Only now did he see that her being here had given them a chance to become a real family with a closeness they'd never before experienced.

Dan whistled as he once again picked up his tablet. The Lord sure did work in mysterious ways.

～

"Come in," Katie Ruth called out at the knock on the door.

When Oaklee had told her that she was making salads for Dan's party, but didn't know how to begin, Katie Ruth had invited her over.

Gladys and her cohorts were bringing the entrées—fried chicken, sloppy joes and baked ziti. Ami was baking Dan's favorite cake—double chocolate with sour cream frosting. Oaklee and Katie Ruth were in charge of salads.

"Your postal carrier is super friendly." Oaklee set several Tupperware bowls on the table. "Ours in Lincolnshire never stops to chat."

"She's very nice." Katie Ruth studied the bowls and nodded approvingly. "I made a list of—"

"I don't think Dan suspects."

Katie Ruth stilled. "Suspects?"

"About the party." Oaklee plunked herself down in a chair. "When he started asking me about the food, I thought he might."

Katie Ruth took her time taking the lids off the bowls. "What did he say?"

Oaklee waved a dismissive hand. "Something about not making too much food. I'm thinking it was just my overactive imagination."

When Oaklee's gaze settled on her, Katie Ruth realized the conversational ball had been passed. "I found out the entrées

Gladys is making and came up with three salads that go well with those food types."

"Whatever you want to make is fine with me."

"He's your brother." Katie Ruth pulled out a chair and sat beside Oaklee. The last thing she wanted was to barge in and take over. "These are what I had in mind. If you don't like these, or if you think Dan wouldn't be a fan, let me know, and we'll move on to something else."

Oaklee studied the first page.

"Blue cheese potato salad." She wrinkled her nose. "I don't think Dan likes blue cheese in his potato salad."

"I wondered about that." Katie Ruth pushed the alternate recipe in front of the girl. "What about this?"

"Yes." Oaklee nodded. "Deviled egg potato salad, for sure."

"We've got a winner." Katie Ruth set the recipe aside. "What about a fruit salad to go with the sloppy joes?"

"Pineapple, cherry pie filling, whipped topping..." Oaklee's smile widened with each ingredient. "Dan will love this. My mouth is watering just reading the recipe."

"Good." This recipe went on top of the other keeper.

"Tell me you're having chips. Dan loves chips."

Katie Ruth gestured to several large bags on the counter. "Covered."

She started to pull out the last side recipe when she felt Oaklee's hand on her arm. "Thank you."

"I love cooking and—"

"I don't mean about making the salads, although I am eternally grateful for the help." Oaklee's gaze remained riveted on hers. "What I meant was thank you for caring for my brother. He acts big and tough, like he's got everything under control. But he needs someone like you. He lights up when you walk into a room. I can't be the only one who notices that big, goofy grin."

"Dan is an amazing man."

"Don't break his heart."

"You mean like Lindsay—"

"No. Dan never loved Lindsay. If he did, he'd still be sad. When my brother loves, it's with his whole heart." Oaklee paused for a moment. "I can tell that's how he feels about you."

Katie Ruth's heart swelled. "He means a lot to me, too."

"I thought so." The sass was back in Oaklee's voice. "I can't wait to see the surprise on Dan's face when he walks in. You're clear about how this is going down?"

"Dan comes to pick me up. I suggest a short walk before driving to the restaurant. I make sure we're in the car at six." Katie Ruth could recite the scenario in her sleep. "A few minutes later, you call and tell him the dishwasher has sprung a leak and you need him at home. When we get there and he opens the door, everyone yells, 'Surprise!'"

Oaklee nodded her approval. When she bent to move her purse out of the way, she straightened with something in her hand. "I'm sorry I didn't already give this to you."

Katie Ruth saw she held a letter.

"I signed for it when I was talking to your mail carrier. It's for you."

"It's a certified letter." Katie Ruth noticed the name in the return field, and her heart froze. It took everything she had to keep her fingers from trembling as she lifted the envelope from Oaklee's hand.

Opening a drawer, Katie Ruth shoved it inside.

"Don't you want to open it?" The puzzlement in Oaklee's expression put Katie Ruth on alert.

*Play it cool.*

"It isn't anything important. What's important is getting the salads made." Katie Ruth smiled at Oaklee. "Which one do you want to tackle first?"

By the time Oaklee left to take the salads to the Living Center where they would be eventually transferred to Dan's home, Katie

Ruth was tired of pretending that hearing from Judd again wasn't a big deal.

What was it with Judd? Why, oh, why, when her life was going so well, did the past have to rear its ugly head? What could he possibly want with her after all these years?

Katie Ruth pulled out the envelope and collapsed in one of the kitchen chairs. It had been eight years since she'd last seen him. Even then, they'd known each other for only a weekend.

She stared at the envelope. She could open it. See what he had to say. As tempted as she was, it felt as if she'd be bringing the past into the present by reading whatever words he'd written.

Like releasing a genie from a bottle...

Katie Ruth couldn't do it. She would not bring even a sliver of Judd Stevens into her life with Dan.

Ripping the envelope in half, she tossed it in the trash.

# CHAPTER EIGHTEEN

"Happy birthday." A dozen voices shouted out the words.

Katie Ruth had to give Dan credit. He did an amazing job of acting surprised. She'd been worrying on the way over that she had ruined the party for him. He'd reassured her, reminding her again that he didn't like surprises.

Dan glanced around, a broad smile on his face.

Oaklee stepped forward. "We wanted to celebrate your birthday in a big way."

Dan turned to Katie Ruth and inclined his head. "Did you know about this?"

"I did." She rose on her tiptoes and brushed his lips with hers. "Happy birthday."

Heat flashed in his eyes, but when he slung an arm around her shoulders and turned to face the crowd, he was in total control.

"Thank you for this." His hand encompassed all his friends as well as the table containing more food than a group twice this size could eat. "It reminds me how much I love Good Hope and all of you."

"Happy birthday to you…" Gladys began to sing, and everyone joined in, ending the song with applause.

"We've got plenty of food." Oaklee's voice was loud enough to reach the back row of any theater. "Birthday boy, will you start the food train?"

Dan chuckled, but when they reached the table, he gestured for Katie Ruth to go before him.

As she filled her plate, going sparse with the food in order to allow room for the cake to follow, she forgave herself for telling Dan about the party.

His relaxed posture told her that, because he'd been ready, he would fully enjoy this evening with friends.

Katie Ruth hadn't been sure about the high tables that Oaklee had brought in, but it had been a good call. The tables gave everyone a place to set their plates while socializing.

"I didn't expect to see you tonight." Katie Ruth gave Lindsay a quick hug. "Who's watching the baby?"

"Anita and Len are watching her," Owen said, referring to Lindsay's mother and her boyfriend.

"My mom has been begging for a chance to watch Olivia." Lindsay rested her head against her husband's shoulder. "We didn't really want to leave, but decided this one hour away would give my mom her baby time and allow us to celebrate with Dan."

"We can't stay long, but," Owen slanted a glance at Dan, who was engrossed in a conversation with David and Hadley Chapin, "Dan was so good during Mindy's illness. He means a lot to both of us."

"I know your friendship means a lot to him."

Dan strolled up, the smile he offered Lindsay and Owen warm and friendly.

"I didn't expect to see you today." Dan chuckled. "Then again, I never thought I'd see all these people today."

"Happy birthday, Dan." Lindsay met his gaze. "I think of birthdays as a time to reassess where we're at in our lives. I believe you and I are just where we're meant to be."

Dan's gaze stole to Katie Ruth before returning to Lindsay. "I couldn't agree more."

The rest of the party flew by with people coming and going.

Katie Ruth nodded approvingly. "It was smart of Oaklee to make this party more of an open house. Less people in your home at one time."

"My sister has done a lot of growing up in the short time she's been in Good Hope." Dan finished off his piece of cake.

"She feels your love and support." Katie Ruth sighed. "That makes the difference when you're young and trying to figure out where you belong."

"My parents haven't been the most supportive. For me, but not for her."

"That's unfortunate." Katie Ruth didn't say more. These were, after all, his parents they were discussing.

"Your parents were supportive."

He said it as a statement, but Katie Ruth heard the question. Katie Ruth thought of the struggles she'd had in college. She remembered the long conversation she'd had with her mom from that hotel room in Vegas.

"My parents are amazing. Warm, accepting and supportive." Katie Ruth forked off another bite of cake. "Despite the issues when their extracurricular activities came to light, I feel blessed."

Dan studied her for a long moment, for so long she felt her face heat.

"Do I have frosting on my face?"

He shook his head. "You're amazing. You talk about your parents being accepting and supportive. You possess those same wonderful qualities."

"I don't know about that," she demurred.

His hand closed over hers, and he brought it to his lips. "Trust me on this."

Katie Ruth's breath caught. She was fighting for composure

when she spotted Gladys munching on a carrot stick, studying the two of them with her pale blue eyes.

When their gazes locked, Katie Ruth didn't know what to think when Gladys gave her the thumbs-up.

It must be the older woman's way of saying Katie Ruth had done well at keeping Dan away from home while they readied the house for his party.

By the end of the evening, Katie Ruth had nothing but admiration for Gladys and her friends. The three stayed until the end, then spent the next thirty minutes cleaning up and putting away the leftovers.

Once they left, Oaklee retired to her room. Katie Ruth and Dan were finally alone.

"You have a lot of birthday cards to read." Katie Ruth let her gaze linger on the basket placed on a barstool near the front door.

The wicker basket overflowed with envelopes much like the one she'd received earlier today. Katie Ruth shoved the memory aside. She refused to let anything ruin this evening.

"You and I could go through them tomorrow after church."

Katie Ruth saw the question in his eyes. "I'd like that."

"Good."

She took a step closer. "Did you have a nice birthday?"

"I did." His fingers played with the ends of her hair. "Thanks to you."

"Don't you mean thanks to Gladys and Oaklee?" Credit where credit was due. "They did most of the work. And all of the planning."

"You were the one who gave me the heads-up." His voice lowered. "I was prepared. I mean, I can roll with the punches, but I prefer not to be blindsided."

He tugged her to the sofa. They sat next to each other, his arm around her shoulders. Katie Ruth decided this was her favorite part of the day. "I love this."

He inclined his head.

"Sitting with you. Relaxing." She snuggled against him and expelled a happy sigh.

"I love this, too." His lips brushed against her cheek. "I love you."

Katie Ruth's lips paused midsmile. She turned to him.

Dan angled toward her. He took her hands, his gaze never leaving her face. "I love you, Katie Ruth. I know we've only been dating a short time, but I know how I feel. I'm in love with you."

Katie Ruth had never said the words to any man. But, like Dan, she knew her heart. Knew that what she felt for this wonderful man was honest and true. She moistened her lips, swallowed against the lump of emotion clogging her throat.

"I love you." Katie Ruth's voice shook. She raised a hand and cupped his cheek. "So very much."

The emotion in his eyes took her breath away, and when his mouth closed over hers, she was ready.

Ready to love this man for the rest of her life.

Katie Ruth had seen Dan every day since his birthday. The fact that they'd declared their love added a new ease to their relationship.

Dan still hadn't heard about the Lincolnshire position. He mentioned his father had called him several times this week, asking for an update.

Katie Ruth knew they would both have decisions to make when the offer came through. For now, she was enjoying spending time with the man she loved. With the man who loved her.

Tonight, she and Dan would be supervising a group of teens at the church for something new, a Friday Night Coffee Shop.

There would be games, and Ryder had offered his coffee cart and his services as a barista.

While Katie Ruth had always been active in the church, she'd been there every day this week. It felt right. Maybe she *should* consider a career in youth ministry. She enjoyed her work at the Y, but she loved working side by side with Dan.

Today, she'd taken the afternoon off, using the time to get her hair trimmed. She showered again when she got home, then reapplied her makeup. She was spritzing on perfume when she heard a knock at the door.

Oaklee had mentioned she might drop over, but Katie Ruth expected that would have been several hours ago.

Casting one last look in the mirror, Katie Ruth smiled at her reflection. Her hair was curled and hung loose to her shoulders. She liked herself in blue, and the sparkly superhero headband would likely be a hit with the teenagers.

She didn't bother to look through the peep, just opened the door. "You could have just come in—"

Katie Ruth froze as the man she hadn't seen in eight years brushed past her and stepped into her living room.

He turned, studying her for a long moment. "You haven't changed. You're as beautiful as ever."

Tall with short-cropped blond hair and bright blue eyes, Judd had classically handsome features that were enough to make any woman lose her head.

Which was what she'd done for forty-eight hours all those years ago.

"What are you doing here?" she demanded.

He dropped down on her sofa. "Thanks. I will have a seat. I suggest you do as well."

Katie Ruth sat in the chair, keeping her gaze fixed on him. "I repeat, what are you doing here?"

"I had to come." Judd's tone was matter-of-fact. "I tried to message and text. You never responded. I sent a certified letter in which I asked you to call. You never did."

"When we left Las Vegas, it was with the understanding—on both of our parts—that that crazy episode was over."

He raked a hand through his hair. "If only that were true."

A chill traveled up Katie Ruth's spine. What she saw in Judd's eyes had alarm bells ringing. "Just say it."

"We're still married."

Katie Ruth was glad she was sitting. She wasn't sure her knees could have held her. "That's not possible. The minister said he wouldn't file the paperwork. That meant the wedding never happened."

"I thought that, too. All these years, I never gave that weekend a second thought." Judd surged to his feet as if he couldn't stand sitting for another second. He began to pace the small living room, gesturing with his hands as he explained, "Like you, I thought it was over. Done."

Katie Ruth clutched her hands together in her lap. She tried to slow her breathing. "Tell me what happened."

"I'm getting married."

"Congratulations."

"The wedding is set for next fall. Steph is a wonderful woman."

"Does she know about Las Vegas?"

"I told her. She thought it was funny." His mouth quirked up for a moment. "Neither of us is laughing now."

"I don't understand." Katie Ruth's voice shook.

"Steph's brother is an attorney in Tahoe. The Las Vegas wedding came up, and he told us it doesn't matter whether the paperwork was filed or not. It was a legal ceremony, done by a valid minister. Filing makes no difference. He confirmed you and I are still legally married."

Katie Ruth was on her feet now, though she didn't remember standing. "We'll get an annulment. That should be simple, right?"

"That was my first thought." Judd raked a hand through his hair. He looked so miserable that any anger she had toward him disappeared. Besides, she couldn't be mad at him when all he'd done was make the same mistake she had in assuming the wedding hadn't been official.

"The thing is, Katie girl, you can't annul a marriage that's been consummated. We have to get a divorce."

"That's why you were trying to contact me."

"We need to get moving on this divorce." His expression searched hers. "I assume that's what you want, too?"

"Of course. The sooner, the better."

Judd expelled the breath he'd obviously been holding. "Thank God."

Katie Ruth offered him a wan smile. "I'm going to make us coffee, and you're going to tell me what I need to do."

She felt his eyes on her as she started the coffee, then poured two steaming cups, setting one before him.

"I brought papers for you to sign." He pulled an envelope from his pocket, removed some papers and spread them out on the table in front of her. "Simon, Steph's brother, had an attorney friend out of Milwaukee draw them up. There's another form in there saying we're not claiming any community property, or something to that effect."

Judd was back on his feet again. "We're running out of time. The wedding is set for October nineteenth. Once you sign off, he can push for a judgment."

"I'll sign right now," Katie Ruth assured him. "But why the rush? Your wedding isn't until the fall."

"The divorce judgment is immediate but, since we're getting a divorce in Wisconsin, neither you nor I can marry again for six months." Judd puffed out his cheeks. "If Steph and I have to reschedule the wedding, we will, but the church, the reception venue…all of that is already booked. I'd really like to make this work."

"I don't want to cause you any grief." Katie Ruth sighed. "I'm sorry I didn't get back to you."

"I only wish I'd found out sooner."

"Marrying someone you'd just met, well, I don't know what got into me."

"Steph asked me why. I didn't have a good answer for her either." Judd shoved his hands into his pockets, rocked back on his heels. "Maybe it was that I'd just got back from the Middle East. You were so fresh and pretty and sweet. You brought light into my darkness."

Katie Ruth sipped her coffee. "I don't know what my excuse was. Other than you were cute."

"Were?" he teased.

The spark in his eyes had her remembering how he'd thoroughly charmed her and had her forgiving herself, just a little.

"I'm glad you found someone who makes you happy."

"It took a long time. Steph is the one for me." He inclined his head. "What about you? From the research I did, it didn't appear you ever got married."

"I'm still single."

"Don't tell me I turned you off of marriage."

"Who is this?"

Katie Ruth jumped to her feet.

Oaklee stood in the doorway to the kitchen, which meant she must have come in through the back. Katie Ruth had told the girl many times she didn't need to knock, but wished this time she had.

Forcing a smile, Katie Ruth gestured to Judd. "Oaklee Marshall, this is an old friend of mine, Judd Stevens. Judd was in town and thought he'd stop by and say hello."

"You're the one who sent her the certified letter." Oaklee crossed the room and dropped down on the sofa. "Did you used to be Katie Ruth's boyfriend?"

Katie Ruth exchanged a glance with Judd and shook her head slightly.

"What are these?" Oaklee picked up the papers. Her eyes grew wide. "OMG. You two are married?"

"Yes, but no." Katie Ruth found herself floundering.

Judd lifted his hands as if to say, *I got nothing.*

Katie Ruth realized, just like he'd had to explain the Las Vegas craziness to his fiancée and her family, it would be up to her to explain the unexplainable. Not only to Oaklee…but to Dan.

# CHAPTER NINETEEN

The explanation of what went on in Vegas, Katie Ruth decided, would have to wait.

Katie Ruth signed the papers, her trembling hand making a mess of the signature. She looked up at Judd, her lips twisted in a wry smile. "The judge will look at this and think you married a kindergartner."

Her effort to lighten the mood must not have been as successful as she'd hoped, because Judd placed a hand on her shoulder.

"You're doing great." The blue eyes that gazed into hers were kind and filled with understanding. It was almost as if he sensed the effort it took for her to keep her composure. "I'm sorry. I knew me showing up like this after all these years would be a shock."

"I never thought I'd see you again." Katie Ruth ignored Oaklee's curious stare. Right now, dealing with Judd was all she could handle.

"I wondered if you'd changed much." His blue eyes warmed. "You're as pretty as ever."

He wasn't coming on to her. The compliment was clearly designed to put her at ease. Even though it didn't work, Katie Ruth appreciated the effort.

"I'm sorry I ignored your text and email." She shook her head. "I should have known there was a good reason for why you were trying to get in touch."

"I'd probably have blocked you if you'd contacted me." He gave a humorless chuckle. "The thing is, I've never been the kind of guy who does impulsive shit, ah, stuff. I still don't know what got into me."

"I'm not sure why I did it either." Katie Ruth waved a hand in the air. "Young and stupid, I guess."

"I hope this doesn't cause problems for you. I mean, my coming here like this." He slanted a glance in Oaklee's direction, appearing startled when she gave him a thumbs-up.

"I'm sure it'll be fine." Even as she said the words, Katie Ruth knew it wouldn't be.

Though Judd was kind and respectful, she watched him leave with a sense of relief.

There had been no desire on either of their parts to reminisce about the past. They'd been strangers when they married. They were strangers now.

Oaklee stationed herself on the sofa. Her eyes danced as if she'd been watching a particularly engaging movie.

"This is super juicy." Oaklee rubbed her hands together. "I've pieced together some of it, but there are still gaps."

Sighing, Katie Ruth dropped into the chair. "What do you want to know?"

"How did you and Mr. Studly meet?" Oaklee fanned her face with her hand. "That man is so hot he's on fire."

Katie Ruth acknowledged Judd was cute, though not nearly as attractive as Dan.

"When I was about your age, a friend had her bachelorette

party in Las Vegas." Katie Ruth met Oaklee's gaze. "Let me just say that the people I was hanging out with at the time were not ones I'd be with today. We lived on the edge. I was trying to figure out who I was and what—"

"You were a wild woman." Oaklee leaned forward, interest snapping in her blue eyes.

"If by 'wild' you mean I lost my focus and did things I'm ashamed of doing, then yes." Like a movie reel, images flashed before her. The drinking. The partying. The—

"Did you know Judd well before that weekend?" Oaklee leaned forward, resting her elbows on her thighs. "Was he a friend of the groom's?"

Katie Ruth shook her head. "No connection. I ran across him at a club. We danced and—"

Oaklee squealed. "You married someone you just met."

Katie Ruth winced. "I did."

"Your own version of a girls-gone-wild trip." Oaklee sounded impressed.

The phrase reminded Katie Ruth of what Dan had once said, causing her spirits to plummet even further. "We both regretted the marriage the next day and asked the person who married us not to file the papers. We thought that would prevent the marriage from becoming official. According to the attorney Judd consulted, that isn't true. We're legally married, which means we have to be legally divorced."

"This is epic." Oaklee howled with laughter, slapping her thigh. "Vintage rom-com material."

"This isn't a romantic comedy, and none of this is remotely funny." Katie Ruth thought of the crimp this had put in Judd's wedding plans. She tried not to think how this would affect her relationship with Dan. "Who marries a guy she just met?"

"Not just any guy. A smoking-hot one," Oaklee reminded her.

Guilt flooded Katie Ruth. "It doesn't matter what he looks like."

"It does when you're twenty-one." Oaklee's expression softened as she finally appeared to notice Katie Ruth's distress. "Lighten up. It's not as if your dog died. You were young. You made a mistake. Big friggin' deal. None of this changes who you are now and all the good you do."

Something in Oaklee's eyes had Katie Ruth pausing. Knowing the girl had a few of her own regrets had Katie Ruth carefully choosing her words.

"You're right. This doesn't change who I am now. In fact, I believe learning from my mistakes shaped me into who I am today. It also helps me understand the struggles we all have and how sometimes we make bad choices." Katie Ruth spoke firmly. "I also know God has forgiven me, and I've forgiven myself."

The trouble, and what Katie Ruth didn't say, was this wasn't just about her. This development could impact Dan's career. The thought made her feel sick inside.

Katie Ruth moistened her lips. "I'd like to ask you a favor, Oaklee."

A watchful waiting filled the girl's blue eyes, all humor gone. "Anything."

"I'd appreciate it if you wouldn't say anything to Dan—or anyone else—about this." Katie Ruth met her gaze, willing the girl to see she was serious. "It's best he hears this from me."

"I forgot about my brother." Oaklee's expression turned somber. "How do you think he'll take the news? I mean, it isn't as if you're an ax murderer or anything."

Why did Katie Ruth suddenly think that if she had a good excuse for a murder, that would be easier for Dan to swallow than finding out she was married?

*Married.*

Katie Ruth didn't know whether to laugh or cry.

"Katie Ruth?" Oaklee touched her arm, her brows pulled together in worry. "You don't think he'll be angry, do you?"

She shook her head. "I don't think he'll be angry."

Katie Ruth would almost prefer anger to the disappointment she was likely to see.

"Good." Relief lightened Oaklee's voice and erased any lingering shadows from her eyes. "My brother loves you. I know he does."

Despite her heavy heart, Katie Ruth forced a smile. No need to look for trouble. Though she didn't say this to Oaklee, she had a sinking feeling that, in this situation, love might not be enough.

～

"How did Katie Ruth look to you?" While Dan was happy to have his sister help him with Coffee Shop Night, he couldn't hide his worry. "Do you think someone should check on her?"

Oaklee looked up from the sheet Katie Ruth had given her. The kids were currently on a scavenger hunt in the church. They had another fifteen minutes to report in.

"She looked pale, but I'm sure she'll be, ah, feeling better by tomorrow."

Dan nodded, resisting the urge to call her again. They'd spoken shortly before the youth activity began. After apologizing for not being able to make it, she'd updated him on everything she'd set up.

He'd been so eager to see her and to tell her about the call from Ted. Not just that, but the ring he'd purchased for her was burning a hole in his pocket.

This was to be a night of celebration. But that didn't matter. What mattered was she was alone and not feeling well.

Dan glanced at the clock. Nine fifteen. Less than an hour to go until the parents would arrive to pick up their teens. The time couldn't go by quickly enough.

He should go to her, see for himself that she was okay.

*You must avoid even the hint of impropriety.*

He should send Oaklee to her. It was the smart, rational choice, but his heart rebelled. He had to see for himself that she didn't need anything.

Dan told himself he didn't have to stay long. Even one quick conversation at the doorway might be enough to ease his fears.

Yes, that's what he would do. As soon as the kids were picked up, he'd go to Katie Ruth and make sure all was well.

~

Though it wasn't particularly cold in her house, Katie Ruth had pulled on her softest flannel pj's and a favorite chenille bathrobe.

The end of her relationship with Dan was in sight. She felt it in her bones. It would have been easy to drown her sorrows in a bottle of wine. She settled for hot cocoa, wrapping her cold fingers around the oversize red mug covered in snowflakes. As tonight was her night to grieve, she let the tears fall unchecked.

When she thought of losing Dan, the crushing pain in her chest stole her breath. Was this what a heart attack felt like? The sobs began again. She set down the mug and wrapped her arms around her knees, rocking herself on the sofa.

The ringing doorbell seemed to come from far away. She stopped rocking and listened. There it was again.

Katie Ruth sniffled and swiped at her cheeks. She already knew who it was...Oaklee. Undoubtedly, the girl had come to make sure she was okay.

If she'd texted, Katie Ruth would have told her not to come. She needed this night alone. Needed to get all these feelings out so she could be strong when she faced Dan tomorrow.

She hadn't considered how she would break the news to him. Thankfully, she didn't need to worry about that right now.

Padding to the door in her tiger-paw slippers, Katie Ruth opened the door. "You didn't need to—"

She blinked. Was she hallucinating? She had to be. Dan would never come to her house this late at night, and certainly not alone.

When she blinked again, he didn't disappear from her porch.

Instead, the worry lines on his face etched only deeper into his skin.

She didn't invite him in, but suddenly he was in her living room, shutting the door behind him and pulling her into his arms.

Though it was weak of her, Katie Ruth closed her eyes and let him hold her one last time. The feel of his strong arms around her and the scent of his cologne were so familiar and so dear. The ache in her heart returned, and tears began leaking from her eyes. She buried her face against his chest and wept.

Dan murmured soothing words and stroked the back of her head. "I was so worried about you."

Didn't he know how much harder he was making this? Of course he didn't. Dan had no clue he was holding a married woman in his arms.

Calling on every bit of strength left in her, Katie Ruth drew a shuddering breath and took a step back.

"I'm sorry." Despite her best efforts, her voice shook and more tears slipped down her cheeks.

He brushed them away with the pads of his thumbs. "Don't worry about tonight. Oaklee stepped up. You'd have been proud of her."

She gave a hiccupping sob. He thought she was upset about missing the youth group activity. If only it was that simple.

Dan's caring gaze searched her face. "Is there anything I can do? What can I get you?"

The concern in his warm brown depths nearly undid her. She feared after she told him her story, he'd never look at her in that loving way again.

*You have to tell him now.*

Katie Ruth gestured to the sofa. "There's something I need to tell you."

His momentary hesitation told her he knew he shouldn't be here. Not alone with her. Not at this time of night.

She should tell him to leave, but she couldn't let him go. It was difficult to find a time and place where they could be alone. Katie Ruth needed to tell him where she didn't have to worry about their conversation being overheard.

Dan sat on the sofa, appearing surprised when she dropped into the chair rather than sitting beside him.

"Before you start," he said while she was finding her voice, "I got a call from Ted today."

Katie Ruth inclined her head.

"They narrowed the search down to three. They're asking each of the finalists to spend two weeks at the church, preaching and interacting with the congregation and other staff."

Katie Ruth didn't know how she managed it, but knowing this was such a big deal, she managed to inject some enthusiasm into her voice. "That's exciting."

"I wanted you to hear it before anyone else."

"When does your two weeks start?"

"I'm the first one up. I'll take a two-week leave beginning on Monday."

*For the best*, Katie Ruth told herself.

"Congratulations." She forced the word past dry lips.

"I'd like you to—"

"We can talk more about that in a minute, but what I have to say is really important."

"I'm sorry." He offered a sheepish grin. "I couldn't wait to share this with you."

"What I have to say is difficult for so many reasons."

Dan's smile disappeared. "What is it? You know you can tell me anything."

"There was a guy I met years ago, on a weekend trip to Las Vegas."

Katie Ruth watched the shutter drop over his eyes. Was he thinking about how it had been when Lindsay told him she wanted out of their engagement? This was different, Katie Ruth told herself. She didn't want out of her relationship with Dan. The decision would be his.

"I hadn't thought about Judd in years. Out of the blue, I got a Facebook message from him. I didn't read it. He was part of my past. I blocked him."

The tense set to Dan's shoulders eased. He blew out a breath.

"I don't know how he got my phone number, but I received a text from him." Katie Ruth's voice sounded foreign to her own ears, cool and composed, like a person relaying a business report. "Again, I deleted the message without reading it and blocked him."

Dan frowned.

"He sent me a certified letter," Katie Ruth continued. "I tore up the envelope and tossed it in the trash."

"There are laws against stalking." Anger flashed in Dan's eyes as he leaned forward. "If this guy is—"

"He showed up at my door today."

The words had Dan springing to his feet. "We need to call Cade. Tell him what—"

"Judd came to tell me we're still married."

Dan froze. His dark brows slammed together. "What did you say?"

"Sit down."

He shook his head and paced to the window, bracing both hands on the sill. His gaze remained focused into the darkness. "I don't think I can."

She waited. For what, she wasn't sure. But when he said nothing, she continued. "Eight years ago, I met Judd in Las Vegas. He was just out of the military, and I was there with friends for a bachelorette party."

Turning abruptly, Dan returned to the sofa, his face expressionless, his jaw set in a hard line.

"There were two years in college that I sort of lost myself. I did a lot of stuff I'm not proud of, but those times have given me a heart for those who struggle."

"Go back to the married part."

His voice held no emotion but still cut deep.

"Judd and I got married. It seemed like a crazy lark." Katie Ruth gave a nervous laugh. "The next morning, we realized what we'd done."

"You were drunk when you married him."

Katie Ruth wished she could use that excuse, but this was about being honest. "No. I'd had a few drinks, as had he, but neither of us was intoxicated."

"Go on." Dan ground out the words between clenched teeth.

"We contacted the 'minister' who married us. I use that term loosely. The guy wasn't affiliated with any church, and we learned he'd only gotten the credentials the previous week that allowed him to perform marriages." Her mouth had turned dry as dust. Katie Ruth gulped the now lukewarm cocoa before continuing. "The minister listened and sympathized and agreed not to file the marriage license. Judd and I went our separate ways. I hadn't seen him since."

"What is this about you still being married?" Dan's face gave her no clue what he was feeling.

"Judd is getting married next fall." This time, it was Katie Ruth who had to stand, who needed to move. She began to pace. "In speaking with a Nevada attorney, he discovered that even if the license isn't filed, the marriage is still legal. Judd brought me divorce papers. I signed them."

Katie Ruth studied Dan's face. She could almost see his analytical brain sorting through the information she'd given him.

"Why not an annulment? Why do you need to get a divorce?"

Katie Ruth took a breath, let it out slowly. "You can only get an annulment if the marriage wasn't consummated."

Dan nodded, but appeared to be avoiding her searching gaze.

"Apparently, Wisconsin recognizes no-fault divorces, and although it's a community-property state, Judd had his attorney draw up a form where we agreed to simply keep our own assets." Katie Ruth tried to smile. "The judgment will be effective immediately, but neither of us can marry for at least six months."

Dan extended his hands, palms up, a look of bewilderment on his face. "I've been dating a married woman."

"Technically, but—"

He surged to his feet. "I've been dating a married woman."

"Don't say it that way."

"It's true, isn't it?" The eyes that bore into her held little trace of the gentle man she'd fallen in love with over the past weeks.

"I explained how it was." She stiffened under his unyielding gaze. "I was young. I was stupid. I regret my actions. None of that changes who I am now."

"You're married." He raked a hand through his hair.

"Just until the papers are filed."

He shook his head, his lips pressed together.

"I'm doing everything in my power, and so is Judd, to undo this mistake. I'm an imperfect person who made a mistake." Katie Ruth realized she had to take this a step further. "I didn't even know until Judd just told me. I thought our marriage wasn't official. I understand the position I've put you in, but other than your sister, I promise you no one will ever know."

"My sister?" His words were harsh, filled with anger. "How did Oaklee get dragged into this mess?"

"She signed for the certified letter last week." Katie Ruth held his gaze. "She was here when Judd arrived earlier today."

Dan expelled a harsh breath. "Great."

"She promised not to say anything."

"Oaklee?" Dan made a rude noise. "She doesn't know how to keep her mouth shut."

"You're upset, but that's unfair and you know it."

"Is it? When you asked my sister to withhold the truth from me, it was the same as asking her to lie." The voice in which she'd heard anger only seconds before was now laced with pain. "I wanted you to go with me to Lincolnshire. Not as my girlfriend, but as my fiancée. Now—"

He'd planned to propose.

She would have said yes.

Katie Ruth waited for him to tell her they could make this work. But as the silence lengthened, she accepted that it was over. "I guess we'll be just another couple who couldn't go the distance."

Dan nodded, his eyes hooded. "If I take the job, it'll put even more distance between us."

She wished she could see beyond his stony countenance. Was his heart shattering along with hers?

"Don't take it if it's offered simply because of me." Katie Ruth's voice softened. "I promise to stay away. If it's difficult for you to see me in church, or work with me on the youth activities, I'll find another church. I'll resign my volunteer position."

Instead of protesting that that wouldn't be necessary, he appeared to be considering the options. "I don't want you to have to do that."

"It may be for the best anyway." Katie Ruth tried to smile, but couldn't pull it off. "It'll be difficult to see you and not be with you. I-I love you, Dan."

"I love you, too, Katie Ruth." His gaze grew puzzled. "But this, well, this makes me wonder if I even know you."

"Finding out I'm married was as much a shock to me as it is to you. I didn't deliberately keep it from you."

There were dozens of things Katie Ruth could have added.

She could have told him that the woman she was now was the sum total of all her experiences, both good and bad.

She could have reminded him that it wasn't what she'd done but how she felt about what she'd done that mattered.

She could have asked him how God could forgive her, but he couldn't.

Instead, she walked him to the door and said good-bye to the only man she would ever love.

# CHAPTER TWENTY

On Tuesday, Gladys and her friends lingered in the Good Hope Living Center's spacious dining room. They'd been in church on Sunday, when Dan had announced his two-week "trial" at the church in Lincolnshire.

"I think it's a bad sign that Katie Ruth wasn't in church on Sunday." Katherine lifted the china cup to her lips.

Gladys pursed her lips. "When I stopped by the Y to see her yesterday, her coworker said she'd taken a few days off."

"It's obvious he's planning to make this move without her." Katherine motioned over one of the teenagers who worked the dining room. "My coffee has gone cold. Would you be so kind as to get me a fresh cup?"

Ruby waited to speak until after the young girl had hurried off. "I could have sworn he'd fallen in love with Katie Ruth."

Gladys tapped a finger against the linen tablecloth. "I feel as if we're missing a piece of this puzzle. Everything was right on schedule, and now it's fallen apart."

"Oddly reminiscent of what happened between him and Lindsay." Katherine smiled her thanks as the girl set a steaming cup on the table.

"I disagree. While the sudden nature of the split is similar, Dan seemed much more," Gladys waved a hand, "oh, what is the word, *into* Katie Ruth."

"We need to speak with Oaklee." Ruby, giving in to temptation, stuck her fork into the marble cake she'd been avoiding. "How can we bring the two back together if we don't know what pushed them apart?"

"Excellent point." Gladys nodded approvingly. Her eyes grew sly. "Oaklee, dear. Come join us."

The other women turned and smiled in unison as Oaklee crossed and took a seat at the table.

"The administrator told me I could find you in the dining room." Oaklee glanced around the now empty room. "Are you guys planning to graze all day?"

"We have a lot to discuss." Gladys kept her tone mild. "We're puzzled by something and think you might be able to cast light on the matter."

"Sure. If I can." Oaklee eyed an extra piece of cake and pointed. "Is anyone eating that?"

"You are." Katherine set the dessert plate in front of Oaklee.

"This looks great." Oaklee immediately dug in.

"I imagine it's strange being alone in the house, what with Dan off in…" Gladys pretended to be fumbling for the location.

"Illinois. Lincolnshire." Oaklee spoke around a mouthful of cake. "That's the same town where my parents live."

"Of course. I remember now." Gladys sipped her water and considered the proper strategy. She didn't want to—

"We noticed Katie Ruth wasn't in church on Sunday for the announcement," Ruby said. "Did they break up?"

If Ruby hadn't been on the other side of Katherine, Gladys would have given her a swift kick to the shin.

Oaklee lowered her fork. Her eyes held the look of a trapped mouse as three hungry cats closed in.

The girl knew something, that was for certain. What did she know?

"Katie Ruth and Dan remain good friends." Oaklee refocused on her cake.

Gladys couldn't help it. Well, she *could* have helped it, but she didn't bother to try. She arched a dark brow. "Is that the *official* response?"

Oaklee's gaze darted from side to side. "I don't know what you mean."

Gladys had the feeling if Oaklee *would* have been a trapped mouse, she'd have gnawed off her leg to get away.

"Oh, Oaklee. We're all friends here." Gladys spoke in a soothing tone. "We love Dan and Katie Ruth. I don't know about you, but I was convinced we'd be hearing wedding bells soon."

Tears filled Oaklee's eyes. "I thought so, too."

When she sniffled, Katherine handed her a napkin, but wisely said nothing, letting Gladys take the lead.

"You two are like sisters." Sympathy, real not fake, oozed from Gladys's voice.

"I love Katie Ruth." Tears slipped down Oaklee's cheeks. "Dan talks about forgiveness, but..."

As if realizing she'd said more than she'd meant to say, Oaklee pressed her lips together. "I'm sorry. I promised not to say anything."

"Of course. And you're a person who keeps her word." Gladys reached over and patted her hand. "That's commendable."

"Would anyone like more coffee or water?" The young girl had been replaced by a woman whose name Gladys couldn't recall.

All Gladys knew was she was Ron and Edna Peabody's middle daughter.

"We're fine here, thank you." Gladys offered a polite smile and made a shooing gesture with one hand.

She waited until the woman stepped away to refocus on Oaklee.

"I can see this is difficult. You likely have no one to talk to about your feelings, or even to bounce ideas off of for how you could possibly make this better."

"I can't talk to Katie Ruth because she already feels bad enough." Oaklee inhaled deeply, then exhaled a ragged breath. "My parents, well, they'd have a field day if they knew."

Gladys nodded sympathetically. "Dan isn't here, and you can't speak with him."

"I tried." Oaklee began shredding the napkin in her hand. "I tried to tell him that she was getting a divorce, and then they could be together. But he—"

"Katie Ruth is married?" Ruby spoke loudly, as was her habit when startled. "Are you saying Dan was dating a married woman?"

"Lower your voice," Gladys snapped. Thankfully, a quick glance around the area showed only the Peabodys' daughter filling salt and pepper shakers at a table across the room.

"Now I've done it." Oaklee put her head in her hands. "I promised I wouldn't tell, and I did."

"Just to us." Gladys hated seeing the girl so distraught. "We're your friends. We're on Katie Ruth and Dan's side. We want to help. Tell us what happened."

"I don't know if I should." Oaklee's voice trembled.

"We can't help if we don't have the details." Gladys glanced at Katherine and Ruby. "Nothing you say will leave this table."

"Just be sure and keep your voice down." Katherine cast a furtive glance at the woman working diligently at the far table.

"I was at Katie Ruth's house and—"

Gladys listened to Oaklee's every word, knowing that sometimes small details made the difference. Though Oaklee kept her voice low, Gladys heaved a relieved sigh at the sight of the Peabody woman leaving the dining hall.

~

"Are you sure I can't get you anything?" Dan's mother stood in the doorway and studied her son.

Dan had papers spread out across the small kitchen table in the alcove off the kitchen. He'd considered spreading out at the dining room table, but his dad was watching television in the living room.

"I'm doing fine, Mom. Just working out a few kinks in my sermon for tomorrow night." Dan hadn't expected to take the pulpit so soon after his arrival.

He should have known he'd be thrust feetfirst into the fire. The committee had chosen three of the applicants for a closer look, and he was the first to do a trial run. Since Ted wanted to preach on Easter Sunday, and the committee wanted to give the congregation a chance to hear each potential minister twice, Dan would speak on Good Friday and then the Sunday after Easter.

"I'd ask if there was anything I could do to help, but sermons aren't really my area of expertise."

The words struck a familiar chord. It was what Lindsay used to say when he asked for her assistance. His efforts to convince her that he just wanted her impression, her feedback on whether the message touched her heart, had fallen on deaf ears.

Dan knew it would be the same with his mother. His father, well, he knew better than to ask. While supportive of what he considered a "step up" in his son's career, John Marshall made no bones about not being a particularly religious man.

"I enjoyed having dinner with you and Dad." Though Dan wanted to get back to his sermon, he reminded himself that he was a guest in his parents' home.

"We're both looking forward to having you closer." His mother hesitated, and Dan could almost recite the question before she said the words. "What happened between you and

Katie Ruth? You seemed so infatuated with her the last time we spoke."

Infatuated? He'd been in love with her.

*Married.* Dan found it difficult to wrap his mind around the fact that she'd left out such a significant part of her past. What else didn't he know?

His fingers tightened around the pencil he still held in his hand. "Several things came up. I realized I don't know her as well as I thought I did."

"For the best." His dad, who often feigned poor hearing, seemed to hear quite well at the moment, even one room away. "Concentrate on your career."

Dan didn't bother to correct his father, who continued to insist on calling his ministry a career.

"I'm sorry." Sandra crossed the room and laid a hand on his shoulder. "I can see you're hurting."

"Thanks, Mom." He glanced down at the papers. "I'll be better once this sermon comes together."

"I'll leave you to it." She planted a kiss on the top of his head and left him alone.

Once his mother had disappeared from sight, Dan set down his pencil.

His sermon centered around God's power to forgive and reconcile. The content was appropriate for a Good Friday sermon, and Dan knew the emotion he wanted to convey.

The trouble was, when he thought of forgiveness and God, he thought of Katie Ruth.

Dan knew Katie Ruth would have had lots to say about his message. She'd realize it was an important one. Unlike his father, who usually saw things in black and white, Katie Ruth understood people's complexities, their weaknesses, and had compassion for them.

He could almost hear her voice urging him to put more emphasis on God's power to forgive. No matter how horrible your sins might seem, you could lay them at the cross and be forgiven.

Dan told himself he'd forgiven her for withholding information about her marriage. Reconciliation, well, that was a whole different story.

The fact that he had dated a married woman went against every belief he held.

Would Katie Ruth ever have told him about her Las Vegas marriage if her husband hadn't shown up wanting a divorce?

He thought of Lindsay. She hadn't told him about her feelings for Owen until they'd become so apparent, she could no longer deny the truth.

Was it him? Did he make it difficult for people to confide in him?

Dan rested his head in his hands, the sudden pain in his head matching the one in his heart.

This position in Lincolnshire had come at exactly the right time for both him and Katie Ruth. They needed distance to get their heads straight.

Heck, who was he kidding? *He'd* needed the distance.

Except the miles separating them scarcely mattered, considering he couldn't get her off his mind.

Katie Ruth stepped into the Daily Grind the Friday before Easter for a quick cappuccino. She smiled, happy to see Cassie behind the counter. With her wedding fast approaching, Cassie had been working only a handful of hours at the coffee shop.

Though she normally didn't drink caffeine this late in the day, Katie Ruth needed the jolt. She barely slept at night, and when she did sleep, her dreams were filled with Dan.

"A cappuccino wet, please." Katie Ruth smiled at Cassie. Next month, Cassie would wed a man who'd only recently come back into her life. Despite their short time together, it was obvious the two were meant to be together. "Ready for the big day?"

The second she asked the question, Katie Ruth realized that an odd silence had descended over the shop. The dining area had gone silent. When Katie Ruth turned, she found all eyes on her and Cassie.

No doubt hanging on Cassie's every word, since the woman was marrying former NFL superstar Krew Slattery.

"There's something I want to show you." Cassie motioned to Katie Ruth, then turned to Ryder, who'd stepped out from the back. "Could you watch the counter for a few minutes?"

Ryder glanced at Katie Ruth, then back at Cassie. Something seemed to pass between them. "Take your time."

Only when they were seated in the back office, with the door closed, did Katie Ruth apologize. "I'm sorry about asking about your wedding. I know you and Krew are—"

"Is that why you think everyone was looking at us?" The kindness in Cassie's eyes had Katie Ruth shifting in her seat. "Because they were hoping for wedding details?"

Katie Ruth nodded. "Why else?"

"The news is out."

"What news?"

The pity on Cassie's face told Katie Ruth her and Dan's breakup had become public knowledge.

"They know about Dan and I breaking up, don't they?"

"That's not what has the gossip mill churning overtime."

"What, then?"

"They know about your marriage."

Katie Ruth remembered vividly the day her parents had told her about their lifestyle. The air had simply left her lungs. She hadn't been able to catch her breath. She felt that same way now.

"My marriage?" Her words seemed to come from far away.

Cassie reached over and took her hand. "Look at me."

Katie Ruth did as Cassie ordered, gazing into the soft blue

eyes. If anyone knew what it was like to be the subject of gossip, it was this woman.

"Take it from me, the best thing you can do is hold your head high and ignore them." Cassie shook her head as if banishing bad memories. "Your friends, those people who you can count on, will stand with you until the talk dies down."

"How-how did you find out?" As far as Katie Ruth knew, only two other people knew of the situation, and neither of them would talk.

"It's all over Good Hope."

Katie Ruth flinched, realizing the look Ryder had exchanged with Cassie told her that even he knew.

"Hey, think of it this way. The secret is out there. No need to worry about people finding out."

Katie Ruth gave a little laugh. "Because they already know."

"Exactly." Cassie squeezed the hand she still held. "You're a strong person, Katie Ruth. You'll get through this and be better for the experience."

"How do you figure?"

"You'll know firsthand what it's like to have people spread lies and half-truths about you. This experience will give you even more empathy for the kids in your youth group and at the Y." Cassie sat back. "You got through the gossip about your parents. You'll get through this as well."

"I didn't think the marriage was valid." Katie Ruth found herself wanting to explain even though Cassie hadn't asked. "Until Judd, he was the guy I married in Vegas, came and told me we needed to get a divorce."

"I figured you didn't know." Cassie paused for a long moment. "I imagine it came as quite a shock to Dan."

The lump pressing against Katie Ruth's windpipe had her clearing her throat before speaking. "I understand why he didn't want to be with me any longer. Still..."

"Given time, sooner or later, everyone we love will disappoint us." Cassie's eyes took on a faraway look. "Because they, like us, are human."

"He didn't even try to understand my side."

"Dan is a wonderful minister. A fine man. But I'm betting he hasn't dealt with situations like this in his personal life."

"How many situations can there be when you find out the woman you love...I mean, the woman you've been dating is married?"

"Not many, hopefully." Cassie's smile flashed before her expression turned serious. "But this isn't about facing crazy telenovela situations. This is about tossing aside your pride and your hurt and trusting your heart. It's easy to talk about forgiveness, to tout putting aside the past because we've been forgiven. It's a lot harder to do when your own heart is hurting."

"I don't want to be angry with him."

"Then don't be. But don't let him off the hook entirely. He may be hurting, but you're dealing with your own pain."

"He won't be back." Then Katie Ruth added, "Maybe to Good Hope, but not to me."

"Then he isn't the one for you. Remember what I said. Keep your head up." Cassie stood and flashed a grin. "Refusing to play the guilty party drives judgmental people crazy."

CHAPTER TWENTY-ONE

Katie Ruth was prepared to walk out of the shop with her head held high. The mental practice took her back to her middle-school years immediately after her parents had been the ones feeding the gossip mill.

*You got through that time. You'll get through this.*

With each step toward the door, she felt more determined. She would not apologize to strangers for a youthful mistake. Granted, this was a big one, but it was innocuous if you considered its impact.

"Have a good day." Katie Ruth nodded in Ryder's direction as she rounded the counter, the glass door in sight.

There were several people pushing inside, so Katie Ruth slowed her steps.

The smile faded when she saw Mitch, a city parks supervisor. Now paunchy and balding, he'd been one of the boys who'd made her life hell as a teenager. In high school, he would jangle keys in front of her when she walked down the hall, asking if she'd be up for a threesome in his car.

Despite the pleasant aroma of coffee and cinnamon in the air,

Katie Ruth's stomach turned over. Running into him was definitely not what she needed.

Instead of looking away, she met his insolent gaze full on, visualizing him as a bug under her shoe. She'd learned long ago to show no fear.

"Hey, Katie."

That was another thing about Mitch. He'd always insisted on calling her by the wrong name.

Not about to engage, she ignored him as if he was someone on the street she didn't recognize.

"You know, unlike our esteemed preacher, I don't mind dating a married woman."

His leer had bile rising. Katie Ruth wished she was like Eliza, who never seemed at a loss for a quick comeback. She settled for rolling her eyes.

Before she could take another step, Mitch reached out. Quick as a snake, his fingers closed around her arm.

Startled, she let out an involuntary cry and tried to jerk away.

He held tight and stepped closer.

Then he was stumbling back, and Ryder was in his face.

"Get out of my shop." Ryder ground out the words through clenched teeth.

Mitch held up his hands and took a step back. "Hey, I'm a customer. You can't toss me out."

"This is my place, and I *can* toss you out." Ryder pointed to the door. "Don't come back. You're not welcome here."

Mitch opened his mouth as if to protest.

Ryder held up a hand. "Say one more word, and I'll call Cade and have you arrested for assault."

"I didn't want any damn coffee anyway." He turned and strode out the door, slamming his palm against the jamb.

The buzz of conversation became a groundswell.

Ryder turned to the patrons in the dining area. "Show is over, folks."

When Katie Ruth left the shop, Ryder was at her side. She was grateful. Not that she expected Mitch to be waiting for her outside, but still...

"I didn't mean to cause a scene."

"You didn't. He did." Ryder's gaze narrowed when Katie Ruth continued to rub her arm. "That's going to leave a bruise."

She shrugged. "He's a jerk. Always has been."

Despite the casualness of her tone, Katie Ruth once again felt tears pushing at her lids. Determinedly, she blinked them back. "Thanks for what you did back there."

He fell into step beside her as she continued down the sidewalk. "I know Cassie already spoke with you and probably said as much, but we've all got stuff in our past that creeps up on us. I know I do. But it doesn't define us, so don't let anyone treat you like it does."

"Thanks, Ryder." Katie Ruth touched his hand. "You're a good friend."

"Dan is a lucky guy."

Katie Ruth nodded. Apparently, Ryder hadn't heard the news and still thought they were together. "He is."

"When will he be back?"

*Never.* The thought was like a knife to her heart.

"He'll be preaching the Good Friday service tonight in Lincolnshire and then the Sunday service after Easter, too." Katie Ruth stopped. "You should go back. Cassie is swamped."

His dark eyes searched her face. "If you need anything, I'm here for you. You have friends in Good Hope."

"As do you."

"That's why I stay." He flashed a smile. "Take care of yourself."

Oddly, despite the encounter with Mitch, Katie Ruth felt better. Cassie and Ryder had reminded her that she wasn't alone.

She had friends in Good Hope. She would get through this the same way she'd gotten through the talk about her parents... one day at a time.

~

The Good Friday sermon at First Christian, by a retired minister out of Eau Claire, centered around forgiveness and God's love. While the man's oratory skills were not on Dan's level, the message was just what Katie Ruth needed to hear.

"Wow. That's some bruise." Oaklee leaned down to get a better look when they paused in the vestibule after the service.

"It's nothing." Why, oh, why, Katie Ruth thought, had she pushed up her sleeves when the room got too warm?

Cade and Marigold stopped on their way to the exit.

"I heard what happened with Mitch today. I want you to know I'll be speaking with him." The sheriff's gaze dropped to her arm. "Ryder was right. It did bruise."

"It's okay—"

"It isn't okay." A muscle in Cade's jaw twitched. "If you want to bring charges—"

"I don't," Katie Ruth spoke quickly. "Just tell him to stay away from me."

"What's this about?" Oaklee's brows pulled together in concern.

"I heard about the incident at the Grind." Hadley placed a hand on Katie Ruth's shoulder. "If you ever need to talk, I've had experience with angry men."

Katie Ruth looked around the circle of friends that was growing by the second, and a warmth filled her body. One thing all this had taught her was she was surrounded by people who cared.

And then one sour voice broke through.

"I can't believe you're in charge of our youth programs." Edna paused a few feet from Katie Ruth, pulling away when her husband attempted to hurry her along. "Once we get a new minister, I'm going to make it my mission to get you out. You should be ashamed of yourself. A married woman dating around. I—"

"Edna Peabody." Eliza, part of the group gathered around Katie Ruth, stepped forward. Despite the baby strapped to her chest in a pink carrier covered in frolicking lambs, Eliza remained an impressive force. "It's you and that daughter of yours who should be ashamed."

Edna's sharp chin lifted so high it appeared to be reaching for the heavens. "We only spoke the truth."

If she thought she could intimidate Eliza Kendrick, the woman was mistaken.

"Judge not." Eliza's gray eyes turned to steel. "Go home and read your Bible."

"I didn't know I was married, Edna. That situation is being remedied." Katie Ruth would explain, but she was done apologizing. "I was young and foolish. I made a mistake. That doesn't change who I am now. I think we can agree there's not a person in this church who doesn't fall short of the glory of God."

Despite Eliza's steely gaze, Edna opened her mouth.

Katie Ruth plowed ahead. "Eliza's suggestion was a good one. Perhaps when you do go home and open your Bible, you should pay special attention to John, chapter eight, when Jesus talks about letting he who is without sin cast the first stone."

"Mom." One of Edna's daughters stepped forward and took her arm. "We need to go."

Minutes later, Katie Ruth and Oaklee said good-bye to their friends and strolled into the warmth of the lovely spring evening.

"I'm going to miss you." Katie Ruth slanted a glance at Oaklee as they took the sidewalk toward town. Dan had gotten his dad to agree to let Oaklee join the family for Easter. "I'm sure you'll have a wonderful time."

Oaklee's gaze remained focused straight ahead. When a tear slid down Oaklee's cheek, Katie Ruth stopped.

"Sweetie, I know you're still angry at your parents, but try not to be upset."

"No, it's not that."

"Then what's wrong?"

"It was me."

"I don't understand."

"It was me who blabbed." Oaklee went on to explain about the conversation in the dining room at the Living Center.

Not only had she told Gladys, Katherine and Ruby a secret she'd promised to keep, but Edna Peabody's daughter had apparently heard every word.

"I understand if you hate me." Oaklee sniffled. "I know you'll never trust me again."

"Oaklee."

Katie Ruth's firm tone stopped the girl's tears.

"You needed someone to confide in, so you spoke with people you trust. You couldn't know that Edna's daughter was listening in and would repeat what you said in confidence."

"But—"

"There's no buts about it." Katie Ruth softened her tone. "It's okay."

"You-you forgive me?"

"Yes, I forgive you."

"I wish you could be my sister."

The words punched her heart. "We're sisters of the heart. I'll always be here for you. Just like you'll always be here for me."

Oaklee flung her arms around Katie Ruth's neck. "I love you."

Katie Ruth closed her eyes for a second. "I love you, too."

After a few seconds, Oaklee released her choke hold and blinked away the last of the tears. "Is there anything you want me to say to Dan?"

Katie Ruth's smile faltered for just a second before she steadied it. "Tell him to just be himself. I know he'll do awesome."

~

Dan's mother had Easter dinner catered. The china and crystal were out, perfectly spaced on the Irish linen tablecloth. The fact that Oaklee had come was what made the day special for Dan.

His mother had raved so much about his sister's new haircut and color, Dan wondered if Oaklee would change it as soon as she got back to Good Hope.

"Have you been keeping yourself busy?" Sandra asked her daughter as she passed the potatoes.

Oaklee slapped a dollop of potatoes on her plate and handed the china bowl to Dan. "I've been making quilted place mats and table runners, as well as some stuffed animals, for Lindsay."

"Dan's Lindsay?" His mother raised a brow.

"She's not my Lindsay." Dan passed the potatoes on to his father without taking any. He hadn't much of an appetite lately. "She's married with a child."

"She *was* yours," his mother said pointedly.

Despite what his mother thought, Lindsay had never been his. The connection had been tenuous at best. Not like it had been with Katie Ruth...

"Yes, I've been working with Lindsay Vaughn." Oaklee's tone was matter-of-fact. "In addition to her floral shop and work, she contracts with several artists for specialty items that—"

"Artists." His father snorted. "Sewing place mats doesn't make you an artist."

"You haven't seen what your daughter can do." Dan shot his father a warning look. "Her work is beautiful and creative."

Oaklee favored him a smile as she reached across the table and grabbed a bun from the bread basket.

That earned her a censuring look from her mother.

*The kid can't catch a break*, Dan thought.

"I assume you're staying away from that woman."

Oaklee cocked her head. "What woman would that be, *Father?*"

"The one who nearly ruined your brother's chances for career advancement." John stabbed a piece of ham and placed it on his plate. "Your mother has stayed in touch with several women she met during our visits to Good Hope. Apparently, the news that my son was dating a married woman is all over town."

"Don't you dare say anything bad about Katie Ruth." Oaklee tossed her head, and Dan saw the defiant gleam in her eyes. "We're besties."

"Why doesn't that surprise me?" A muscle in John's jaw jumped. "Still, I can't believe that after what she did to your brother, you—"

"What did she do, Dad?" Oaklee tore the bun in half instead of splitting it with a knife, her eyes never leaving her father's face.

"You know very well—" Sandra began, but one sharp look from her daughter had her going silent.

"She made a mistake when she was young. Big deal." Oaklee shifted her attention to Dan. "You're all about forgiveness. Or that's what you preach. Despite all the bad things that are happening to her, do you know what she said when I asked her if I could pass along a message to you?"

Dan's heart gave a leap. When he spoke, his voice sounded raspy. "What did she say?"

"She said to tell you to just be yourself. You'll do awesome." Oaklee narrowed her gaze on her father. "That's the kind of caring person she is, so I don't want to hear another word about me being friends with her."

"Fine with me." John lifted his hands. "It's not as if I want to discuss the woman. I'd much rather celebrate that your brother will soon have a new job."

Dan didn't bother to correct his father. They knew the position wasn't yet his. He didn't even know if he would accept it if a call were extended. And it wasn't a *job*, it was a *ministry*.

None of those things mattered as his mind latched on to something else Oaklee had said. "What do mean, the bad things that are happening to her?"

"The fact that she was married got out." Oaklee set down the half-eaten bun. "Everyone in Good Hope knows."

"How?" Dan asked. "You and I were the only ones who knew."

Oaklee's face took on a dejected look. "I said something to Gladys about her being married. Edna Peabody's daughter overheard."

"Oh, Oaklee, how could you be so careless?" Sandra huffed out a breath and glanced at her husband.

John's face was set in hard lines.

"You may have just cost your brother his promotion." John turned to his son. "You need to find a way to tell the search committee about this before they hear it from someone else."

"I agree." Sandra shot her daughter a disapproving look.

"What bad things?" Dan repeated. His sister still hadn't answered his question.

"Mitch Peskin confronted her at the Grind. What a loser." Oaklee's upper lip curled. "He grabbed her arm and told her he didn't mind doing it with a married woman."

Dan shoved back his chair with a clatter and sprang to his feet.

"Sit down, son," his father urged. "This isn't your battle."

"He left a big bruise on her arm." Oaklee's comment added kerosene to the fire scorching Dan's veins.

"I can't believe everyone just stood around and let him—"

"Ryder stepped in. Ordered him out of the Grind. Told him not to come back." Oaklee paused. "People stood up for her when Edna started in on her after services on Good Friday."

Dan closed his eyes for a second. He couldn't believe this was happening.

"Sit down, Dan. There isn't anything you can do about this now."

For a long moment, Dan simply stood there, and anger surged.

Anger at Mitch and Edna.

Anger at himself for leaving so that Ryder and others had to be the ones to stand by her side.

Anger at himself for abandoning her to gossip.

He dropped back into his seat.

"Your father and I are excited that your new church is so close." Apparently, his mother had decided the best course of action was to ignore the past minute. "I can already tell you're going to love—"

"You're running." Oaklee ignored her father's sharp glance and kept her gaze on Dan. "You're hiding from the real work that needs to be done. You make a difference in Good Hope, Dan. Can you really say you'll be able to make that same difference here?"

Dan didn't answer. He had no answers.

Not about the position in Lincolnshire.

Not about the feelings he had for Katie Ruth.

And not about the guilt that gnawed at him, that told him his actions had disappointed not only himself and Katie Ruth, but God as well.

# CHAPTER TWENTY-TWO

Katie Ruth's phone dinged as she was climbing into bed. Though part of her wanted to ignore the text, curiosity wouldn't let her stay under the covers.

Casting the lightweight quilt aside, she padded across the floor to the dresser where her phone was charging. When she saw who the text was from, her heart gave a leap.

*How are you? I've been thinking about you.*

Pleasantries, Katie Ruth told herself, nothing more. Still, her fingers trembled as she texted back.

*OK. Keeping busy. Oaklee said you preached on Good Friday. How was your sermon received?*

There was a long pause. Katie Ruth wondered if she'd made a mistake in being so wordy. Perhaps all he was looking for, all he was wanting, was something quick that told him he didn't have to worry about her. Not that he was likely worrying about her.

Dan was a minister, a caring guy. This reaching out was just another example of that caring.

*I heard from quite a few who said they "enjoyed" the sermon, but that didn't tell me if they understood the passages better, or if I enabled them to see their problems in a clear light.*

Katie Ruth smiled. *Classic Dan*. Always pushing himself harder in an effort to offer truth that could be applied to the daily lives of the members of the congregation.

*I say "enjoy" when I get something out of the sermon. Glad it went well.*

There were so many other things that Katie Ruth wanted to tell him. In the weeks they'd been together, he'd become her closest friend and confidant. She reminded herself that those days were over.

Another long silence.

*Oaklee told me about the problems with Mitch and Edna.*

This, Katie Ruth realized, was why he'd texted. She'd known there had been a specific reason for his concern.

*Don't worry. I can handle myself. I have friends here who have my back.*

Just before she hit send, Katie Ruth thought about deleting the last sentence. Would he see it as a jab? Think that she was being passive-aggressive and telling him that he hadn't had her back? She sent it the way she'd keyed it in.

*I'm sorry you have to go through this.*

Yeah, Katie Ruth thought, me, too.

*What doesn't kill us makes us stronger. It's late. Gotta go.*

Then, before she could be tempted to continue the conversation, she shut off her phone and put it back on the charging pad.

She wished he hadn't reached out.

She wished she hadn't responded.

Most of all, she wished she didn't love him still.

While the other ministers and key support staff filled their coffee cups, Dan remained seated around the oval conference table. His thoughts, as they had so often during the past week, drifted to Katie Ruth.

After Sunday's dinner, he'd gone for a run, hoping to clear his head after Oaklee's troubling comments. Thirty minutes later, he was exhausted, but the exercise hadn't eased the ball of fury in his gut. In his head, he had no trouble seeing Mitch accost Katie Ruth or picturing Edna Peabody in action.

He'd been glad to hear that Katie Ruth was staying strong, that she had friends around her who cared. Friends who, unlike him, had rallied around her in her hour of need...

When Ted began the meeting with a prayer, Dan added his own silent prayer for Katie Ruth.

"Our goal for this year is to reach more people in our community."

Dan perked up. That had been his goal for First Christian ever since arriving in Good Hope. But in the years he'd been there, the congregation had remained stable, with no appreciable uptick in numbers.

Ted turned to Dan. "We discovered the main factor limiting church growth is pastoral care."

Whatever limiting factor Dan had expected Ted to give, it hadn't been this one. "Are you referring to having pastors who don't connect with their congregation?"

"Not at all." Ted's gaze turned sharp and assessing. "You're currently the pastor of a small congregation with less than two hundred members. Correct?"

Dan nodded, not sure where Ted was going with this, but interested in the possibilities.

"I'm going to list some of the duties a pastor in such a congregation takes on. Stop me if I mention something that isn't part of what you consider your duty."

Feeling like a runner poised at the starting block, Dan nodded.

"Visit every hospitalized member. Perform every wedding and funeral. Make regular house calls to shut-ins. Attend every meeting."

"Not every meeting." Dan thought of Katie Ruth and how she took personal ownership of the youth group. Then there was Jackie White, who managed the Little Fishes day care program. "I have wonderful coordinators and volunteers who handle the programs from preschool through high school. They provide me with the minutes of their meetings. We consult over any program changes, but I don't usually attend their meetings."

"Excellent." Ted made some notes on the notepad sitting in front of him. He looked up. "Do you lead every Bible study?"

Dan shook his head. "Again, I have very committed volunteers in that area."

"You're doing many things well, but there is room for improvement." Ted smiled. "Just like here. We're doing some things well, but there is definite room for improvement."

Ted went on to explain that when a pastor tried to do it all, sermon preparation and organizational leadership suffered, and that inhibited growth. "Both seminaries and congregations have unrealistic expectations of their ministers. Pastors in small congregations and in large ones burn out because they can't keep up."

"What are you suggesting?"

"That's what this meeting is about." Peter answered the question, but Ted didn't seem to mind. "We get together regularly to discuss potential changes that need to be made to make Christian leadership more strategic."

"To grow, congregations need to understand that their pastor might not be the one to do it all." Ted met Dan's curious gaze. "It sounds as if you've set that expectation in your programs for children. More of your care duties need to be shifted to the congregation."

Dan inclined his head to show he was listening, but said nothing.

"It's really a win-win. You have more time to focus on duties only you can provide, while shifting others. This allows people to care for each other."

First Christian was filled with loving, caring individuals. Would Gladys and some of her friends be interested in visiting shut-ins? Dan thought of Floyd and Len and other retirees who could visit the hospitalized.

His mind began to hum with possibilities. Katie Ruth, he knew, would find this topic fascinating. He couldn't wait to talk to her—

He pulled back his thoughts. They weren't a couple anymore. Were they even friends? His heart sank.

"Do you do the counseling yourself?"

Dan jerked back to attention. "Yes."

"That's another area we've outsourced, so to speak, to trained Christian counselors." Ted paused. "I realize you're in a small community. Would you have someone you'd feel comfortable referring to?"

"We have a clinical psychologist in our congregation who specializes in children, but who also has a thriving adult practice." Dan didn't know Liam Gallagher well, but Cassie had sung his praises. "I believe he might be interested."

Ted nodded approvingly and made another notation on the pad.

Dan realized suddenly that this discussion was part of the interview process. Reviewing these options was a way for those around the table to see how open he was to doing things differently.

What Dan found particularly interesting was that he wasn't looking at how *this* church could best implement these suggestions, it was how he could implement them at First Christian.

Maybe that was because the church in Good Hope was what he knew.

Or maybe he'd been put in this situation so that he could take back the lessons he'd learned and better serve the population of Good Hope.

That might end up being the most interesting lesson of all.

～

Gladys didn't often get discouraged. In fact, she could count on one hand the number of times she'd felt the way she did right now. It was as if she was traveling down a familiar path when suddenly she'd been forced to veer right even though she preferred to continue straight ahead.

Gladys placed the clear glass vase tied with raffia and over-flowing with sunflowers on a table in the Hill House parlor and pursed her lips. "Dan Marshall is a thorn in my side."

"You have a thorn in your foot?" Concern furrowed Ruby's brow. Her gaze dropped from the arrangement in her hands, this one destined for the mantel, to Gladys's stylish heels. "How are you even able to walk with a thorn?"

"Oh, for goodness sake." Gladys huffed out the words, then spoke through gritted teeth. "I said that Dan Marshall is a thorn in my side. I have no idea how you got 'a thorn in my foot' from that comment."

Ruby placed the arrangement she held on the mantel, then fussed with it for a second. Once her hands were free, she tapped a finger against one ear. "My hearing isn't what it used to be."

Though Gladys could hear a pin drop at fifty feet, she understood some people weren't as blessed. "What I was saying…"

She motioned Katherine over, not in the mood to repeat the conversation. Thankfully, they were the only ones in Hill House decorating for Cassie and Krew's bridal shower.

In a matter of minutes, the catering staff from Muddy Boots would arrive with the appetizers, and Anita, the mother of the bride and a superb baker, would show up with the cake. These few minutes were likely the last time today that Gladys and her friends would be alone.

"I find Dan Marshall to be the most frustrating man we've ever attempted to match." Gladys looked to Katherine and Ruby for confirmation and received nods of agreement. "First, there was the situation with Lindsay."

"That wasn't Dan's fault," Ruby protested.

No surprise, Gladys thought. From the time she'd been a little girl, Ruby had stood up for the underdog.

"Lindsay broke off their engagement," Ruby said, as if they needed a reminder.

"He didn't seem to try too hard to keep her, did he?" Gladys blew out a frustrated breath.

When Ruby opened her mouth, Katherine shot her a warning look. Ruby closed her mouth without speaking.

"Now we have this thing with Katie Ruth." Gladys gave one of the table centerpieces a half turn so that the sunflowers were shown to their best advantage. "I'm beginning to think the man has commitment issues."

"He's a minister." Katie Ruth's voice echoed in the nearly empty Victorian. "A pastor is held to a higher standard, as are the women they marry. Or even date."

Gladys froze. She'd known Katie Ruth, who was hosting the shower, would be arriving shortly. She hadn't known she had a key to the back door.

"Don't blame Dan." Looking adorable in a black dress covered in oversize orange poppies, Katie Ruth strolled across the polished wood floors to Gladys. "If anyone is to blame, it's me. I should have told him about Judd and the sham wedding ceremony. A ceremony that turned out to be real."

"You had no way of knowing that episode would come back to bite you in the backside," Gladys pointedly reminded her.

"No. I didn't." Katie Ruth shrugged. "I still should have told him."

"You look different today." Katherine studied Katie Ruth thoughtfully. "Zen."

"You do appear very relaxed." Ruby smiled. "When you startled us by sneaking up on our conversation, it was the first thing I noticed."

Gladys stifled a curse. She would have swatted Ruby in the side if it wouldn't have made their conversation look even more subversive.

Katie Ruth didn't appear to take offense. Her expression turned thoughtful as she touched the soft green leaves that added an elegant element to the sunflower arrangement. "I've been pretty stressed since Dan and I broke up. Then, last night, I did what I should have done all along."

"You called him?" Ruby asked with a hopeful expression.

"I prayed." Katie Ruth's voice softened. "I turned my fears and grief over to God."

Gladys could only nod, for once at a loss for words.

"I felt an immediate sense of relief wash over me."

"I understand." Ruby placed a hand on Katie Ruth's arm. "When my Eddie died, I was heartbroken. I felt so sad and alone that I didn't think I could go on. Only when I turned my sorrow over, did I begin to heal."

Katherine inclined her head, her eyes narrowed on Katie Ruth. "You're giving up on Dan?"

The question might have been a tad abrupt, but Gladys was glad Katherine asked. The same question had been pushing against her lips, waiting for the right time to be voiced.

"I'm no longer going to worry about the future." Katie Ruth sighed.

The fact that she couldn't quite muster a smile told Gladys the young woman wasn't nearly as Zen as she appeared.

"All things work together…" Katie Ruth continued, but didn't finish the Bible verse that happened to be one of Gladys's favorites.

"If there's anything we can do, anything at all, please let us know." Gladys realized that, during the course of the conversation, something had changed. This was no longer about her own determination to make another successful match. This was about something more important. Friendship.

"Thank you." Katie Ruth's gaze traveled around their small semicircle. "You remember the incident with my parents. I harbored this rage inside because of the gossip and the actions of a few."

"I'm sorry you're experiencing some of that again." Katherine's normally unflappable countenance turned stern. "It isn't fair."

"It's okay." Katie Ruth offered a reassuring smile. "You know why? Because I've felt this outpouring of love from the three of you and so many more. It took something like this to make me realize how truly blessed I am. Sometimes, it takes the bad times to make you appreciate the good."

"He'll come around," Ruby said, sounding surprisingly confident.

"God's hands," was Katie Ruth's response.

Though Gladys wasn't nearly as positive as Ruby that Katie Ruth and Dan would end up together, she *was* positive about one thing.

Dan was missing out on an amazing woman if he let Katie Ruth Crewes slip through his fingers.

# CHAPTER TWENTY-THREE

Katie Ruth stood back and felt a surge of satisfaction. The couple's wedding shower appeared to be a huge success. Though, *family* wedding shower would be a more accurate term.

Ami, Eliza and Lindsay had brought their babies as well as their husbands. As had other guests. For a few moments, it had seemed that the children outnumbered the parents. Having someone to keep an eye on the children had been the one thing Katie Ruth had overlooked.

Thankfully, Cassie's daughter, Dakota, home from college for the shower, teamed up with Oaklee to keep the younger ones in check.

Cassie and Krew stood surrounded by family and friends, holding flutes of champagne. When Cassie leaned into Krew's broad shoulder, Katie Ruth's heart gave a lurch.

How many times had she done that with Dan?

Cassie must have caught her staring, because she handed her flute to Krew, brushed a kiss across his lips and hurried over. She caught Katie Ruth's hands up in hers.

"Thank you for this wonderful party." Cassie's face glowed nearly as bright as the large diamond on her left hand. "Initially, I didn't want any fuss. Krew encouraged me to give myself, to give us, the hoopla. I'm glad I agreed."

"The wedding isn't far off."

"Less than a month. Then we move to Green Bay." Cassie's expression faltered for a second. "I know it's the right move for all of us, but I'm going to miss everyone so much. I'm going to miss you, Katie Ruth."

"You're going to be too busy with your new home and launching that real estate career to even think of anything else."

"Not true."

"Well, Green Bay isn't that far." Katie Ruth met Cassie's eyes. "You can come back for the big Fourth of July celebration and the Harvest Festival. All your friends will still be here."

"Will you stay?"

The question took Katie Ruth by surprise. "In Good Hope?"

Cassie nodded.

Katie Ruth had already decided that Dan would probably take the position in Illinois. Even if he stayed in Good Hope, she'd manage...somehow. "Your husband's job is the reason you're relocating. There isn't any reason for me to leave Good Hope. My life is here."

Surprised voices calling out had both women turning.

Katie Ruth's heart gave a solid thump against her ribs when she saw who they were greeting.

*Dan.*

"He made it." Happiness ran through Cassie's voice like a pretty ribbon. "I hope you don't mind that we invited Dan. I didn't think he'd be able to make it, but he did."

Giving Katie Ruth's hands another squeeze, Cassie hurried over to greet the minister.

Katie Ruth remained where she was, unable to move. Unable to take her eyes off him.

His dark hair gleamed in the light, and when he smiled at Cassie and Krew, his whole face lit up.

A warm, sweet mass filled her chest. He was such a good guy.

"I can take care of this." Gladys reached to take a discarded plate from Katie Ruth's hands. "You go over—"

"Dan isn't here for me." Katie Ruth kept a firm grip on the plate. "He's here for Cassie and Krew."

When Gladys's fingertips tightened on the edge of the plate, Katie Ruth met her gaze. "I need to keep busy."

After a second, Gladys released her hold and stepped back. "I understand."

Katie Ruth cleared tables, chatted with guests and avoided looking in Dan's direction. The clock ticked slowly toward five o'clock, when the shower would end.

Shortly before, Katie Ruth looked up and realized the crowd had thinned considerably.

"Hey, got a minute?" Krew's deep voice had her looking up into his handsome face. "Thank you for doing this, Katie Ruth," his arm swept the room, "for me and Cass. It means a lot."

"It was my pleasure. I have no doubt that you and Cassie will be deliriously happy together."

"Deliriously?" Dan's voice held a spark of amusement.

Katie Ruth stiffened, but managed to keep a smile on her face. She turned toward him and raised a brow.

"It's a tall order," Dan said.

"Not too tall for me and Cassie." Krew's fiancée appeared at his side, and he pulled her to him.

"What are you talking about?" Cassie asked, her smile as bright as a thousand suns.

"How happy we're going to be." Krew grinned.

"We're already happy," Cassie told him, lifting her face to gaze into his amber eyes.

"Oh geesh." KT, one of Cassie's sons, rolled his eyes. "They're going to start kissing again."

Krew laughed. "Kissing your mother is one of my favorite pastimes."

"I think it's cute," Dakota smiled, "how much you love each other."

"Thanks again for everything." Krew smiled at Katie Ruth before his gaze shifted to Dan. "Tomorrow night at seven?"

"You got it," Dan said. "Your last premarital session."

"I told you we'd manage somehow to get them all in." Krew shot his fiancée a teasing look.

After a minute more of conversation, Katie Ruth found herself alone with Dan. "I thought you'd still be in Illinois."

"I preached my second sermon this morning." Dan's eyes remained focused on her face. "One of the other finalists for the position arrives tomorrow."

"Well, good luck to you."

She turned, searching for more cleanup to do.

"Katie Ruth. Would you have a few minutes so that we could talk?"

She closed her eyes briefly, then turned back to him. "Sure. I need to finish cleaning up first."

"We can take care of the rest." Gladys waved a dismissive hand.

"Don't worry about anything," Oaklee called out. Now free of the childcare responsibilities, Dan's sister was removing the centerpieces from the table.

The flowers would be delivered to church members who were currently hospitalized or ill at home.

"I guess we can talk now." Katie Ruth motioned to one of the tables.

"I've been sitting a lot today." Dan's tone was casual and offhand. "Would you mind if we took a walk?"

Katie Ruth glanced down at her heels, then remembered the gym bag in her car. "Give me a second to change my shoes."

She thought he'd wait inside. Instead, he followed her to her car and talked about the weather, while she sat on the passenger seat with the door open and changed into her sneakers.

Standing, she smiled ruefully. "I won't be making any fashion statement in these, that's for sure."

His gaze never left her face. "You look lovely."

She ignored the warm tingle his compliment set off in her body. "Where do you want to walk?"

"This way." He gestured in the direction of the residential area, rather than the path that would lead them to the business district.

Katie Ruth told herself it was understandable that he didn't want to be seen with her. Still, the realization stung. "How was your time in Lincolnshire?"

"Illuminating."

Okay, so he obviously didn't want to discuss his new job, or what would soon be his new job.

"I'm sorry Mitch and Edna caused problems for you."

"Mitch has always been a jerk. He used to harass me in high school." Katie Ruth waved a hand in the air. "I can handle him."

"Ryder got in his face?"

"He did." Katie Ruth smiled at the memory. "Mitch is now permanently barred from the Grind."

"Edna?"

"She's the same." Katie Ruth kept her voice even. "Once the church calls a new minister, I'm sure she'll be in his office urging him to get rid of me. Whether he does or not will tell me what I need to know about his heart."

"There isn't going to be a new minister."

Katie Ruth stopped in front of a Cape Code home with black shutters and a couple of bikes on their sides in the front yard.

"Even if it's offered, I'm not accepting the call."

She inclined her head. "Why not?"

Dan shoved his hands into his pockets. "It didn't feel right."

"You have time to think about it. You might feel differently in a week or so."

Without any further prompting, he began telling her about the meeting he'd attended last week.

She listened for a few minutes without interrupting. "Sounds like they were seeing how open you are to change."

"Exactly what I thought." His voice held a note of triumph. "The crazy thing was, I got really excited. I started thinking of all the possibilities, not in terms of their church, but the one here."

After a long pause, he added, "This is where I'm meant to be."

Katie Ruth thought how much harder it was going to be to have Dan in Good Hope. To see him in church, to run into him in the bakery, to watch when he fell in love with someone else.

*All things work together…*

"There's something I need to say," she told him. "One final thing to clear the air."

"Okay."

"I was wrong not to tell you about Judd. Because he was a part of my past, however brief. But you were wrong, too."

A flicker of emotion, one she couldn't quite identify, flashed in his eyes.

"You said you loved me." When her voice trembled, she paused to steady it. "Yet, you walked away from me without a backwards glance. Why? Because you were afraid I'd sully your reputation?"

When he started to speak, she held up a hand. "I understand the need for a minister to try to avoid even a hint of impropriety, but this was an unusual situation. There was no malice on my part, no desire to hide something from you, other than that I'm imperfect."

There was more she could say, but it would only be covering old ground.

"You're right." Dan cleared his throat. "I let myself get caught up in 'What would people say?' Instead of thinking, 'What would Jesus do?' I'm embarrassed and ashamed of my behavior, and I'm deeply sorry. Will you forgive me?"

Katie Ruth wondered why his apology didn't bring her comfort. "Yes. I accept your apology, and I forgive you."

"Would you like to go out sometime this week? For dinner? We could—"

"I can't step back and pretend things are the same as they were before."

"You forgave me."

"I did. I do." Katie Ruth tried to make sense of the emotions vying for dominance inside her. This was what she'd wanted. Now that renewing a relationship with Dan was in reach, why was she hesitating? "I need time. When you walked away from me, it was as if you were saying to me—and to the community— that I'm not good enough. Or at least, that's how it felt to me."

"When we start dating again, people will see—"

"If we start dating again, everyone will think, 'Oh, look, that wonderful pastor was able to forgive the poor sinner.'" Katie Ruth waved a hand in the air and fought the tears that wanted to fall. "I'm probably not making any sense. I can't even figure out what I'm saying."

"What I'm hearing is that I hurt you." His gaze dropped to the sidewalk. When he finally lifted his eyes, the dark depths blazed with determination. "I love you. If this time apart showed me anything, it's how much you mean to me."

"I love you, too, Dan." She lifted her shoulders and let them fall. "I just don't know what to do about it."

The following Sunday, Dan spotted Katie Ruth seated near the front next to his sister. This past week had been the longest of his life.

He couldn't believe he'd been so arrogant as to assume Katie Ruth would simply fall into his arms when he returned. It was another difficult lesson he'd had to learn.

Knowing Katie Ruth still loved him kept him going. He had to figure out what he could do to not only show her his love was true, but show the community he'd been wrong to walk away.

Whatever he did, it needed to be a grand gesture. One that would put to bed any doubts that Katie Ruth harbored.

The problem was, he wasn't a grand-gesture kind of guy. Or he never had been. But if that was what it took to convince Katie Ruth, Dan would figure out a way.

All week, he prayed.

On Friday, as he set aside his Bible, he ran across the deck of relationship cards. Alone in the house, he pulled a card from the middle of the deck and read the question.

It was as if God had spoken directly to him.

After the benediction on Sunday, Dan picked up the cordless microphone. "I have a few announcements to make. However, the children are released to Sunday school."

Dan wiped his sweaty palms against his robe and waited until the mass exodus of young people was over.

"Some of you may have already heard the news, but I wanted to announce that I have notified Pastor Martelle in Lincolnshire that I will not be accepting a call there should one be extended."

The unexpected applause that filled the sanctuary warmed Dan's heart.

"I believe Good Hope is where the Lord wants me to be. I came back from my short time away with new and exciting ideas for this congregation. Ideas that I'll be proposing in the weeks and months ahead."

He saw the polite smile on Katie Ruth's lips, but the only thing he cared about was that he had her attention.

"I also came away with a new understanding of what I'd like to change about myself. Contrary to what is commonly assumed, your minister is not perfect. Far from it."

As he expected, laughter rippled through the congregation.

"I discovered that I was so conscious of pleasing others and so determined to not let any scandal touch my position, that I hurt someone who matters very much to me and to you."

The room grew so quiet he could hear the fans whirring overhead.

"Katie Ruth Crewes is a wonderful, caring woman. She has re-energized the youth programs at First Christian. She prays and shows compassion for everyone. She trusts in God's plan for her life." Dan met her gaze. "Katie Ruth, would you join me here at the front, please?"

With a wary look on her face, Katie Ruth slipped out of the pew and covered the short distance to him.

He turned to her. Only years of public speaking kept his voice from shaking. "I want to publicly commend you for the wonderful work you've done both here at First Christian and in your outreach on behalf of the congregation."

Dan held out his hand. She stared at it for what seemed an hour—but was likely only a couple of seconds—before taking it.

"Thank you, Pastor." She smiled at him, then turned to the congregation. "It's been my pleasure to learn and grow spiritually with all of you."

Thirty minutes later, Dan sat with Oaklee in his office.

Oaklee frowned, appearing annoyed. "I thought you told me you were going to propose this morning."

Dan raked a hand through his hair and pushed back from his desk. "That was the plan. Then I remembered the scene with Lindsay. I put her on the spot that night. I didn't want to do that to Katie Ruth. I've already hurt her enough."

Oaklee offered a grudging nod. "In front of a congregation isn't the best place for a proposal. You're right, she would have been on the spot."

Dan studied his sister. "Do you think you can handle a group of middle schoolers for," he glanced at his phone, "fifteen minutes?"

"Easy-peasy." Oaklee's eyes sparkled with interest. "What are you going to do?"

He stood. "I'm going to propose to Katie Ruth."

When Oaklee informed Katie Ruth that Dan was having a quick meeting of department heads and she was to go to his office, Katie Ruth was certain Oaklee had gotten the time wrong.

There was no way Dan would schedule a meeting while she was in the middle of leading youth group. But Oaklee was insistent, so Katie Ruth made her way to Dan's office.

She knocked on the closed door.

"Come in."

She stepped inside and immediately realized his welcoming smile still had power over her. She glanced around. "Where is everyone?"

"We're alone for now." He gestured to a chair. "Please have a seat."

Once she had, she cleared her throat. "Ah, thanks for the nice things you said about me. You didn't have to do that."

She'd quickly realized it had been his way of making it clear to everyone that he held her in the highest regard.

"Everything I said was true." He pushed to his feet. "I didn't say everything I wanted, so if you don't mind, I'd like to say the rest now."

"Okay."

Dan half sat on the corner of his desk, his gaze firmly fixed on her. "I ran across the deck of relationship cards this week."

Startled, she blinked. "Did you?"

"I opened the deck to a question, and it was a timely one. 'What is the best gift your partner could give you?' It's the one thing I didn't give you. The gift of trust. I didn't trust that there was a good explanation. I didn't trust that, no matter what happened in Vegas, we would deal with it together."

Dan leaned forward. "I'm telling you now, and I promise that I will show you in the weeks, months and years to come that you can trust me. You can trust me to never walk away from you, to always have your back and to always love you."

Katie Ruth hesitated. "I was wrong, too. I thought I was protecting you by not telling you. But I promise you can trust me to always tell you the truth."

"I almost proposed this morning."

It took Katie Ruth a moment to find her voice. It came out in a high-pitched squeak. "Proposed?"

"I didn't want to put you on the spot."

*Like he did with Lindsay.*

"I-I appreciate that."

"Right now, it's just you and me." Dan rounded the back of her chair to close the door. It was a signal everyone knew that said he was in conference and didn't want to be disturbed.

When he tugged her to standing, Katie Ruth's heartbeat quickened.

He held her hands in his. "You, my sweet Katie Ruth, are a wonderful woman who inspires me to be a better man. I realize I disappointed you. I disappointed myself. But if you'll give me another chance, I promise no one else will ever love or cherish you more than I do."

Katie Ruth licked suddenly dry lips. "What are you saying, Dan?"

"I love you. Your patience and kindness amaze me. I can't imagine growing old with anyone else." Dan dropped down to one knee and pulled a jeweler's box from his suit jacket. "Katie Ruth Crewes, will you marry me? Will you give me the chance to make you deliriously happy?"

She stared at the sparkling diamond, then lifted her gaze to the man she loved. Yes, he'd made mistakes, but so had she. She firmly believed they could move forward from this time, stronger and wiser than they'd been before.

Katie Ruth had turned this over to God.

Now, He'd turned it back over to her.

"Yes." The word came out on a choking sob. Katie Ruth found herself laughing and crying at the same time.

When Dan slipped the ring on her finger, Katie Ruth had only a second to breathe a prayer of thanks before he stood and closed his mouth over hers in a soul-shattering kiss.

*Deliriously happy?* Katie Ruth held him tight. *Guaranteed.*

I hope you enjoyed reading Katie Ruth and Dan's story as much as I enjoyed writing it. It was a challenge to write a minister hero but I hope this book gave you insight into Dan, the man. When Lindsay broke up with Dan in an earlier book, he was sad but as with all of us, sometimes we realize what happened really was for the best. Lindsay belonged with Owen (Tie the Knot in Good Hope) the same way Katie Ruth was Dan's perfect match.

The next book in the series brings together Greer Chapin and a newcomer to Good Hope, Wyatt McConnell. Not just any man will do for headstrong Greer, who holds her feelings close. Sparks Fly in Good Hope is a reader favorite and once you read it, I think you'll understand why.

Pick up your copy of Sparks Fly in Good Hope now and enjoy another heartwarming romance and a return to Good Hope today. Sparks Fly in Good Hope Or keep reading for a sneak peek.

## Chapter 1

"You're trespassing."

Greer Chapin's hand froze on the tree branch. She'd come to the peace and solitude of Cherry Acres to steady herself after a distraught customer had lunged across her desk at her.

She'd needed time alone. Time to think. Time to settle.

Since she was sixteen, the cherry orchards on the outskirts of Good Hope had been a sanctuary. Only now did she realize she'd been foolish to come here...

No. Not foolish. This was Roy's land. At least until the estate was settled. The old man had made it clear she was always welcome here.

"What do you have to say for yourself?" The hard edge to the unfamiliar male voice sliced the cool spring air.

Rather than cowering like many might have—or apologizing when there was no reason—Greer lifted her chin. Her fingers tightened around the sprig of cherry blossoms she'd been admiring, snapping off the branch.

She turned, blossoms in hand, thankful she'd changed out of

her suit and heels before driving here. If she had to make a run for it, at least she stood a chance in sneakers.

Keeping her face expressionless, Greer surveyed the stranger. As she'd lived in Good Hope for her entire life—save for her college years—she knew most everyone in the area. Especially those close to her own age.

The man's classically handsome features might have caused her heart to skip a beat if there'd been the merest hint of a smile on his lips.

The scowler stood over six feet. He was dressed casually in jeans and a Henley, his chestnut hair looking as if he'd just run his fingers through the wavy strands.

"Who are you?" Her cool tone demanded an answer and conveyed she wasn't the least bit intimidated. Her brothers called it her "snooty tone" and usually laughed when it was directed their way.

"I ask the questions." His dark eyes narrowed on the branch she held before returning to her face. "You're on my land."

*His* land? Yeah, right.

"Even if this property is yours, what do you think I am? Some kind of cherry spy?" The thought was so ridiculous Greer nearly smiled.

While the man was definitely imposing, with his broad shoulders and lean, well-muscled frame, Greer felt no fear when she looked into his eyes. There was no mean or crazy lurking in the dark brown depths.

Still, Greer wasn't foolish. The trust she placed in her instincts went only so far. She kept enough distance between them so he couldn't reach out and grab her.

"Who are you?"

Greer lifted her chin another inch. "I believe that was my question."

This guy's demanding tone grated against nerves already on edge. The day had started badly when her water heater conked out right before her morning shower. It continued downhill when she'd had to turn down a loan request from Tom Jenkins, a longtime customer.

The nasty words Tom had shouted as the security guard escorted him from the bank had shredded Greer's heart and threatened her composure.

It appeared her bad-luck train continued to roll down the tracks. She'd come here for solace and ended up in a confrontation with her second surly male of the day. Come to think of it, this guy was her third. The water-heater repairman hadn't been all that pleasant either.

She chuckled and shook her head. Bad things really did come in threes.

"You think trespassing is funny?" The guy slipped the phone from his pocket, his gaze never leaving her. "We'll see what you think when the sheriff arrives."

He paused and stared at the screen, as if not sure of the number.

"Would you like Sheriff Rallis's cell or the official department number?" As Cade was practically one of the family, Greer had both numbers.

For a second, he looked uncertain and not so intimidating. Taking pity on him, Greer decided to give him a break.

"Listen, I think we got off on the wrong foot. I am, or I was, a friend of Roy's." Emotion rose inside her unexpectedly. Greer cleared her throat, but didn't say more.

She didn't know this man and certainly didn't need to explain further.

"Roy is dead." Those eyes, dark as Venezuelan chocolate, were as flat as his voice.

"I'm aware of that fact. I attended his memorial service." Any regret over her bad behavior disappeared. "I don't recall seeing you there."

"Why would I attend?" A muscle in his jaw jumped. "I didn't

know him."

His dismissiveness about someone she'd cared about was like a slap. "Yet here you are, ordering me—a friend—off his land."

His jaw jutted out. "It's my land now."

The last puzzle piece dropped into place. The whereabouts of Roy's daughter had been unknown, so the estate's executor had hired a private investigator to track her down. When Chicago records showed Shannon Davis was deceased, her share of the estate had gone to her son.

"You're Wyatt Davis." Greer had read in the Open Door, Good Hope's online newsletter, that Roy's grandson—and heir—had been located. "I was sorry to hear of your mother's death."

She thought of her father's unexpected death when she'd been sixteen and added, "It's never easy to lose a parent."

"My mother died a long time ago." He spoke matter-of-factly. "You still haven't told me who you are or why you're in my orchard."

*His* orchard. Greer knew for a fact the estate was still in probate. Granted, since he was the only heir to the property, the process should go smoothly, but the orchard wasn't officially his. Not yet.

"Well?" he prompted.

Greer wasn't certain why she hesitated. She should simply introduce herself. It was the polite and neighborly thing to do. Getting off on the right foot also made good business sense.

As a landowner, there would be times in the future where he might need the services of a bank. *Her* bank.

It wasn't like he was asking for her life story. She could keep it brief. She'd been missing Roy and had come to the orchard, where she'd spent many happy afternoons.

The words wouldn't come. Maybe because her pleasant memories of Roy were tied to the dark days when her family's banking empire had been threatened. Maybe because Greer had little tolerance for arrogant men.

Roy's grandson was not only arrogant, but rude. "I don't appreciate your manner, Mr. Davis. Or the inquisition."

Without another word, Greer whirled and headed down the row away from him.

"Hey, you can't leave."

Greer continued walking, each step taking her farther from Mr. Insufferable.

If the man spent any time in Good Hope, he would quickly learn that no one ordered Greer Chapin around.

No one.

～

Wyatt McConnell's gaze lingered on the woman's shapely form as she ran from him. No, he instantly corrected, that wasn't accurate. She didn't *run*. In fact, if he had to hazard a guess, he'd say this dark-haired beauty didn't run from anything or anyone.

There hadn't been an ounce of fear in her steel-gray eyes. The only flicker of emotion was when she'd mentioned his grandfather.

It appeared someone had cared about the old guy. His mother certainly hadn't, if the fact that she'd never mentioned him and hadn't seen him in the twelve years before her death was any indication.

Roy was a stranger to Wyatt, someone he hadn't known existed until he was dead. His mother had always insisted she didn't have any family.

Now, Wyatt stood on land that had been in the family, *his* family, for generations.

His phone rang, and when he glanced at it, he saw it was his sister Trinity, wanting to FaceTime.

He accepted, and a pretty face with a mass of blond hair filled the screen. "Hey, bro."

"Hey, baby sis," he shot back, knowing that would get a rise out of her.

She lifted an eyebrow. "If I recall correctly, you and I are the same age."

"Nope." Wyatt settled the phone more securely in his hand. "I'm the older, prettier one."

"Only by three months." She flashed a smile. "As far as prettier, I'll just say, in your dreams."

Wyatt enjoyed sparring with her, but pulled his next shot. She looked tired today. He didn't doubt that worry over her job situation had put those lines on her face.

The last time they'd spoken, his sister had told him the small clinic in Omaha where she was practicing was in danger of being absorbed into a large health system.

He cocked his head. "How's the job?"

"Even as we speak, the minnow is being swallowed by the big fish."

Though Trinity kept her tone light, Wyatt saw the disappointment in her eyes. "I'm sorry."

"It hasn't been just a job to me, you know. It's a place where I can really help people, where I could belong." She gave a little laugh. "Sounds silly, I know."

"Not to me." Wyatt expelled a breath. "I still hope to find that sense of belonging someday."

"Don't you have that now?" Confusion skittered across her face. "Look at those beautiful trees behind you. It's gorgeous where you are. And whether you knew your grandfather or not, he was blood, which means you have a tie to that town, that land."

"I know, but—"

"Didn't you also say you'd inherited a big company?"

"I did."

"Maybe you can think about running it in a way that helps employees instead of being like the soulless corporation that's forcing me out." Passion wove through her words, but the serious set of her mouth was softened by a small smile playing at the corners of her lips as she continued. "Plus, if the Hallmark Channel has taught me anything, it's that small towns always have ways for you to get involved. You just have to open your eyes to opportunities."

Wyatt thought about everything he'd discovered so far about Good Hope. "Because of the tourist industry, Good Hope is a thriving town. It also appears to be a tight-knit community. More than one person has told me that 'neighbors helping neighbors' isn't just a slogan, but a way of life here."

The people Wyatt had met were interesting and friendly. Except for the woman he'd just confronted in his orchard.

"Good Hope sounds amazing." Trinity's clear blue eyes searched his face. "Yet, you still don't appear convinced that it's the place for you. Why is that?"

Wyatt hesitated. There weren't many people he could admit this to, but he knew Trinity would understand. "I feel like an outsider. I realize that in a town where everyone has always known everyone, it's impossible not to, but I'm tired of feeling that way."

"I understand." A thoughtful look blanketed his sister's face. "Remember, though, it's only been a couple weeks. Plus, it goes both ways. You'll always be an outsider if you never let anyone in."

She really did know him, he thought.

"I'd love it if you'd come visit me." His tone turned persuasive. "You could stay with me while you weigh your options."

She smiled. "I may just take you up on that offer one of these days."

"I hope you do."

When Trinity ended the call, Wyatt started down the row in search of the smoky-eyed intruder.

He'd barely taken a step when he heard his name. He whirled

to find Beckett Cross, the attorney for his grandfather's estate, striding toward him from the opposite direction.

"Beck." Wyatt smiled in welcome. "What brings you out this way?"

The attorney with the intelligent brown eyes and easy smile had been the one who'd notified him that his grandfather had passed away. Beck had explained that, as Wyatt's mother was deceased, the bulk of Roy's estate now passed to him. An estate that included a large sum of cash, a processing plant and nearly a thousand acres of red tart cherries.

"Things were running smoothly at Muddy Boots," Beck said, alluding to his café on Good Hope's Main Street, "and it was a nice day."

The attorney gestured with one hand to the trees covered in cherry blossoms. "Looks like you're going to have a good crop this year."

"It would seem so." Wyatt didn't know much about cherries, but he'd learned that lots of blossoms equaled an abundance of cherries. Which meant this would be a good time to sell the orchards. Unfortunately, the estate was still tied up in probate.

From a distance, the sound of a car motor split the quiet, rural scene. The brunette was leaving.

Wyatt could almost hear his mother chiding him for his poor manners. After spending four years in foster care following his mother's death, he'd been given a second chance with a new family. Eileen McConnell and her husband, Jerry, had adopted him when he was fourteen. They'd taught him everything he knew about being an honorable man.

Beck's gaze turned thoughtful. "Was that Greer Chapin I saw you speaking with?"

Wyatt offered a noncommittal nod, reluctant to admit the woman had refused to give him her name.

His parents, and likely Beck as well, would not be pleased with how he'd treated Ms. Greer Chapin. Wyatt couldn't even mount a proper defense. He didn't understand himself why he'd been so short with her, so accusatory.

"Greer is a good friend." Beck's lips lifted in a fond smile. "In fact, she's practically family."

Wyatt raised a brow.

"Her mother is married to my wife's father."

It took everything in Wyatt to keep his expression impassive. He was urban to the core. Coming here had been a shock to his system. Forget six degrees of separation. In Good Hope, it was down to three.

When Wyatt realized that Beck was waiting for an answer, he struggled for something to say about *Greer*.

He rolled the name around in his head. It fit the fiery brunette. "She mentioned she and Roy were friends."

Beck paused, clearly startled by the comment. "If Greer says they were friends, it must be true. He did leave her money in the will."

Wyatt had paid scant attention to the other beneficiaries when he and Beck had gone over the terms of Roy's will. "Thanks for the pictures."

Changing the topic back to business was deliberate, a way to put his encounter with Greer in the rearview. Unfortunately, the second the words left his mouth, Wyatt realized he'd made a mistake.

Going through the personal contents stuffed into Roy Davis's safe-deposit box had thrown Wyatt off-kilter and unearthed more questions than answers. As the house where his mother grew up had burned to the ground, the pictures stored in the box were the only remaining records of her life in Good Hope.

There were pictures of Shannon as a young girl, pails of cherries in each hand, smiling brightly for the camera. There was even a family picture with Roy and a woman Wyatt assumed was his grandmother. The woman looked a lot like her daughter.

"I'm sorry there wasn't more." Beck studied him with a sharp-eyed gaze that missed nothing. "It didn't give you much."

Wyatt shrugged. "It isn't as if I knew any of these people. My mother never spoke of her parents. You said they were divorced a long time ago."

"I've only been here a handful of years, but my father-in-law knew Roy and Paula. Apparently, Paula left Roy for a man who was in the area working on one of the road projects. Steve—that's my father-in-law—said Shannon was seven or eight at the time."

Wyatt thought of his mother's tough exterior and her insistence that you should look out only for yourself. That had been his attitude as well...until he'd moved in with the McConnells. "Did Paula and Roy share custody?"

Beck shook his head. "If the information I received is accurate, neither Shannon nor Roy heard from her again."

Though Wyatt had loved his mother, he wasn't blind to her faults. She'd been quick-tempered and moody. The smiles he'd seen in the pictures had been in short supply during his childhood.

Was that because her mother had deserted her? Undoubtedly, her contentious relationship with her father also factored in.

"I wonder if that's why she cut herself off from her life in Good Hope." At Beck's speculative look, Wyatt continued. "Too many bad memories here."

Wyatt inhaled the sweet scent emanating from the flowering trees. The sky overhead was a brilliant blue, and the sun warmed his cheeks. He lifted his face for a second and felt himself relax.

When Wyatt turned back to Beck, he shook his head. "I think of some of the places we lived, the urine stench in the halls and the gangs roaming the streets. It had to be bad for her to willingly exchange this life for that one."

A smile lifted Beck's lips. "Sounds as if you're starting to like it here."

Wyatt chuckled. "Good Hope is growing on me."

When he'd arrived on the Door County peninsula, the plan had been to sell all the assets. After his conversation with Trinity, he was having second thoughts.

"Good Hope grew on me, too," Beck admitted. "I came here to start over, but never intended to fall in love with the town. Or the people. Now, I can't imagine living anywhere else."

Wyatt considered how to respond. He'd read the online account of Beck's pregnant wife dying in an accident caused by a drunken driver back in Georgia. He knew Beck remarried a local woman and had two young children with her.

Beck's eyes took on a distant glow. "I planned to leave the practice of law behind and run a small café, all the while keeping to myself."

"Seriously? You thought you could keep to yourself in a small town?" Wyatt chuckled. "Even I know that if you want privacy, live in a city."

"Looking back, I believe I wanted the connection." Beck's eyes softened. "Ami owned the bakery down the street from my café. We started sharing coffee and doughnuts every morning, and our relationship developed from there. I tried to put her off, but Ami can be very persistent."

Wyatt had the feeling Greer could be as stubborn, er, persistent, as Ami.

"Am-mee." Wyatt repeated the name, wondering if it was simply Beck's Southern accent that made the common name sound unusual.

Beck smiled. "That's right. Am-mee, short for Amaryllis. Her maiden name was Bloom. She and her three sisters all have flower names."

Wyatt nodded, wondering how they'd gotten so off track. "I've been meaning to ask if you know of a house or apartment I could rent on a month-to-month basis? Until I decide if I'm going to stay."

Beck's gaze turned sharp and assessing. "You're still considering selling?"

Wyatt heard the surprise in the attorney's voice. He understood. Seconds ago, he'd practically waxed poetic about life in Good Hope, and now he was talking about leaving.

"I'm keeping the option on the table. For now." Wyatt studied the endless row of trees. "I've spent my professional life involved in city government. I'm not sure I'm cut out to be a farmer."

"There are plenty of opportunities for civic involvement in Good Hope." In that moment, Beck sounded like Trinity. "There's a budget meeting in the courthouse tomorrow night at seven. You might want to attend. With your background, I bet you'd find it interesting."

Wyatt nodded. He walked past the building every night on his way to Beck's café.

Beck's watch pinged. He glanced down and expelled a breath. "Duty calls."

The wind picked up, and pink flowers rained down on them as Wyatt walked with Beck between the row of trees. "Was there a specific reason you stopped out today?"

Beck stopped abruptly and shot him a rueful smile. "Thanks for the reminder. Ami and I are hosting a barbecue on Saturday."

"What's the occasion?"

"Just Memorial Day weekend." Beck smiled. "You should come. It'll be a good opportunity for you to get better acquainted with everyone."

Though Wyatt's first instinct was to accept, he hesitated. He wasn't sure it was smart to get involved locally until he decided if he was staying.

If not for the election of a new mayor, he'd still be enjoying his work as a city manager in a community on the outskirts of Minneapolis. As his position had been appointed, when a mayor of the opposing party was elected, he was out.

Wyatt had been considering several opportunities when Beck

notified him of his grandfather's death and his inheritance. Instead of pursuing those leads, he'd come to Good Hope.

"I appreciate the offer." Wyatt chose his words carefully, not wanting to appear ungrateful. "But—"

"There will likely be someone at the barbecue who will know of a place you could rent." Beck smiled. "The Sweet Dreams motel is nice, but I understand wanting more space."

Wyatt grinned. "You should be selling cars."

"I'll take that as a yes." Beck chuckled. "See you Saturday."

The attorney drove off in a vintage truck painted a bright cherry red. As Wyatt watched him go, Trinity's words came back to him. *You'll always be an outsider if you never let anyone in.*

An image of Greer in her red shirt flashed before Wyatt.

He wondered if she'd be at the party.

Wyatt grinned, suddenly eager for the weekend.

This is just the story that will have you staying up WAY too late at night and closing the book with a smile. Grab your copy and dive into this uplifting story now. Sparks Fly in Good Hope

# ALSO BY CINDY KIRK

### *Good Hope Series*

The Good Hope series is a must-read for those who love stories that uplift and bring a smile to your face.

Check out the entire Good Hope series here

### *Hazel Green Series*

Readers say "Much like the author's series of Good Hope books, the reader learns about a town, its people, places and stories that enrich the overall experience. It's a journey worth taking."

Check out the entire Hazel Green series here

### *Holly Pointe Series*

Readers say "If you are looking for a festive, romantic read this Christmas, these are the books for you."

Check out the entire Holly Pointe series here

### *Jackson Hole Series*

Heartwarming and uplifting stories set in beautiful Jackson Hole, Wyoming.

Check out the entire Jackson Hole series here

### *Silver Creek Series*

Engaging and heartfelt romances centered around two powerful families whose fortunes were forged in the Colorado silver mines.

Check out the entire Silver Creek series here

Made in the USA
Las Vegas, NV
02 March 2021

18908480R00152

Made in the USA
Las Vegas, NV
02 March 2021